Loving HELEN

A COMPANION NOVEL TO *SAVING GRACE*

Loving HELEN

A COMPANION NOVEL TO *SAVING GRACE*

Michele Paige Holmes

Mirror Press

Copyright © 2015 Michele Paige Holmes
Paperback edition
All rights reserved

No part of this book may be reproduced in any form whatsoever without prior written permission of the publisher, except in the case of brief passages embodied in critical reviews and articles. These novels are works of fiction. The characters, names, incidents, places, and dialog are products of the author's imagination and are not to be construed as real.

Interior Design by Rachael Anderson
Edited by Annette Lyon, Cassidy Wadsworth, and Kelsey Down
Cover design by Rachael Anderson

Cover Photo Credit: Andreea Retinschi/Trigger Image
Cover Photo Copyright: Andreea Retinschi

Published by Mirror Press, LLC
ISBN-10: 1941145531
ISBN-13: 978-1-941145-53-1

To Mom—

*For all those times you let me keep reading
instead of doing my chores.
And for your encouragement and faith
that helped me believe I could do anything.*

Other Books by Michele Paige Holmes
Counting Stars
All the Stars in Heaven
My Lucky Stars
Captive Heart

Between Heaven and Earth (Power of the Matchmaker)

First Light (Forever After)

A Timeless Romance Anthology: European Collection
Timeless Regency Collection: A Midwinter Ball
Timeless Romance Single: The Heart Only Grows

Hearthfire Romance Series:
Saving Grace
Loving Helen
Marrying Christopher
Twelve Days in December

Hearthfire Scottish Romance Series:
Yesterday's Promise
A Promise for Tomorrow

CHAPTER 1

Yorkshire England, October 1827

Helen Thatcher gathered the voluminous skirts of her silk gown as she tiptoed across the small foyer. Stopping outside the double doors that led to the sitting room of Mr. Preston's guesthouse, she peered through the crack between the doors and spied her lady's maid, Miranda, busily folding linens at the table. Just as this room filled so many purposes—they visited, dined, read, and sewed here—her maid had taken to doing many tasks outside her usual duties as well. Helen wished it was otherwise, though it did seem that both her servants, Miranda and Harrison, were happier here than they had been since her guardian and grandfather, the late Duke of Salisbury, had died, shortly after which the new duke had summarily dismissed them from his residence.

We might all have stayed and continued on in comfort. The guilty thought plagued Helen, as it had every day the past several months. Had she only accepted the new duke's marriage proposal, she and her siblings, Grace and

Christopher, along with their servants, would still be at the grand estate, with everything they needed—everything they desired—at their disposal.

Yet because I did not desire marriage, we've become little more than penniless outcasts.

It had been more than a simple lack of desire that had spurred her refusal—a rejection that the new duke had neither expected nor accepted. At their first acquaintance, it had become apparent that he was a man used to getting what he wanted. And along with her grandfather's vast estate and wealth and title, the duke had wanted Helen as his wife. He had told her it would be so, rather than asking, much as he told Grandfather's servants what they were to do and how they were to do it, then disciplined them harshly when they deviated in the least—often simply because they were used to different ways. Helen had seen him throw a pitcher of just-boiled water at one of the maids and kick a young stable boy and had made up her mind that she could not bear to be the duke's wife. Returning to their estranged father was the lesser of the two evils, for evil was what she believed Grandfather's heir to be. Grace and Christopher had supported her decision, and they had returned to their father's home—and a new set of troubles.

After six years away it had been difficult to live again with their father, whose only ambition had been spent in marrying a duke's daughter—an act that never yielded the fortune or life of ease he had hoped for. They discovered him to be in more debt than ever. In his children he had devised a means of income, intending to marry his daughters off to the highest bidder.

A situation gone from bad to worse. Helen suppressed a shudder as she recalled the events of the last few months. *I am safe now,* she reminded herself. Yet it might not always be so. It would not be so now, if not for Grace's unselfish sacrifice.

Because of my cowardice in refusing to marry Grandfather's heir, Grace has endured much. After offering to take Helen's place and be married, Grace had been forced to meet with suitors of their father's choosing, each of whom proved to be wretched, lecherous men. That is, until the last, Mr. Samuel Preston, had surprised Grace with genuine friendship and a concern extending beyond her welfare to that of her siblings.

Helen's mouth curved in a smile as she thought of Mr. Preston—so gentle and kind to them all. She had never met a man quite like him. It seemed terribly unfair that Grace had met him last and not first. But by the time of their meeting, Grace had already taken drastic action, making certain her reputation was ruined by spreading the tale of a most unfortunate middle-of-the-night mix-up in the bed chamber of Lord Nicholas Sutherland, Mr. Preston's closest neighbor, former brother-in-law, and sworn enemy.

From what Helen had learned of him, Lord Sutherland did not appear to be much better than some of the other men whose company Grace had suffered, *and now she is betrothed to him.*

But even amidst the worst of circumstances, Grace worries about us. And so Mr. Preston had arranged for the four of them—Christopher and Helen, and their servants, Miranda and Harrison—to reside at his guest house until the matter of their inheritance could be favorably settled or until Grace was suitably wed.

Would that I had a shred of her courage or selflessness, Helen thought, frustrated with herself yet again. She smoothed the front of her gown, knowing that what she was about to undertake would require at least one of those valiant qualities. She desperately hoped she possessed courage somewhere.

As for selflessness, the plan she'd conceived seemed rather the opposite.

But what else am I to do?

Grace's betrothal to Lord Sutherland had begun badly, and perhaps it yet might end the same, terminating what little protection it had bought them for the time being. The new duke seemed determined to see that they did not get a penny of their inheritance, while debt collectors banged down her father's door.

It is only a matter of time before Father thrusts me out to meet them. I will be forced to marry. Marriage was the very last thing she wished. *But if I am to be forced to it...* At least there was now one option that might be bearable.

Grasping the doors, Helen pulled them open and stepped inside the drawing room. "Good morning."

Miranda did not look up from folding the linens, and Helen realized she'd spoken too softly. Christopher was forever chiding her about whispering, but it wasn't something she did intentionally. After so many years spent avoiding Father and the vile men he associated with, whispering was simply something that came naturally. If she'd acquired any talent at all in her eighteen years, it was knowing how to keep quiet and remain unseen.

But now, she was about to attempt the very opposite.

She cleared her throat and tried once more. "Good morning, Miranda."

"Miss Helen?" Miranda glanced up from her task, then straightened to her full height, her spine as rigid as her rules of etiquette. "What are you doing up already—and dressed without my help?" Her lips turned down in disapproval. "And suddenly out of mourning, I see."

"I mean no disrespect to Grandfather. Please don't scold," Helen said, guessing the direction of Miranda's thoughts. The poor woman had faced an arduous task from the beginning, taking two girls used to a life of poverty and struggle and turning them into ladies. With Grace, it seemed, she'd nearly had success. Only Father's debts had forced

Grace back to her independent, rash ways of survival.

"You've been working so hard lately," Helen said. "I wanted to save you some time." A partial truth, but Miranda need not know that. "What do you think?" Helen held out the sides of the cream gown and turned a slow circle. "I know it is a drastic change from black, but this *was* a gift from Grandfather. Did I do all right?"

"That depends," Miranda said, hands on her hips, "on whether you are planning to attend a breakfast or a midnight ball."

Helen's fragile confidence slipped a notch. It had taken quite a lot of maneuvering to get herself into this dress with only the chambermaid to assist. And she'd spent over an hour with the curling tongs and burned a few fingertips to achieve the ringlets in her hair. Still, she'd felt pleased with the reflection staring back at her in the glass. But Miranda's obvious disapproval weighed heavily.

"I know this gown is a bit fancy for breakfast," Helen said. "But I so seldom go anywhere that I thought it would be all right to wear it." The gown had been one of the last gifts Grandfather had given her before his passing. Grace owned a similar one and had worn it to Mr. Preston's, though that occasion *had* been a ball.

Miranda let out an exasperated sigh. "It is not breakfast attire, but I suppose this one time won't hurt. At least let me put your hair up properly." She started toward Helen.

"I—I wish to wear it down." Beneath the dress, Helen's heart pounded. She'd never disagreed with Miranda before, had never done other than what her maid told her was proper and fitting.

Miranda's brows furrowed. "Why?"

"My hair took a great deal of time," Helen said. "And—I think it looks pretty this way." She did not mention the information she'd gleaned from Grace's letters—that Lord Sutherland had ordered her to wear her hair *up*, though

Grace secretly believed that he might admire it on the occasions she left it down. If so, Helen hoped that keeping her hair down as well might capture the attention of a certain gentleman. She needed to use every resource available to her, limited as they were.

"It does look pretty." Harrison's rasping voice and hacking cough filled the room as he came through the doors to stand behind her. "Leave her be, Miranda. Miss Helen's a rare beauty, and there's no reason to hide it by keeping her in black and tucking away her curls."

"Thank you, Harrison," Helen murmured. From the corner of her eye, she saw Miranda marching toward them.

"When you become a lady's maid, you'll be allowed an opinion on the subject," Miranda said, wagging a finger at him. "Until then, I'll thank you to keep your nose where it belongs—outside and pointed toward the backside of a horse."

"It doesn't take a maid to appreciate beauty." Harrison cleared his throat and sounded a bit better. "There's no time for her to change, anyhow. Ladies—" He bowed gallantly. "Your carriage awaits."

Miranda scoffed. "What nonsense is this? We don't need a carriage. We can see Mr. Preston's house from here. It's but a short walk."

"Over a dewy lawn," Harrison said. "It could ruin her fine gown."

"Well, we don't need to leave now. We're not expected for another hour," Miranda argued.

"Breakfast won't be served until then, but that does not mean Miss Helen cannot enjoy visiting before." He winked at Helen.

She worked to contain a smile—a task easily accomplished when Miranda turned a severe gaze upon her.

"You two are up to something," she accused. "I

wouldn't have believed it of you, Miss Helen. Your sister, easily, but never of you."

Helen's smile broke free. "Why, thank you." She felt giddy with confidence. For once she had exerted her will, and Miranda thought she'd acted like Grace—the highest compliment Helen could think of, and it boded well for the adventure ahead. After all, Grace had captured the attention of several men without even trying.

I need secure only one.

Helen had learned from weeks of silent observation that the *one*, Mr. Samuel Preston, strolled in his garden at precisely nine o'clock every morning. He always walked alone and always appeared somewhat solemn. This morning, Helen intended to join him and attempt to distract him from his melancholy.

Mr. Preston had invited her to breakfast, but she hoped to make much more of the morning than that. Her skirts swished about her ankles as she followed Harrison outside to the borrowed phaeton. He held out his hand and helped her up. Miranda came running behind them, carrying a wrap.

"You'll catch your death of cold with this nonsense. And Grace barely well herself. I'll not have another foolish girl to care for." Ignoring Harrison's hand, Miranda hoisted herself onto the seat and settled beside Helen. "Let's get this on you," she said, laying Helen's wrap across her shoulders.

"Oh, Miranda," Helen said. "You needn't worry so much. The sun is out. It's a lovely day."

"Hmpf." Miranda sat straight. "I wish your brother was here to see what you're about."

"Well, he isn't," Helen said a little too pertly. Christopher had stayed only one night at Mr. Preston's estate, just long enough to see that he was a gentleman and that she was safely settled, before returning to London to attempt to work out the matter of their inheritance.

Miranda's gaze grew calculating as she appraised Helen.

"A girl who wants nothing to do with men suddenly does an about face and goes out of her way to dress up for one—"

"A page you might consider taking from her book," Harrison said, climbing up on the other side of Helen, so she was sandwiched cozily between them.

"And why should I want to do that?" Miranda asked, looking positively affronted by such a suggestion.

"So that the man who favors you—" Helen looked sideways at Harrison—"might take more notice of you and take more *care with his words.*" She shifted in her seat, giving Harrison a not-so-subtle nudge.

"First there would have to be a man who I would *wish* to notice me." Miranda's words were tart, but Helen thought she saw a faint blush stealing across the older woman's cheeks.

Helen sighed inwardly, wishing Grace were here, so they could discuss—as they had previously—what might be done for their servants to be more amiable to each other. Grace had often said it was as plain as the nose on her face that Miranda and Harrison cared for one another. What Helen could not understand was why they did not simply admit their feelings and enjoy friendship, at least.

She could not begin to understand it, but then, she also didn't know the first thing about relationships between a man and a woman, her only example being a vague knowledge of her parents' ill-fated marriage.

So much I have missed by not having a mother. Grace had done her best as a substitute, but at times—like now, when Helen was about to attempt to gain a man's interest—it would have been a fine thing to have access to some motherly advice.

Harrison slowed the horses and brought the phaeton to a stop well before they reached the front entrance to Mr. Preston's mansion. He jumped out and held his hand up to her.

"Thank you," Helen said, smiling at him as he helped her down.

"What are you doing?" Miranda demanded. "I thought you were worried about spoiling your gown outside."

"I will help you wash it if it becomes stained," Helen promised.

It isn't as if I am unfamiliar with such work. She'd survived her first twelve years by helping Grace launder other people's clothing. Miranda wouldn't allow such a thing now. Even with their changed circumstances, she was most adamant that their lifestyle, inasmuch as was possible, remain as it had been while living at Grandfather's. Helen pulled Harrison aside, waiting a moment for him to cease his wheezing. "Take Miranda for a nice, long ride. And say something kind to her."

"If that is your wish, Miss Helen." He bowed before climbing back into the carriage.

"It is," she said, trying not to laugh when he winked at her again. "Goodbye. Have a lovely time." She waved them off, watching until the carriage had gone down the curved lane and out of sight. Then, much more slowly than she usually walked, Helen made her way toward the entrance of the garden on the side of the house.

Many mornings from her upstairs bedroom of his guest house, she had watched Mr. Preston as he strolled in his garden. He was always alone, and he always walked bent slightly forward with his hands clasped behind his back, as if considering a great many things. Helen hoped he would not mind her company and that he might even enjoy it enough to invite her to walk with him again.

Since their first introduction at her arrival, she'd found herself thinking of Mr. Preston frequently. He'd proven to be kind and soft-spoken. He was pleasant to look upon and not more than nine or ten years her senior, she guessed.

And he has money enough to save us. It was a terribly

selfish thought, but she could not seem to keep herself from thinking it. *If I* must *marry, why can it not be to a man who is gentle as well as generous?* In her heart she cared more about his demeanor than whatever wealth Mr. Preston was in possession of, but her dire circumstances dictated that she also consider his fortune.

A dismal reality, with no help for it. Such was the lot of females: to do their best to marry well. Now that she was a grown woman of eighteen, the time had come for her to join the hunt. She had set her cap for Mr. Preston and must go about securing his interest.

Helen had never expected to find herself in pursuit of any man, yet she could not deny a certain thrill—and a definite terror—to the process. At night she thought of Mr. Preston, oft as she sat at her window, looking out at the lights glowing from his house, wondering which room was his and what he was doing. New feelings stirred within her, emotions she had never expected to experience for any man, and she found them both frightening and exhilarating. As her older brother Christopher had remarked at dinner that first night here, she was growing up.

And so I must act like it. No more hiding. To get Mr. Preston's attention, she must look pretty and smile and be pleasant, as Grace had witnessed other young ladies doing to gain the attentions of their potential husbands. How difficult could it be?

Crossing the drive, Helen walked beneath the neatly trimmed arbor, still abundant with blooms late in the season. She thought Mr. Preston's gardeners must be very good, as she had never seen such lovely flowers with such enormous blooms, bright color, or sweet fragrance.

In addition to the yellow roses lining the drive, the garden boasted plants and flowers in what seemed to be every hue of orange, red, and gold. Helen had viewed them from her window, but standing among them, she realized that the labyrinth she'd spied from above would be more difficult to navigate than she'd anticipated. Multiple paths spread in various directions, tall hedges lining many of them. She paused before starting down any as she tried to recall where she had most often viewed Mr. Preston.

After a moment's contemplation, she remembered that he usually ended up in one of the two courtyards with a fountain. Helen set off on the path she hoped would lead her to the nearest one. As she walked, she rehearsed in her mind what she would say upon meeting him.

Good morning, Mr. Preston. Pleasant day for a walk, isn't it?

He would agree, compliment her on how fine she looked, and invite her to stroll with him. She would inquire after Grace, as he saw her when he delivered their letters, and Mr. Preston would then inquire as to how she and Christopher were faring. They would stroll and visit politely—about what, Helen wasn't quite certain, but she supposed an appropriate topic would manifest itself at the right time.

At breakfast she would employ all of the manners instilled in her while living with Grandfather, and Mr. Preston would find her so charming that by noon their courtship would be well underway.

Helen clasped her hands in front of her, pleased with the imagined scenario and feeling certain that the events would transpire in just such a way—if only she could locate Mr. Preston.

She reached the first courtyard and found it empty. The fountain spouted no water, and the bench sat vacant. No footprints marred the dew upon the moss growing between the stones. It seemed unlikely that Mr. Preston had visited here this morning.

Resolute in her cause, Helen gathered her skirts and marched on, toward the back of the house along a path she hoped would link the west garden to the east. She passed the gazebo, which was centered in the middle of the vast back lawn, and found it deserted as well. The path forked, the right heading in the direction Mr. Preston walked most afternoons when he went to exchange letters with Grace. Helen chose the other path, following the flagstones around the eastern corner of the mansion. She'd taken but a few steps when voices—or rather, one voice, Mr. Preston's—reached her.

"More and more I feel I cannot continue as I have been. I am at a loss to know what to do with Beth. She needs a mother, and I . . ." His voice trailed off, and Helen waited expectantly for a response from whomever he was speaking to.

None came. But Helen imagined that she heard a wearied, despondent sigh.

"It is a wretched thing for me to bring up today, of all days," Mr. Preston continued. "But I cannot seem to help myself. I beg your forgiveness, though I have already asked it far more than I deserve."

His earnest plea received no response. Helen crept closer, feeling a vague sense of annoyance and desperation on his behalf. Who would not forgive him? Would not even deign to respond?

The second courtyard came into view, and Mr. Preston with it, hunched forward on the bench, head in his hands.

He is upset. This unsettled her. She had expected his mood to be contemplative but not so sad or serious as he appeared now. She had also—foolishly, she worried—imagined that he would be pleased by her unexpected arrival. Never before had she witnessed Mr. Preston display any emotion aside from joviality. The change left her uncertain how to proceed.

Everyone has problems, her grandfather had once told her. *Do not ever consider yours to be greater than those of others around you. Be compassionate—a lesson I wish I had learned much earlier in life.*

Helen felt compassion stir within her now, though she felt at a complete loss as to what to do about it. Biting her bottom lip, she alternately hid behind the hedge and peeked around it as she pondered what course of action to take. She did not wish to abandon her plan—it had taken courage to come this far—but to continue seemed beyond self-serving. Mr. Preston obviously had something pressing on his mind, and she should show him respect enough to postpone her attempts to gain his attention.

Having decided this, she felt relief. She let out a breath she had not realized she'd been holding, and her hands unclenched. Parting the bushes, she peeked into the courtyard one last time before returning down the same path she'd come. Aside from Mr. Preston, the square was empty, so whomever it was he'd been speaking to must have left already, by the opposite path.

Odd, Helen thought, that he'd been with anyone at all. She'd watched him for nearly three weeks, and never once had she seen anyone accompany him on his morning ramblings.

It was a mystery she would have to consider later. For now, she wished only to leave before she could be seen. Moving quietly, she began her retreat but had taken no more than five steps when Mr. Preston spoke again.

"Miss Thatcher?"

Helen stopped, pinned in place by his voice. She turned slowly and found him still hunched on the bench, now with his head turned sideways toward her. He'd caught her during the few seconds the path crossed his view.

"Hello." She did not attempt a smile. Somehow, as she noted his solemn look, smiling did not seem appropriate.

"Have you been here long?" he asked. "Did you hear—"

"Not long," she rushed to assure him. "I heard you

speak briefly but did not hear your companion at all. My apologies. I did not mean to eavesdrop."

He sighed, then straightened on the bench, tilting his head back as if searching the sky. After a few seconds looking heavenward, he lowered his head, braced his hands on his knees, and stood.

"I'm sorry to have disturbed you," Helen said, glancing over her shoulder at the path behind her. "I'll go now."

"Don't—please." He crossed the courtyard and came to stand before her. "You needn't leave on my account."

"I should not have come." Helen could not meet his gaze, shamed that she'd ever had the idea to disrupt him on his morning walk.

"Nonsense," he said, a hint of his usual good humor in his tone. "The gardens are meant to be enjoyed, especially by my guests. You are free to walk here whenever it pleases you."

It is you I wished to walk with. Helen kept her gaze averted, feeling her face warm with the thought.

Mr. Preston glanced about as if expecting to see Miranda accompanying her.

Perhaps he will think me as scandalous as Grace, walking without a chaperone.

"I came early," Helen said.

His brow furrowed.

"For breakfast," she clarified.

"Of course." He broke out in a smile. "Goodness. Is it that time already? He withdrew a watch from his vest and looked at it. "But no." His gaze was questioning as he met hers.

"I came early," Helen said once more, wishing very much she had not.

"You are hungry," he assumed, stepping forward and offering his arm. "We'll go right in and get you something."

"I am not," Helen protested. "Hungry, that is. I only

came to walk—with you." There. She'd said it. And what an eloquent speech it had been. She closed her eyes briefly, wishing the earth would open up and swallow her.

When she dared peek at Mr. Preston again, she thought he looked rather perplexed, and perhaps even a bit put out.

This was a terrible idea.

"Well then—" He still offered his arm. "Of course you may join me. That was very—thoughtful—of you."

"I have seen you alone in the mornings," Helen blurted, then wished she had not, as his gaze strayed in the direction of the guesthouse. "You are always alone, and I thought you might enjoy company."

Or, perhaps being alone is to your liking, she realized too late. *Or perhaps you are not usually alone at all, as you were not today.* "But if you would rather be by yourself—" She stepped back, preparing to flee.

"Not at all." He shook his head a little too vigorously to be entirely believable. "Stay. And allow me to explain."

Explain what? Why you prefer to be alone? Why you are sad? Who you were talking to? Helen did not ask what he meant; neither did she agree to stay. But instead of leaving, she moved to stand along the far edge of the path. He did not offer his arm again, for which she felt grateful. She'd only wished to walk and talk with him, not touch him.

"I must confess that you startled me," he said as they began to move awkwardly along the path, she trying to stay a step ahead so they did not accidentally touch, while looking back at him as they walked.

"I do walk alone every morning."

"But not today. You were talking to someone."

He grimaced. "You are as direct as your sister." It did not sound like a compliment.

"I am sorry. I should not have said that. I should not have intruded upon your privacy." She glanced about, looking for a break in the hedge where she might make her escape.

"My privacy, or my insanity?" he said, almost more to himself than to her.

Helen looked back at him, astonished to find him smiling, albeit rather sadly.

"You have discovered my secret," he said. "And I must beg you to keep it."

She nodded, fearful of what he was about to say. She had believed him to be so nice, so kind—she should have known he was too good to be true. All men, excepting Grandfather, Christopher, and Harrison, had some fatal flaw about them. If insanity was Mr. Preston's, should she fear him?

Should I run?

He caught up with her so that they stood quite close. Helen's pulse quickened. She took a step backward, then another, and her heel slipped from the path. She fell back into the hedge but quickly righted herself, though not before thorns caught in the lace of her dress.

"Don't move," Mr. Preston ordered.

She froze, too paralyzed with fear to do anything else. He reached over her shoulder and brushed her curls aside. Moving even closer, so close she felt his breath upon her ear, he worked, carefully freeing her gown from the bush.

"There. No harm done, I believe. That is a very pretty gown." He stepped back, a curious expression on his face as he studied her. "Is it your sister's?"

Helen shook her head, more confused than ever at the turns their conversation was taking. *But he did not hurt me.* Her heart began to slow as the distance between them grew again. "Grace has a similar gown. Grandfather had them made for us." She prattled on, attempting to hide her nervousness. "He knew I would not be wearing mine to any balls, so he had it designed in a more medieval style, like the gowns the heroines wore in the stories we read together."

"It does have a hint of Camelot about it," Mr. Preston said, a smile curving his mouth. "It looks quite lovely on you, and I recall that your sister looked very pretty, too, the night she wore hers to my ball."

"Grace is very beautiful," Helen agreed, not knowing what else to say.

"Why is it that your dress will never be worn to a ball?" Mr. Preston asked. "Do you not dance?"

Helen shook her head. "I do not care for dancing."

I do not care to be near so many people, so many men.

"Only strolls in the garden," he mused, glancing down at her perfectly normal feet.

She did not offer further explanation, and they started off again.

"I was about to confess my madness a moment ago," he said.

Does that make him madder yet, that he has reminded me? He needn't have told her. She had forgotten already. But then, it seemed she could hardly recall her own name in his presence. "As you caught me," he said, "I feel I must offer an explanation."

"You don't have to," she hurried to assure him. *I really don't want to know.*

"It is all right. I feel that for some reason, I can tell you. I trust you will not go running about the neighborhood sharing my secret."

"Not at all," Helen said, feeling her eyes widen. What awful thing was he about to confess? She glanced about for a side path once more.

"Every morning I walk in the garden and speak to my wife, Elizabeth." His lips pressed together, and he paused, as if waiting for a reaction of shock or disapproval.

"But isn't she—dead?" Helen whispered, then wished she could take it back.

"Deceased sounds so much better," Grace had said when people came to offer their condolences after Grandfather's funeral.

"She is." Mr. Preston gave a tight-lipped smile. "She died in childbirth over three years ago. What I meant is that I *imagine* I speak with her. I share with her my problems and concerns. I tell her the amusing things Beth has said or done. It is only a pretend conversation—annoyingly, Elizabeth does not respond—but I find that it does me a great deal of good—most days."

"Oh." Helen looked at the ground, fighting a swell of emotion. Relief, sweet and refreshing—*he is* not *mad*—was followed almost instantly by the realization that her plan to catch Mr. Preston's interest had ended before it began. His wife had been gone for three years, and still he spoke to her in the garden every day. It was the most tragically romantic thing Helen had ever heard.

"I'm sorry. I did not mean to upset you. Are you quite all right?" he asked, concern in his voice.

She nodded her head and forced herself to look up, not wanting him to misunderstand. "You are not insane at all."

So why did she feel so sad? Helen swallowed painfully as his face blurred from the moisture building in her eyes. "I think that your talking to your wife is the most beautiful thing I have ever heard. I am so sorry to have interrupted." She turned and fled the way she had come, wiping at her eyes as she went back along the path, past the bush that had caught her dress, and onto another path.

Mr. Preston's situation *was* beautiful and tragic. Beautiful because of his continuing devotion. Tragic because he was still in love with his wife.

CHAPTER

Forty-five minutes later, Samuel sat down to breakfast alone, though the table was set for two. He supposed he'd frightened his guest off and told himself he must ask Grace, when they met later today, more about her sister. Perhaps he would learn something that would allow him to remedy the situation. Miss Thatcher was such a young, timid thing; he supposed he oughtn't have told her about speaking to Elizabeth.

But Miss Thatcher had overheard him, so he'd had to tell her something. *Why not the truth?* He hadn't intended to send her fleeing.

No doubt her sister would have reacted very differently. He guessed it would not have upset Grace in the least. *Indeed, she might have jested with me about it, until I was able to laugh at myself.* Grace had a way of making his worries feel lighter—possibly because her own were rather burdensome at present—and Samuel found he had begun to crave her company and to wish he had not been so quick to help along the situation that had ended with her betrothal to Nicholas Sutherland.

When he had first learned that Grace was to be offered up for marriage, he'd requested an audience with her excuse of a father. *I should have been bolder, should have paid the man right then and there.* But Samuel held Grace in higher esteem than that. He hadn't wanted to purchase her affection, though he was quite willing to pay her father for the privilege of marrying her, had it come to that.

And it might have, he thought ruefully, were it not for a storm and a broken carriage that had landed Grace in the wrong bedchamber of the house just up the road.

And now I am here alone, while Nicholas is blessed with her presence daily.

Grace looked nothing like Elizabeth, but Samuel felt she had a similar spirit. Setting out to purposely ruin her reputation so she and her younger sister might both avoid marriage had required gumption, the likes of which he had only witnessed in his wife. He still loved Elizabeth and felt a constant ache in his heart for her. But for the first time in over three years, he'd felt hope that he might yet have another chance at love, that the spirited lady currently betrothed to his former brother-in-law and current enemy might have been the one woman who could fill the void in his life and bring him happiness again.

We could have been happy together. We still might be, if all does not go well with Nicholas. Such a thought courted disaster, but Samuel could not stop himself from thinking it anyway.

"I'm sorry I'm late." Miss Thatcher stood in the doorway, wringing her hands and looking generally miserable. He could tell she'd been crying, and he worried it had been because of their earlier encounter. He rose to greet her.

"Please don't trouble yourself." She hurried forward to the seat with the other place setting, seating herself before he could come around to pull out her chair.

"I'm glad you've joined me," Samuel said. "I worried that I'd offended you."

"No!" she exclaimed, a little too loudly. "Nothing of the sort." She took her serviette and unfolded it.

Samuel glanced at the sideboard where the food was located and waited for Miss Thatcher to notice it. When, after an awkward, silent moment of her repeatedly smoothing and adjusting the cloth across her lap, it did not appear she would, he brought everything over to the table, placing it well within her reach. Only when he'd sat again and started eating did she begin to serve herself; but even then she still did not look at him.

He searched his mind for a safe topic of conversation. "I believe Grace continues to fare well at Sutherland Hall."

Miss Thatcher looked up, hope alight in her expression. "Have you another letter?"

"Not yet. But I plan to see her today. If she has written, I will bring the letter directly to you."

"Thank you," Miss Thatcher said. "You are far too kind to us all."

Samuel scoffed. "There is no such thing as too much kindness."

Miss Thatcher made no response to this, and again Samuel was left wondering if he had said something wrong. He remembered her being shy during their few, previous interactions, but never so quiet as she was now. Their meal continued in uncomfortable silence. He asked himself why it was he'd felt the need to invite her to join him.

Because Grace continuously asks of news about her family. Samuel could not yet tell Grace of her siblings' presence here. Her situation with Nicholas was still tenuous at best, and Samuel had promised himself that he would allow their relationship to develop without providing Grace a way out—yet.

But he'd thought he could at least look after her sister for her and perhaps learn something that would ease Grace's mind about the girl's welfare. So far, all he had discovered this morning was that Miss Thatcher did not care for conversation. Or she did not care for him. Or possibly both.

"I hate porridge. I won't eat it. I won't! I won't!" Beth came screaming into the room right on schedule.

Samuel sent a silent plea heavenward as she launched herself at him, not quite clearing the corner of the table and sending the platter of eggs tumbling to the floor.

Miss Thatcher gasped. Beth clapped her hands over her mouth, then buried her face in his shoulder and sobbed, just as her distraught nanny appeared in the doorway, out of breath and looking rather disheveled with her cap tilted to one side.

"Can we not have one morning of peace around here?" Samuel asked, uncertain whether he felt more exasperated with his daughter or her nanny.

"I'm so sorry, sir," the latter said between gulps of air. "She got away again, and once more, she's refused to eat her breakfast." She thrust a filled bowl forward, evidence of her charge's disobedience.

"It's mush again, Papa. Why must I eat it?" Beth placed her little hands on his cheeks and looked at him directly, her large, blue eyes imploring him to understand. Samuel felt himself wavering. How could he deny her anything when he had already denied her a mother? Yet something must be done. Her behavior was becoming entirely out of control.

"Beth, look at this mess you've made." He spoke in the sternest voice he could muster, which sounded rather soft to his own ears.

Her face crumpled. "I'm sorry, sir." She climbed down from his lap and began gathering the eggs from the floor.

He was at once suspicious of her contrite behavior. Generally Beth was only apologetic or agreeable when she wanted something.

"That will be all, Mary," Samuel said wearily. "I'll return her to the nursery shortly. Thank you."

Mary gave a curt nod and stepped forward to place the bowl of mush on the table, then turned on her heel and exited the room. Samuel leaned back in his chair and sighed, only then remembering his guest.

Miss Thatcher was smiling at him—the first smile he'd seen from her all morning. He frowned, displeased at being the object of her amusement. He opened his mouth to excuse himself and put an end to their awkward breakfast, when she surprised him again by speaking without prompting.

"May I?" She stood and reached for Beth's bowl of porridge before he could answer. She pulled it toward herself and poked the spoon around in it a moment. "Mmm. The very best kind."

She wishes to eat Beth's mush?

"You may have it if you'd like," Samuel said, taken aback by such atrocious manners. Grace had said her sister was extremely shy, but she'd failed to mention anything about her being odd. Perhaps she had something amiss in her mind.

Unfortunate.

Like her sister, she was very pretty and might have made a good match.

Miss Thatcher scooted her chair back slightly, leaned forward, and ducked her head under the table. "Your name is Beth, isn't it?"

Samuel glanced down to see Beth drop the handful of squished eggs she had been collecting. She looked curiously at their guest and nodded.

"Would you like to play a game?" Miss Thatcher's voice came muffled from beneath the table.

Beth nodded again.

"Will you come and sit by me?" Miss Thatcher patted the chair beside her.

Without so much as a glance in her father's direction to ask permission, Beth crawled beneath the table to the other side and climbed onto the chair beside Miss Thatcher, who herself was sitting properly again, though, with her hair somewhat in disarray, having brushed it against the tablecloth.

"I like your dress," Beth said, running her fingers over the beads adorning Miss Thatcher's sleeve.

"Thank you."

Samuel noticed that Miss Thatcher did not shy from Beth's touch or seem bothered by it.

Spying the bowl of porridge, Beth made a face and pushed it far away from her.

Miss Thatcher took the bowl and pulled it close to her own plate, out of Beth's reach.

"When I was a little girl, we ate mush like this every morning."

"*Every* morning?" Beth asked, sounding properly horrified.

"Except on those days when we had no breakfast at all," Miss Thatcher said, as if not having breakfast had been an ordinary occurrence.

Beth's eyes grew large. "None?"

"None," Miss Thatcher said dismissively. "But I wish to tell you about the game we played when we did have breakfast."

"What was it? Tell me," Beth demanded. She sat up on her knees and leaned toward Miss Thatcher with rapt attention. Samuel relaxed in his chair, finding that she had captured his interest as well.

"Every morning, we pretended that an evil king had sent us the porridge. Some mornings, we had to eat it quickly before he returned, took it from us, and threw us in a dungeon. Once in a great while, the king was careless, and there would be jewels in our bowls. If we were very careful, and ate very fast, and found the jewels before he returned, then we could keep them."

"Real jewels?" Beth asked, moving closer still. Samuel worried she would fall from her chair if Miss Thatcher's story went much longer.

Miss Thatcher shook her head. "Pretend jewels," she whispered. "But you have them too." She took the spoon and fished a raisin from Beth's bowl. "Right here." She pointed at the raisin. "I think this one is a ruby."

"It's a *raisin.*" Beth giggled, obviously enthralled with the game—*and* with Miss Thatcher. Samuel was too.

"You must use your imagination," Miss Thatcher whispered. "The evil king—" she inclined her head toward Samuel—"has fallen asleep at the table, but his naps are very short."

Samuel closed his eyes, lolled back in his chair, and pretended to snore loudly. Beth's resulting laughter warmed his heart. He peeked through half-closed eyes as the game continued.

"Dear Miss Beth," Miss Thatcher spoke in a distressed voice, "we must hurry to find the jewels before the king awakens. If he finds them first, he will surely take them from us, and we will be punished. But if we discover them all before he awakens, we shall be able to buy our freedom."

Beth reached for the bowl and eagerly grabbed the spoon.

"Wait," Miss Thatcher whispered, glancing at Samuel. "We must eat with care, ever so quietly, if we do not wish to awaken the king. We must take small bites and chew with our mouths closed, or he will hear us."

Samuel watched in astonishment as Beth nodded. "But

what will you eat?" she whispered to Miss Thatcher. "You haven't got a bowl of jewels."

"No," Miss Thatcher said sadly. "The king has only given me this large rock." She poked at her roll with her fork. "He has commanded that it be gone before he wakes, or I shall be in a great deal of trouble."

"If I finish finding the rubies, I'll help you," Beth offered.

Miss Thatcher smiled at her, and they began eating, quickly but with the best table manners Samuel had ever witnessed from his daughter.

A few times during their meal, he snorted or shifted in his chair and pretended to be talking in his sleep. "Jewels. Someone has stolen my jewels."

Beth's whispered admonition for Miss Thatcher to hurry reached his ears.

"You've done it," Miss Thatcher whispered at last. "The king still sleeps, and you've found all the jewels. You are free."

"Oh no, she's not!" Samuel jumped up from the table, arms outstretched. Beth shrieked and leaped from her chair, running from him. He chased her around the table twice before capturing her and tickling her mercilessly. "Where are my rubies? Give me my rubies."

"Papa. It was just a game." She laughed and shrieked, but he refused to put her down.

"You'll never be free. You're mine. Forever." He smothered her face with kisses, and she threw her hands around his neck.

"Can we play this game every day? Can she come to breakfast every day? I like her." Beth looked at Miss Thatcher still seated in her chair, and Samuel realized that his daughter did not know their guest. He'd never felt so remiss; he'd also never been so happy to introduce his daughter.

"Beth, this is Miss Thatcher. She and her brother are visiting for a while."

"Miss Helen, if you please," she said, head bent slightly, looking up at him through long eyelashes, as if she was afraid of his reaction to her request. "Miss Thatcher is my older sister."

"Of course. My apologies." Becoming acquainted with Grace as he had, it seemed his manners had slipped with regards to her sister. "Miss Helen, this is my Beth. Mine forever," he added in his growly king voice as he held her tight. She giggled again, then squirmed out of his grasp and ran to stand beside Miss Helen.

"Will you come to breakfast every day?"

Miss Helen's face flushed red, and she looked down at her lap. "I—"

"Miss Helen has a great many responsibilities." Even as he said the words, Samuel wondered what those were. What *did* she do all day? "But perhaps we can arrange for the two of you to play sometime." An idea formed as he spoke, and he felt the first hope regarding his daughter's behavior that he'd felt for some time. "Run along now and apologize to Mary."

Beth leaned forward, gave Miss Helen a brief hug, then scurried off. Samuel watched her go and found Miss Helen watching his daughter as well. Before she could get all jittery or quiet again, he came around the table and sat beside her in the seat Beth had vacated.

He picked up the empty porridge bowl. "This is impressive. You have quite a way with children."

"I find them easy to talk to," Miss Helen said, her gaze once more directed at her lap.

Samuel wished she would look at him but guessed that doing so made her uncomfortable. For all the ease she had exhibited with his daughter, she seemed to feel none at all with him. "Have you ever considered becoming a governess?"

This got her attention, and she looked up at him with something close to despair.

"I did not mean to offend," he rushed to say. *How many times have I already apologized for that very thing this morning?* Miss Helen was proving as impossible to converse with as her sister was easy to talk to. "I only meant that if your inheritance does not come through, if the court does not rule in your favor, such a position is something you may wish to consider. You have worked no less than a miracle with my daughter this morning."

"She is a delightful child."

"I am afraid that a few in this household would disagree with you. Beth has always been precocious, but lately, it has turned into headstrong stubbornness. I find myself at a loss as to how to handle it—to handle her. That was the very problem I was contemplating in the garden this morning when you came upon me talking to myself."

"Not to yourself. You were talking to Elizabeth," Miss Helen corrected, meeting his gaze directly. "And why shouldn't you speak to her? She is Beth's mother and was no doubt your dearest friend."

"Yes," Samuel said, somewhat astounded at her understanding. He smiled. "I knew I could trust you."

"And am I to trust you by seeking a position as a governess?"

"Perhaps." *A young lady with her education ought to be able to get a good position.* He wondered at what age children typically needed a governess instead of a nanny. "I could help you find a good family."

The distress returned to her eyes, and her gaze flitted to her lap.

What did I say?

"Not right away, of course. So long as Grace is at

Sutherland Hall and your inheritance remains undecided, you are most welcome to remain here. I hope you realize that."

"Thank you."

Samuel heard the relief in her voice. *That's it. She is frightened of leaving.*

"Perhaps, in the meantime, you might spend part of your afternoons here—with Beth."

"I would be happy to." Miss Helen pushed her chair back and rose suddenly. "I should be going."

He stood and moved aside to allow her passage. "Would you like an escort?"

"No, thank you." She continued walking. "Good day, Mr. Preston. I thank you for breakfast."

"Good day, Miss Helen," Samuel said, surprised to realize that it might be good after all.

CHAPTER 3

"I've bungled the whole thing," Helen said to Harrison. "Mr. Preston believes that I am good for nothing but tending children." She stood outside the stable door, her skirts held above the ground as she shared her woes.

"Did he say that exactly?" Harrison removed the bridle from the mare that had driven their buggy.

"He suggested I look for a position as a governess," Helen said. "All because I played a game with his daughter. I was only trying to help." She imagined what Miranda would say about her behavior this morning.

Ladies do not crawl under the table to play games at breakfast. Helen stomped her foot, angry with herself.

"Careful where you're stepping," Harrison warned. He scooped oats into the stall bucket, then backed out and closed the door behind him. "Come. Let's get you out of here before you ruin your pretty dress."

"I *should* change." Helen continued to hold her skirts up as they left the stable and headed across the field. "Miranda was right. This gown was much too fancy to wear today. Whatever was I thinking?"

"What most women do," Harrison said. "That looking your best is the way to a man's heart."

"Isn't it?" Helen asked. "Isn't that why women dress up in lovely gowns and curl their hair and use face powders?"

"Not being a female, I can't say exactly," he teased. "But I expect that is the reason. And it works—to a point."

"What do you mean?" Helen asked.

"Appearances will get you only so far. They may capture a man's interest, but it takes more to hold it."

"*What* will hold it?" Helen asked. "What qualities does a man look for when seeking a wife?"

Harrison glanced at her askew. "A wife, eh? Perhaps Miranda was right to be worried about you. What happened to our little girl who didn't want anything to do with men?"

"I *don't* want anything to do with *men*," Helen said. *Just one man, and he is still in love with his deceased wife.* "I am only trying to understand how this world works."

"Mm-hmm," Harrison said.

Helen knew he could see right through her, but she didn't care. She'd had her one chance to impress Mr. Preston, but she'd done the opposite. Now she wanted only to know what she should have done differently, should the unlikely event occur that she ever met another kind man she need not fear.

"If a man is wise," Harrison began, "he wants a woman he can respect and admire, one who will be a companion in many ways."

"Do men not admire attractiveness?" Helen asked, trying to understand, and wishing Harrison would speak more plainly. "What earns a man's respect?"

"Could be many things," Harrison said. "Take Miranda and me, for instance. We're getting on in years, and neither of us is as attractive as we once were—" He stopped walking and turned to Helen. "Don't you ever let Miranda know I said that."

"I won't. I promise," she said solemnly. She could scarcely believe he was speaking of Miranda at all—she and Grace had attempted to broach the subject with him before, but never had he said so much as a word about their lady's maid.

"A man and a woman at our age can still care for each other, and not many of those feelings will have anything to do with appearances. A man may be attracted to a woman because of the way she does something. He may admire her for her strengths, or her kindnesses."

What did Harrison admire about Miranda? She was very strong—in will, anyway.

"I appreciate people for the way they treat others," Harrison said. "These past years—especially these past months—no one has watched out for you girls more or cared more for you than Miranda has. She'd defend you to her last breath. I don't mind saying that awhile back, I was worried that Miranda might be nearing hers. She was ill, yet still caring for your sister. A powerful spirit that woman has, and I respect her for it."

"Harrison, that is the most eloquent speech I have ever heard," Helen declared. "Why do you not tell Miranda that very thing? You know she cares for you too."

Harrison waved her suggestion away, then coughed into his hand, looking down, but not before Helen caught his face reddening.

"It would seem that I am not the only one around here at a loss as to how to proceed," she said.

"Why should *you* be at a loss?" Harrison said. "You know exactly what to do next. Mr. Preston has paid you a compliment and told you what he values."

"He appreciates my way with children," Helen said. "How is that romantic in the least?"

Harrison shook his head and grunted. "Females. Always making everything more complicated than it needs to be." They reached the front walk leading to the guest house and stopped. He took out a handkerchief and blew into it loudly. Helen felt a moment of pity for him, with his nose red from sneezing and his nearly incessant cough. He didn't take to this part of the country well at all.

"What means more to Mr. Preston than anything in the world?" Harrison asked.

"His daughter," Helen said, remembering the way he'd held Beth close and introduced her as "*my* Beth."

Harrison nodded. "And *you* made a connection with her without even trying. It was the best thing you could have done; Mr. Preston has given you the greatest compliment. The way to his heart may well be through his daughter—but don't you dare use her that way."

"I wouldn't," Helen exclaimed. And while that was true, she could not deny that she had been somewhat set on that path, of using someone—Beth's father—this morning.

That would have been wrong too. No matter that she'd believed she could care for Mr. Preston in return for his name and the money that would save them. *But now . . .*

Now that she'd glimpsed the depth of the feelings he still felt for his wife, Helen could not continue her pursuit. She would not do anything that might hurt him further. But she could befriend his daughter.

"Simply care for her, as you have already started to," Harrison said.

"I shall," Helen said. It was too effortless to possibly work as a ploy to gain Mr. Preston's attention, so she would be free from any worry or guilt there. Befriending his daughter might relieve his burden though. It might be one small way she could repay the kindnesses he'd shown to her family.

"These things take time," Harrison said, still giving her

advice, though she needed it no longer—with regard to Mr. Preston, at least.

"Don't go putting on airs. Any man worth his weight will love you as you are." Harrison smiled at her in a manner similar to that with which Mr. Preston had looked at his daughter. It warmed Helen's heart.

"Thank you." She stepped forward and hugged him impulsively. He patted her back once, somewhat awkwardly then stepped away, glancing over his shoulder.

"Miranda," he whispered as the sound of marching feet approached.

Hugging one's servants was not proper, but Harrison had always seemed more of a friend than a servant. Still, Miranda would disapprove if she saw it.

"Tell her how you feel," Helen whispered back. She turned and once again headed down the lane toward Mr. Preston's house.

"Where are you off to now?" Harrison asked Helen as Miranda opened the door.

"I have been invited to play," Helen called over her shoulder.

"In that dress?" Miranda stood on the step beside Harrison.

Helen walked backwards, watching them both a moment, thinking how fine they looked standing together, and thinking how fine they had been for her and her siblings.

Almost like the parents we never had. How she loved them. How dear they were.

"Beth admired my dress at breakfast," she called. "I am wearing it so we can play Camelot."

CHAPTER

Helen knocked on the door of Mr. Preston's residence and waited until the butler came to admit her.

"I believe Miss Beth is expecting you," he said cheerfully before Helen had a chance to explain the reason for her visit. He stepped aside so she might enter.

"I saw you from the window," Beth said, jumping from the second stair and running across the floor. "Have you come to play with me?"

"I have," Helen said, glancing about the foyer and feeling both relief and regret that Mr. Preston was nowhere to be seen.

"I knew it." Beth beamed. "Papa said you might come. I'll show you the nursery." She took Helen's hand.

"If you wish," Helen said. "Though I thought perhaps you might like to play outside. It is a lovely day, and we won't have good weather much longer."

"Oh, yes." Beth changed direction and headed toward the front doors.

"Shouldn't you ask your nanny first?" Helen suggested. She didn't want to get the little girl in trouble or cause anyone to worry.

Beth frowned. She dropped Helen's hand and retreated across the foyer, dragging her feet. Helen worked to contain a smile. How many times had she seen similar behavior? With her grandfather's permission, she'd first become friends with, then later tutored, many of the children whose parents he'd employed. Many a time, Helen had witnessed feet dragging across a floor and shoes being scuffed as children left their play—or studies—and went to do their parents' bidding.

Perhaps I am qualified to be a governess. The thought of leaving Grace and Christopher to live with strangers rather terrified her, but it did sound decidedly better than ending up married to a stranger like the new duke—or worse.

Behind her the butler closed the front doors, and Helen wandered farther into the circular foyer, to the center of the room, where a table stood with a large vase overflowing with gorgeous yellow roses from outside. She leaned forward, inhaling their sweet scent.

"I cut them myself every morning," Mr. Preston said.

Helen lifted her head and jumped back, feeling very much like a child caught at some mischief.

Mr. Preston strode toward her. "I didn't expect to see you back so soon. Have you a letter you wish me to give your sister?"

"Not since yesterday. I've come to play with Beth." Helen glanced about the room, eager for Beth to return. "I have thought about what you said—about being a governess. It is a good idea."

"And one that took you by surprise," he guessed.

"Yes," Helen admitted. "If you would not mind—" She forced herself to meet his gaze briefly. "I should like to spend a bit of time with Beth each day. Since leaving my grandfather's house, I have not been around any children, and I realized this morning how I have missed it."

Mr. Preston smiled at her so warmly that Helen felt a peculiar fluttering in her stomach. "I would be delighted if you would visit Beth every day. I fear she is often lonely and in want of company."

The subject of their discussion appeared on the stairs, racing down, followed by her nanny. When the latter reached the foyer, she looked from Mr. Preston to Helen and caught her breath.

"Miss Beth says you have come to take her for an outing."

"We shall not go beyond the boundaries of the estate," Helen said, speaking more to Mr. Preston than the nanny.

"Miss Helen will be spending some time each day with Beth from now on," Mr. Preston told her. "She is to be allowed to take Beth outside or to visit with her in the nursery as she wishes."

"Of course, sir," Nanny Mary said, looking rather pleased at the suggestion, Helen thought.

"Thank you." Helen mustered enough courage to smile shyly at Mr. Preston. She held her hand out to Beth. "Shall we be off?"

"Where to?" Beth asked, placing her small hand in Helen's.

Helen looked down at her charge as they turned away from the others. "Why, to Camelot, of course."

Two hours later, Helen limped back toward Mr. Preston's house, her feet protesting the time spent galloping about on imaginary horses while wearing slippers too fancy and uncomfortable for gallivanting. Beth lagged behind her.

Helen stopped to wait for the little girl to catch up again. "It seems I have worn you out,"

"I'm hungry," Beth complained.

"Tomorrow we shall see about a picnic," Helen said, and Beth's face brightened.

"With biscuits? Father and I once had a picnic with biscuits that had little sprinkles of sugar. I would like those, please."

"Since you have asked so politely, I shall see what can be arranged." Helen reached out to take Beth's hand once more. Swinging their arms, they crossed the lawn and made their way through the garden—the great forest surrounding Camelot—to the house—King Arthur's castle.

"If this is King Arthur's castle," Beth said as they approached the door, "who is the evil king who tried to steal our rubies at breakfast?"

Helen considered a moment. "He is Arthur's sworn enemy, Mordred, and he is very jealous of Arthur. While Arthur and his knights were away this morning, Mordred tried to take over his Round Table and kingdom."

"And take our jewels," Beth said.

"Yes." Helen knelt on the top step by the girl. "Thank you for playing today, Miss Beth."

"You are welcome, Miss Helen," Beth said with a curtsy.

Helen smiled. "Very good." She had explained the importance of chivalry and manners in the time of Camelot, just as her grandfather had imparted some of his wisdom, decorum, and expectations to Helen, Grace, and Christopher after they'd come to live with him. Instead of lectures, he'd shared stories, which they'd remembered while trying their best to be like the gallant heroes and noble heroines they'd so admired.

Helen watched to see that Beth was safely inside and met by her nanny, then began the walk to the guesthouse. The day was beautiful, and she found herself reluctant to return inside, where activities limited to reading and sewing awaited her. Instead of following the lane, she decided to enjoy the sunshine awhile longer.

Once more, she stepped beneath the arbor leading into the garden. Bending down behind a tall hedge, she first loosened her slippers, then removed them, along with her stockings. Miranda would disapprove, no doubt, and Harrison would happily accompany her around the garden, but after listening to Beth's chatter all morning, Helen longed for some quiet time to reflect.

How often had she and Christopher wandered in Grandfather's gardens this way, their bare feet running over soft grass as they played? At eighteen, Grace had been too old for such freedoms or frivolities, and much of her time had instead been monopolized by tutors attempting to teach her all she had previously missed—important skills like learning to dance La Boulangere, how to properly carry a reticule and use a fan, and how to address members of the gentry—all so Grace might be considered an accomplished young woman. Helen and Christopher had received instruction, too, but not in the same urgent and rushed manner as Grace. And because of the attention initially focused on her, the younger siblings had been allowed hours of freedom and idleness, for the first time in their lives.

Remembering those times with much fondness, and missing her siblings, Helen crossed beneath the arch and into Mr. Preston's garden for the second time that day. At least one good thing had come of her meeting this morning—Mr. Preston had invited her to enjoy the garden whenever she wished. She intended to avail herself of that offer before the weather forced her indoors for a season—a season sure to be dreary without either Grace or Christopher for company. And now she'd lost her hopes of Mr. Preston's companionship as well.

The day had not gone at all as she'd expected, and Helen realized the fault was hers. For all her preparations at gaining

Mr. Preston's attention with her appearance, she had not taken the same pains thinking over what to say to him. Admiring him from afar was one thing; being near him, as she had discovered today, was entirely different. It had not been unpleasant—she still fancied him as much as ever—but she realized that she did not know the first thing about conversing with a gentleman.

If only Christopher were here. He might have had some suggestions. But his sojourn in London seemed never-ending, as did the fight for their inheritance.

She followed the path to the courtyard where she'd discovered Mr. Preston that morning. In addition to not thinking through what she might say to him earlier, she hadn't considered what *his* feelings might be, either. It had not previously occurred to her that he might still be grieving his deceased wife.

When her mother died, Helen had been too young to remember whether their father had been sorrowful, but she very much doubted it, other than mourning the income Mother had brought in.

But Mr. Preston seemed as opposite a man as one could be from her father, and Helen felt she ought to have known that his heart would still be tender. She knew it now and never would forget the forlorn sight of him this morning.

Instead of continuing around the house, Helen took the second path, taking care with her bare feet and admiring the colors and fragrances of the garden as she walked. Somewhere this direction was the wall separating Mr. Preston's property from Lord Sutherland's.

Grace is on the other side. A longing for her sister filled Helen.

But Mr. Preston had asked that Helen not let Grace know of her proximity. He did not wish Grace to know her family was so close. At first Helen had believed this to be terribly cruel, but then he had explained himself. He wanted to give Lord Sutherland and Grace every opportunity to work their situation out on their own, even to fall in love with each other—a very real possibility, he believed.

From Grace's letters, Helen could see it happening already. In spite of their differences—in spite of Lord Sutherland's ogre-like nature—Grace was coming to care for him.

Helen followed the path around another corner and came to the end of both the gate and the stone path as she nearly ran into the very wall she'd been thinking of.

I didn't realize I was so close. Mr. Preston might be upset to find me here. But Mr. Preston himself sat perched on the wall only a short distance away, his manner quite different from what it had been when she'd discovered him in the courtyard. He sat casually, folded arms propped on his bent knee, his other leg swinging in time to his whistling as he looked down upon—*Grace!* She stood on the opposite side of the fence, her head just visible above it.

"I think I shall lose my mind if I don't find something more to do here."

Helen's heart squeezed at the sound of her sister's voice. *I should go. It is wrong to be here.* But the knowledge could not overcome her desire to stay, to hear Grace's voice and see for herself that her sister was well.

Before she dared another peek, she took two steps back, then pressed herself close to the gate and the brilliant red foliage covering it. Grace had disappeared, but she reappeared again a second later.

"You do realize," Mr. Preston said to her, "that if you fall off that bench and break your leg, I'll have the difficult choice of leaving you here to suffer or facing the wrath of your betrothed and admitting to our trysts."

Trysts? Helen's head jerked upright, her hair snagging in the leaves.

"Don't call them that," Grace said. "This is not a tryst. You and I are but friends."

"So I am reminded every time we part," Mr. Preston grumbled.

"If this is too difficult, I will not come anymore. I can find another way to post Helen's letters."

"No." Mr. Preston's sharp answer made Helen jump; one slipper fell from her hand. She tensed, waiting for him to look her direction and wishing fervently that she'd changed her dress when she had the opportunity. The cream silk provided a glaring contrast to the crimson hedge behind her and might be easily spied through the gate. But Mr. Preston appeared not to have heard her. When he returned his attention to Grace's side of the fence, Helen let out a slow breath and brought a hand to her rapidly beating heart.

"What is wrong with you today?" Grace's voice again. "Are you not the one who has been encouraging me to make the most of my circumstance, to try to be on good terms with Lord Sutherland?"

"Aye." Mr. Preston's response sounded rather surly. Helen watched as he drew his knee to his chest and set his chin upon it. "Perhaps I was too generous in my original advice. Can you not make the man despise you—cause him to throw you out of his house so you come running to mine?"

What? A pang of hurt throbbed in Helen's chest. *Could Mr. Preston care for Grace? When—how . . .*

"And have Father throw Helen to the nearest shark?" Grace asked. "No, thank you. You realize I must stay here—for now," she added, her voice quiet.

Helen's mind reeled. *Mr. Preston cares for Grace. And it sounds as if she may care for him.*

I must leave. She'd heard enough—enough to have whatever faint hope she might have still had concerning Mr.

Preston dashed, and to feel somehow betrayed by both. This was what came of eavesdropping. *Would that I had learned my lesson this morning.* She crouched to retrieve her slipper, taking care to be quiet.

"Don't leave," Mr. Preston called.

Helen paused. *Is he talking to me?*

"I'm sorry," he said.

For what?

"You stay on your side, remember?" Grace's voice rang out, playfully scolding.

"Bossy today, aren't we?" Mr. Preston said. But he didn't sound angry.

They are teasing each other. Helen retrieved her slipper and stood slowly. She pressed a hand to her stomach and turned her head to better listen, telling herself she would stay only another moment, just long enough to understand. She had to have misheard. *I must be wrong in my assumption.* After all, Mr. Preston himself had made it so that Grace was forced to stay at Sutherland Hall.

Their banter continued as they spoke of sewing and a new dress.

"I am not a Sutherland," Grace said. "I do not want him to purchase anything for me—not a dress, not even fabric to make one. He's already spent enough to protect Helen."

Don't blame me, Helen thought, growing more upset by the minute. *I did not ask you to ruin your reputation.* But she might as well have. Her refusal to marry the new duke had cost them all so much. *It is my fault Grace ended up in this predicament.*

A predicament, it seemed, she was rather enjoying at the moment.

"I'll pay for it," Mr. Preston offered, continuing their discussion about a gown.

"Can you imagine Lord Sutherland's expression when he compliments me on my dress and I tell him, 'This gown is courtesy of Mr. Preston'?" Grace said. "You'd hear his shouting all the way in your drawing room."

"Does he still yell a lot?" Mr. Preston asked, sounding worried.

"Not so much," Grace said. "We are learning to tolerate each other and which topics to avoid."

"And does he compliment you on your gowns?" Mr. Preston persisted.

"Yes."

Helen heard wistfulness in Grace's reply, and it was all she could do not to march from her hiding place and demand an explanation. What was her sister thinking? Did she care for *both* men? How could she use Mr. Preston like that, and how did she dare to meet him and converse so, with the temperamental Lord Sutherland lurking about?

What game are you playing, sister?

The entire situation was so utterly unlike Grace. She'd never wanted to marry. None of them did. They had plans for an uncomplicated and happy life together, safely away from their father and his debts. Helen could think only that Grace was enmeshing herself in even more trouble.

"You are lost in thought," Mr. Preston said to Grace. "Apparently his compliments leave you much to contemplate." Now it was Mr. Preston who sounded wistful.

Helen felt ill and promised herself that she would write to Grace today, at once—as soon as she returned to the guesthouse—to tell her sister about Mr. Preston's wife and how he still loved her. Surely if Grace knew and understood that, she would not tease him so.

"Tell me more about Elizabeth," Grace said.

Or would she?

"What would she have done on a day like today?" Grace went on.

"Many things," Mr. Preston said. "Today is her birthday."

LOVING HELEN

Helen's hand fluttered to her throat, which had suddenly constricted. Of all days to interrupt his morning walk! *No wonder he appeared so sorrowful.*

The remainder of their conversation was lost to Helen. She turned from the wall and retraced her steps through the garden, her mind filled only with the image of Mr. Preston, head in his hands, alone in Elizabeth's garden.

On her birthday.

And I believed he would be pleased to see me.

A burst of his laughter reached her ears, and Helen realized that where she had failed, Grace was having obvious success, making his heart lighter on this somber day.

The courtyard came into view as more laughter—a child's—came from the opposite direction.

Helen froze, uncertain what to do. She would not mind seeing Beth, but her nanny would likely be with her, and Helen had no desire to explain her lack of shoes and escort, or her proximity to Mr. Preston, who was still conversing at the wall.

No doubt she had a guilty look upon her face. *Because I am* guilty—*and look what it has cost me.* Ducking into an alcove off the main passageway, she discovered another, less-used path leading from it. This she moved down quickly, until she became aware that the voices had increased volume once more. Though she could no longer view Grace and Mr. Preston, she could hear them again.

He still spoke of Elizabeth, clearly seeking comfort from Grace.

Beth's infectious laughter rang out, followed by her sweet voice calling for her father.

"Do you hear that?" Grace asked.

"I must go," Mr. Preston said, sounding rather alarmed.

Has something happened to Beth?

"Why?" Grace asked. "Who is it?"

"Daddy!"

A commotion followed, which Helen could not quite make out for all of Beth's shouting. When at last the child grew quiet, Grace's voice, subdued now, reached Helen one last time.

"Of course," Grace said. "I give you my word. I will not tell Lord Sutherland of your daughter."

Helen's mind was a whirlwind of thought. Could it be? Had Grace not known of Mr. Preston's daughter before today? Yet clearly, Mr. Preston admired Grace.

And Harrison suggested that Beth might be the way to gaining Mr. Preston's affection. Matters of the heart were not nearly so simple as that—no matter what Harrison said.

How foolish I am, Helen realized, *to have believed that wearing a pretty dress was enough to catch a man's attention.*

That Mr. Preston still loved his dead wife had endeared him to Helen even more, even if it meant his heart was closed. She'd been crushed to learn that the only hope she'd found for a favorable ending to her predicament was not to be.

Far worse than that, however, more devastating and confusing, was that Mr. Preston appeared to have developed an affection for Grace.

Yet she is betrothed to Lord Sutherland—at least in part because of Mr. Preston's actions.

Helen wandered until she found herself in the courtyard again, where she dropped onto a bench and tried to reason the situation out and stop the hurt spreading from her head to her heart.

Mr. Preston had described Elizabeth as strong-willed and vivacious—characteristics Grace was very much in possession of. A realization struck Helen, a painful blow to her already tattered soul. If Mr. Preston were ever to fall in love again—*and quite possibly he already has*—it would be with someone like his wife. *Someone like Grace.*

Never with someone like me.

CHAPTER 5

November

My Dearest Grace,
   In your absence I have become acquainted with a darling little girl...

Helen pulled her cloak tight to ward off the chill as she ran through the garden, searching for a place to hide. She really had to convince Beth that their days of playing outside ought to be over—for a few months, at least—and traded for cozy afternoons in the nursery. But each day was the same, with Beth longing to be outside. Cooped up as she was, with a nanny who understood nothing about evil kings and fairy princesses, Helen could not deny the little girl's plaintive requests. In the month since Helen had started visiting each day, Beth had become very dear to her.

While Helen had come to love Beth, it seemed Mr. Preston had been busy falling more in love with Grace. Helen had not been to the wall again, but she recognized the signs well enough . . . Mr. Preston's particularly cheerful disposition after returning from his afternoon walks, his hints and suggestions of what might be done to free Grace from her betrothal, and the little things about her that he mentioned here and there all indicated that the two of them had grown very close. Helen resigned herself to being nothing more than a friend of his daughter's, or perhaps Beth's aunt, if he married Grace.

Helen's was a romance ended before it had begun, and she could feel only grateful that she had not revealed her true feelings to Mr. Preston.

Beth's tiny voice rang out through the cold, announcing that she was beginning her search. Helen crouched behind a fountain and tucked her cloak around her so as to not be too obvious. She always allowed Beth to discover her, but a few minutes of searching made for a better game.

"Miss Helen! Miss Helen, where are you?" Giggling.

Helen smiled to herself. If need be, she'd call out a clue, but with the parameters they had set for hiding, it was not often necessary.

A noise behind her sent Helen jumping. She bumped against something, then whirled about to find Mr. Preston directly in front of her, holding a bunch of fresh-cut roses.

She brought a hand to her heart. "You startled me."

"As did you me." He smiled. "It is a rather cold afternoon for a walk, isn't it?"

"I am playing with Beth," Helen whispered, glancing over her shoulder. "Hiding."

"Ah," Mr. Preston said. "One of her favorite games of late. I'll be quiet."

Much to Helen's consternation, he crouched beside her. The sweet scent of flowers filled her senses, along with the aroma of cut pine and freshly dug earth. He lifted his arm, wiping perspiration from his brow and inadvertently smudging dirt across his face.

The smudge, when added to his mischievous grin, took

years from his face, making him appear almost boyish. Helen found herself wondering just how old Mr. Preston really was, and about the particulars of his situation—beyond owning a grand house and fine piece of property, and being extremely generous with both. He was not titled, but he did not appear to work for his bread. Curiosity overtook her nerves as she noted his dusty breeches and work worn shirt.

"What have you been doing?"

"Moving some of the roses inside for winter," he whispered. "Two years ago, I had a small conservatory built behind the house. Before winter, I move a dozen or so of Elizabeth's rosebushes inside. It allows us to continue growing them throughout the year, and to ensure that some always survive."

Though Elizabeth is gone, he makes certain her roses live on. "You do this yourself?" Helen asked, again touched by his devotion to his late wife.

"I manage the roses. The gardeners take care of the rest."

"Miss Helen, where are you?" Beth's call came again.

"I suppose you think me odd—doing a gardener's work." Mr. Preston offered a rueful smile. "It is just that—"

"—Caring for Elizabeth's roses is something you can do to show your continued love for her and to keep her memory alive." Helen smiled encouragingly. There was nothing odd about it.

"Yes." His look turned searching. "You have an uncanny ability to understand people, Miss Helen."

Not people. You.

"At times—like this," Mr. Preston began, "I feel, perhaps, that I could tell you anything, even of my loneliness and heartache, and, with more than sympathy, you would understand. Why is that?"

Helen could not seem to pull her eyes from his. "Though our sorrows have been different, the results are much the same. Once experienced, loneliness is not easily forgotten."

His brow quirked. "Who said that?"

"I just did," Helen said, returning his perplexed look with one of her own. What did he mean by such a question?

"Oh."

For some reason he sounded almost disappointed.

"My apologies," Mr. Preston continued. "I thought you were quoting literature, as your sister often does."

Helen swallowed the lump in her throat. "Grace is very well read." The reminder of his relationship with Grace, along with Beth's sudden appearance in the courtyard, pulled Helen's attention back to the game. A good thing.

She ducked lower to avoid being seen quite yet, and Mr. Preston did the same, then scooted closer. His shoulder brushed hers, and it was all Helen could do to keep both her balance and her wits. When he placed his hand upon her arm she jumped and nearly gave up their hiding place. He beckoned for her to follow.

She hesitated, uncertain, but he motioned again. Leaving the fountain, she followed him away from the courtyard, toward the back of the house. Once around the corner, she turned back to watch for Beth.

"Miss Helen?" Beth stood near the fountain and turned a slow circle. "Come out, Miss Helen." She sounded less certain this time.

Mr. Preston cleared his throat as he stepped into view. "The king has stolen your princess." He spoke in a gravelly voice. "You will have to come rescue her." He grabbed Helen's mittened hand and pulled her along. Too startled to protest, she stumbled along after him.

"I'll save you!" Beth cried as Mr. Preston pulled Helen onto the open field behind the house. He continued running, and Helen did her best to keep up until they stopped suddenly at the base of a large ash tree. Mr. Preston pulled her behind it. Helen stood beside him, breathless from her run and his nearness.

"Hold these." He thrust the roses into her hands.

Beth wasn't far behind. "Let Miss Helen go, you evil king!"

Mr. Preston did, popping out from behind the tree and grabbing Beth so that she let out a shriek that was part laughter, part terror.

"I've made a surprise for you," he said, setting her on the ground. Reaching to a limb above him, he pulled a rope looped there, releasing a fine, wood-plank swing. "What do you think?"

Instead of answering, Beth struggled to climb onto the seat. He picked her up and made sure she was settled. "Ready?"

She nodded, and he pulled the swing back, then let it go. Beth's laughter filled the yard, and Mr. Preston stood aside, a satisfied smile on his lips.

This explains the smell of fresh-cut wood—a swing for Beth. Helen buried her face in the roses. *Flowers for his wife.* What kind deeds and gifts would Mr. Preston bestow upon Grace if he married her? Something thoughtful, certainly.

Helen lingered behind the tree, out of sight of both father and daughter, and, she was certain, quite forgotten by both. She considered placing the roses on the ground and sneaking away but could not bring herself to stop watching the two. This was how fathers ought to care for their daughters. Her father had never made her anything or given her any sort of gift. He'd never said he loved her, had never so much as hugged her. The only physical contact she could ever recall had been punishments. She touched her cheek, remembering clearly the sting of his slap.

Mr. Preston stopped the swing and lifted Beth in his arms as she called out, "Miss Helen's turn now."

"All right," Mr. Preston said. "If she wants one," he

added, upon seeing Helen's mouth open uncertainly.

He thinks I will not. Desperate to prove him wrong—to prove that she could be both good company and adventurous like Grace, Helen lifted her chin and stepped forward.

"I would very much like a turn. And what good manners, Beth, for thinking of others and offering to share your new swing."

Beth beamed at the praise. Helen laid the roses carefully on the ground as Mr. Preston set Beth near the base of the tree.

"Stay right there," he said. "Out of the way of the swing."

Beth nodded as she pressed her back up against the trunk. "Go high, Miss Helen. It tickles your tummy."

Helen held onto the ropes and sat on the wood board. "I have never done this before. Is there a trick to it?"

"Never?" Mr. Preston leaned around the front of the swing to look at her. He grinned. "You are in for a treat. Hang on tight, and if you feel I am pushing you too high, let me know."

He grabbed the ropes on either side and stepped backwards, pulling the swing, and Helen with it. He let go, and she flew forward through the air, feet thrust out ahead of her, cold stinging her cheeks, and the breeze sending her hair flying. Like Beth had, Helen let out a squeal of delight. She couldn't help herself. Beth was right; the sensation did tickle.

"Higher?" Mr. Preston shouted behind her.

"Yes, please," Helen said, then felt his hands upon her shoulders, pushing her forward. Her stomach fluttered again, which she could not credit entirely to the new height the swing had attained.

Beth was on her feet, clapping and shouting instructions. "Put your feet out more. Lean your head back."

Helen tried this and for a second found herself looking

up into Mr. Preston's smiling, dirt-smudged face as he pushed her once more.

She laughed, partly at how amusing he looked and partly because she was having so much fun—more than she could ever recall. When, after a few more times, he grabbed the ropes and slowed the swing, she felt keen disappointment.

She slid from the seat and stood, surprised to find that her legs were not shaky at all. "Beth, that is the most marvelous contraption. You are a very lucky little girl to have a father who builds you such toys."

"It's rather the wrong season for it," Mr. Preston said ruefully. "Your nose and cheeks are red with cold, Miss Helen."

"A small price to pay for such amusement," she replied. "Besides, you've dirt smudged on your face. I'd say we are quite the pair."

His head tilted to the side, and his look turned quizzical. Only then did Helen realize what she'd said. "I'm sorry. I did not mean to imply—"

"I know." He reached out, briefly touching her hand and silencing her apology. "But if you would be so kind as to help me rid my face of dirt." He stood still, chin jutted forward, waiting expectantly.

"You've some there—across the bridge of your nose," Helen said, pointing. "And more across your brow."

He wiped at both but only made the smudges worse. Beth giggled.

Mr. Preston turned pleading eyes to Helen. "Won't you help me—please?"

Her hand trembled as she reached out, brushing her fingers across his brow. She had never touched a man's face before, not even Christopher's. She'd kissed Grandfather's cheek on occasion, but that felt different than this. Mr. Preston's eyes closed beneath her ministrations as her mittens gently wiped his nose and forehead. "There. All gone." Her hand fell to her side as she stepped back. His eyes opened with that same inquiring look he'd given her a few moments ago.

"Thank you." His voice was nearly as quiet as hers had been, and for a moment, they simply stood there, lost in each other's gaze. Helen felt the ties of their friendship strengthening.

He trusts me. He had shown some trust on many occasions, from the first morning in his garden to allowing her so much time with his daughter. But this felt like something new, something extraordinary, to be cherished. Helen clutched the moment close to her heart to be remembered and dwelt on many times later.

"Papa?" Beth tugged on his hand. "Can we swing some more?"

He turned to look at his daughter, and Helen felt whatever magic had been enveloping them disappear.

"Not today," Mr. Preston said. "I am going to the churchyard to take roses to your mother's grave. Will you come with me?"

"May Miss Helen come too?" Beth asked.

Mr. Preston hesitated the barest second. "If she would like." He glanced at Helen as he bent to collect the roses. "Come with us?"

It wasn't her place, but Helen felt uncertain how to properly decline. The last time they had discussed his wife—that ill-fated morning in the garden—she'd been so blunt as to be rude.

Misinterpreting her silence, Mr. Preston excused her. "It's all right. You don't have to."

"But I want her to," Beth said. "I want to show her Mommy's grave."

"I—would like that," Helen found herself saying. "Yes, I will come."

Mr. Preston seemed as surprised by her answer as he had been by her enthusiasm for the swing, but not displeased. He nodded, and they set off toward the drive and waiting carriage.

Harrison stood by the landau.

"My man has the day off," Mr. Preston explained. "Harrison kindly agreed to drive us." He gave the roses to Helen, then handed Beth into the carriage. Helen followed, seating herself opposite Beth.

Mr. Preston climbed in, and they were off, down the drive to the road that led to the church. Beth chatted animatedly the entire way, monopolizing Mr. Preston's attention, for which Helen felt immensely grateful. Their quarters were entirely too close for her comfort, and she wondered what had possessed her to agree to this journey, no matter how short.

She looked out the window as they traveled, the barren landscape seeming to reflect the emptiness in her heart. Most of the trees had lost their leaves, and the fields lay fallow, brown until spring, when tender plants would rise from their rows once more. The world felt empty, and she did too, the people most dear to her close but unreachable.

Harrison stopped the carriage in front of the churchyard and climbed down to help them out. As Helen descended, he gave her a tender look and her hand a squeeze. She still held the bouquet of flowers, and since Mr. Preston carried Beth, Helen assumed he wished her to continue holding them.

"Elizabeth's grave is at the top of the hill," he said, nodding toward the back of the churchyard, which rose steeply.

Silently Helen followed. Halfway up the slope, he pointed out Elizabeth's father's grave. Helen looked at the date and saw that he'd died almost two years earlier. Grace had written that Lord Sutherland believed it was from the heartbreak of losing his daughter.

So much sadness for one family.

Grace had also written of Nicholas Sutherland's sorrow and bitterness over both his sister's and father's deaths. If anyone could help him overcome his grief, Helen knew it would be Grace.

But how does Mr. Preston figure into that situation? Helen pushed the question from her mind. It was not her concern.

They left the churchyard but continued to climb. Her breathing became labored as she trudged behind Mr. Preston, and she took care not to step on her skirts. When at last they reached the top of the hill and Elizabeth's grave, Helen took a moment to catch her breath. Then she turned a slow circle, taking in the spectacular view. A patchwork of fields spread out in every direction, dotted by buildings Helen knew to be grand estates, but which from here appeared to be no more than tiny cottages. From here, too, the landscape below appeared brown, but Helen imagined that in spring, summer, and early autumn—even beneath winter snow—it was breathtaking. Above the farmland, the sky seemed to go on forever, its blue deepening to purple at the horizon. She turned to Mr. Preston and found him watching her.

"Beautiful, isn't it?" he said.

She nodded. "Beautiful does not seem to do it justice."

"We had to get special permission to bury Elizabeth up here," Mr. Preston said as he set Beth on the ground. "Elizabeth loved to climb hills. She loved that she could see out in all directions, to possibilities and places beyond her world." He bent to brush fallen leaves from the gravestone.

"She sounds like an extraordinary person," Helen said.

"She was." Mr. Preston stepped back from the grave and

addressed Beth. "Would you like to put the flowers on her grave today?"

Beth held her hands out, and Helen surrendered the roses. "Be careful of the thorns."

Beth took the flowers, pulled one from the bunch, and handed it back to Helen. "For you."

"Oh no." Helen shook her head. "These are your mother's."

"It's not for you to keep," Beth said, exasperation in her voice. "You give it to her and say something. One for you too, Papa." She thrust a flower at him. "I'm first."

She turned. "I miss you, Mama." She placed a flower at the base of the stone. "I wish you were here to play with me." Another flower. "I know you would let me ride your horse and tell Papa that it's all right." Two flowers more, and Beth looked over at her father, her lips puckered, a glint of hope in her eyes.

He mouthed an exaggerated no and shook his head, but Helen caught the hint of a smile turning up the corners of his mouth. She wondered if she'd see Beth sitting atop a horse tomorrow. The little girl did seem to have a way of getting much of what she wanted from her father.

"I wish you were here to tuck me in at night," Beth continued. "And Papa too. He doesn't like to sleep alone either."

Helen kept her gaze down but could not get the image of Mr. Preston, in his room at night—and lonely—from her mind.

Two more flowers lay beside the others. "I love you, Mama." Beth's last rose fell from her fingers, and she stood, rather solemnly, compared to her usual boisterous self.

Unsure whether to go next or what she might say, Helen did not move. After a moment, Mr. Preston stepped forward. "We miss you, Elizabeth." He pressed his lips to the rose and then placed it reverently on top of the others.

Helen felt her eyes clouding with tears for a woman she'd never met and the family left behind.

Crouching beside Elizabeth's grave, Helen spoke softly. "You have a beautiful daughter. Everyone says she is just like you. It is my great privilege to know her." Helen placed the rose on the ground beside the others and stood.

Mr. Preston's gaze, warm and filled with gratitude, lingered on hers as she blinked rapidly, attempting to hide her tears.

"You are very sensitive. That is why you understand people so well." His voice was quiet. "You perceive others' feelings and empathize with them in such a way that it touches your own soul—a rare and admirable talent."

"It is not so much a talent." She brushed hastily at her cheeks but did not take her eyes from his. "I simply prefer to linger in the background, observing people and imagining what causes them to act as they do. Your actions are motivated by pure love and devotion to your family." *Much like Grace.* Helen forced thoughts of her sister aside. "That is to be admired."

"And what motivates you, Miss Helen?" Mr. Preston stepped closer. She did not move, did not back away; she didn't want to. Instead she found herself imagining what it would be like to feel his arms around her. Just once . . .

Beth tugged on his hand. "I'm cold."

Looking somewhat startled, as if he had just remembered she was there, Mr. Preston glanced down at his daughter, then bent to pick her up. Once more the connection Helen had felt with him was broken. She turned away, and, wordlessly, they started down the hill, leaves crunching beneath their feet while Helen fought the tide of confusing emotions rising in her breast.

I cannot care for him. He still loves his wife. He may love Grace.

All good reasons, but she could not seem to help herself.

The walk downhill went much more quickly than the walk up had. They reached the carriage, and Harrison helped her in. Helen settled opposite Mr. Preston and Beth once more.

On the ride home, Beth snuggled into her father's lap. The sunset lit the sky, its orange glow masking the gloom Helen had seen on the ride there.

"We never got to finish hide-and-seek," Beth said sleepily, her head resting on her father's arm.

"Tomorrow," he promised.

"Miss Helen is a good friend," Beth said. "We must keep her."

"I quite agree," Mr. Preston said, his gaze flickering to Helen. "I quite agree."

CHAPTER 6

Helen sat near the fire of the guesthouse, head bent over a handkerchief on which she was embroidering Christopher's initials. It wasn't much of a Christmas gift, but given that the matter of their inheritance had not yet been resolved and their funds were extremely limited, it was the best she could do. The past few days, the last of November, she and Miranda had stayed busy in the evenings, cutting up old clothes that still had wear in them and making them over into new items for Christmas. Helen had pretended not to notice when Miranda embroidered a similar handkerchief with Harrison's initials.

A knock sounded at the door, and both women looked at each other.

"Who could that be at this hour?" Miranda said. Setting aside her work, she stood and left the room. Helen followed, lingering in the doorway. A flood of possibilities entered her mind, making her stomach tighten. Had something happened to Grace? Had Christopher returned from London?

"Good evening, ladies." Mr. Preston stood in the doorway, brushing the first snowfall from his cap and coat. "May I come in?"

"Of course." Miranda stepped aside, and he entered.

"Is everything all right?" Helen asked. "Is it Beth?"

The little girl was forever getting herself into scrapes. Just last week, she'd tried to climb the bookcase in the nursery, and it had nearly toppled over on her. After that, Mr. Preston had seen that all the furniture was secured to the walls.

"Beth is quite all right, at home safely in her bed. To my knowledge, your sister is well too," he added, as if guessing Helen's next question.

Miranda closed the door behind him. "Won't you come in and sit by the fire?"

Helen knew it was she who should have made the offer, and she hurriedly added, "Yes, please," while moving back to her chair near the fire.

Mr. Preston followed, seating himself on the settee across from them. "I've come to ask if I may impose upon you both the use of a section of your sitting room."

"It is *your* sitting room, Mr. Preston," Helen said. "We have been imposing on you these many weeks."

"On the contrary. You have been such a good influence upon Beth that I am in your debt."

"Thank you." Helen looked down, grateful for his praise but not quite sure what to do with it.

"I am making her a dollhouse for Christmas," Mr. Preston continued. "But I fear she will find it, curious as she is. It seems there isn't a room in the house safe from her explorations."

Helen glanced Miranda's direction and caught censure in her eyes. Being everything prim and proper, Miranda disproved of riotous little girls. She'd had enough difficulty training the two older ones entrusted into her guidance and care several years ago.

"You would like to build it here?" Helen asked, redirecting her attention to Mr. Preston. Since their visit to his wife's grave two weeks earlier, she'd felt more comfortable around him. He'd shared a portion of himself with her that day, trusting her even beyond what he'd shown with his admission in the garden that ill-fated morning. Her romantic notions might be dashed, but, like his daughter, Mr. Preston had become a friend, one of the few men she'd ever known whom *she* could trust.

"The outside of the dollhouse is already constructed, but the inside details are taking longer—and require warm fingers." He held up his gloved hands. "If I might be permitted to finish the dollhouse here, it would be safely hidden until Christmas Day, and my hands wouldn't be frostbitten as I complete the work."

"Bring it as soon as you can," Helen said, eager to see his creation. "I can send Harrison to help you tomorrow, if you would like."

A sheepish look stole across his face. "Actually, it is just outside."

"Then let us see it." She clapped her hands and stood. "Do you require help?"

"No. It is a little awkward, is all. I can manage if you will but hold the door for me."

"I'll find a cloth to cover the table," Miranda said as Helen followed Mr. Preston from the room, then held the door after he stepped outside.

He returned a moment later, arms stretched wide as he carried the large, rectangular dollhouse. Turning sideways, he maneuvered it through the doorway. Helen closed the door behind him and followed him into the sitting room, where he placed the dollhouse on the table.

"I've just realized you'll have nowhere to eat," he said.

"You will have to take your meals at the house—all of you."

"That is very kind, but we'll be all right," Helen said. He was easier to talk to now, but not *that* easy. The thought of conversing with him for even one meal a day made her anxious. It was simple enough to hide the attraction she felt toward him when they seldom had interaction. *But if we were to dine together every day...*

"I insist," he said. "It is the least I can do."

"It is not necessary—" The rest of Helen's sentence died on her lips beneath Miranda's pointed look of disapproval and strange gestures, which Mr. Preston, from his place in the room, could not view. "We—would be most grateful?" Helen said with reluctance. Miranda's brief smile and nod told Helen she had answered correctly. *Oh dear. I shall see him every day until Christmas—every day!*

"Good. It's settled, then. A dollhouse at your table in exchange for dinner at mine." Mr. Preston stepped aside, and Helen peered into the miniature house, telling herself that she must remain calm. They would merely be taking meals together. Mr. Preston would see it as nothing more, and neither should she. If only her rapidly beating heart would agree. She studied the house closely, in a desperate attempt to return her mind to safer areas of thought.

The house he'd built had two floors with three rooms each and a sloped attic on top. The rooms were bare, but the staircase was done, and she could see where he was finishing the rail.

"Fireplaces go here." Mr. Preston pointed to walls on the lower and upper floors. "Cabinets on the wall here. Some of the furniture I've ordered, and I'm making some as well."

"You've less than a month until Christmas," Helen said. "You'll need to hurry."

"Do you think you can suffer my company that long?"

Suffer was certainly the right word. It would be torture to be near him so often and reminded that it was Grace—*not*

I—who held his interest. Attempting to pretend that his proximity would have no effect whatsoever, Helen brought a hand to her chin, pursed her lips, and pretended to consider. "I suppose we shall bear it somehow."

Across the room, Miranda rolled her eyes, and Mr. Preston's brows drew together quizzically as he looked at Helen, as if not certain he'd heard her correctly.

"I mean, we will be most happy for your company," she hurried to amend. She'd only been jesting, but he did not seem to realize that.

Because teasing is not my place. I am only Beth's friend. A position she might very well lose if he thought her rude and unfeeling.

She tried once more. "I am sorry. Forgive me. I only meant—"

"I know what you meant." A grin swept the disbelief from his face. "It was an unexpected, but delightful, change, I must say." He folded his arms across his chest and leaned back, his eyes narrowed as if scrutinizing her. "Dare I hope you are no longer afraid of me, Miss Helen—as your ability to tease would suggest?"

"I was never afraid of you. However—" Helen ran a finger along the sloped roof of the dollhouse—"the evil king continues to give me nightmares."

"Does he?" Mr. Preston's voice softened, and his look grew searching. "I am sorry to hear that. I hope it is a situation that may yet be remedied. It is not good to be fearful—of anything, pretend or real."

Beneath her gown, Helen's heartbeat raced. Mr. Preston sounded almost as if he knew what she spoke of—and as if he understood. She turned from his gaze, forcing her attention to the dollhouse before she gave herself away entirely.

"But what about the inside?" she asked. "You'll need curtains and bedding and rugs."

"Yes, well . . ." Mr. Preston leaned a hand on the table.

"Fathers are only good at so many things. I'm afraid that sewing is not one of them."

"I could do it." Helen knelt, peering into the small rooms, imagining how they might look properly decorated like a real house. "Miranda will help me, won't you?" She glanced across the room and smiled encouragingly at her maid.

"If it will keep you out of trouble," Miranda said, sounding more like the mother of an errant child than a lady's maid.

"Perfect. We will begin tomorrow." Helen realized she'd left him no room for argument. *I sound rather like Grace.* Worried she'd displeased him, that she'd been too forward, Helen scrambled to think of an apology as she stood.

But before she could speak, Mr. Preston collapsed on the settee once more, a grin on his face and hands behind his head. "It appears I have come to the right place."

CHAPTER 7

December

My Dearest Helen,
  Lord Sutherland has decided to host a Christmas Eve ball, and his mother said it is for me...

Samuel watched from the hall above as his butler opened the front doors and Miss Helen entered the foyer. Samuel had sent his carriage for her just fifteen minutes earlier, thinking, as he had before, how having her so close was convenient. He could not have chosen a better influence for Beth. Indeed, her behavior and demeanor had changed markedly since Miss Helen's arrival. Their friendship had proved just the thing, and while he knew it wasn't the same as having a mother, Samuel had to admit that his guilt regarding Beth had lessened with Miss Helen's presence.

At the top of the stairs he was joined by Beth dressed in a clean frock with her hair tied up prettily for dinner. Samuel took his daughter's hand, and they hurried down the stairs to greet Miss Helen, eager for her company. They'd dined together for a week now, and he'd found the change a most pleasant one, as were the evenings spent at her side while they worked on Beth's dollhouse.

They reached the foyer just as the butler finished helping Miss Helen from her cloak.

"Good evening." Samuel bent over her hand as he kissed the back of it. As he straightened, he took in her trim figure dressed in an amber gown. It was simple in adornment, yet somehow it gave her face the appearance of glowing, complete with a halo of golden curls on top of her head.

Beth rushed forward to hug Miss Helen, though it had been but a few hours since they'd played together. "You look like an angel."

My thoughts exactly. Samuel glanced at Beth briefly before his gaze slid back to Miss Helen, who looked nothing like a governess at the moment. *How are governesses supposed to look?* He felt suddenly uncomfortable that he had suggested such a path to her. A young woman with her beauty might be seen as a threat by the lady of a house. And Samuel could well imagine a gentleman being distracted by Miss Helen's appearance. *And if that were to happen . . .*

It didn't bear thinking about, but he felt that he must consider it and somehow advise Miss Helen of the potential dangers. Beth had been so taken with her that first morning at breakfast—*as was I*—that he had thought of nothing but Miss Helen's apparent way with children. Only now did he realize there were other, very serious matters to be pondered, if she was to find a suitable and safe position.

I would have to know the couple very well, Samuel realized, feeling an odd surge of protectiveness for the woman before him, busily exclaiming over Beth's simple frock.

"Good evening to you both." Miss Helen curtsied, and a few seconds later Beth, looking remiss, did the same.

Samuel took a lady on either side, holding his arm low for Beth, and escorted them into dinner. Remembering Miss Helen's awkwardness the day they'd breakfasted some two months earlier, he'd come up with the idea to have Beth join them the first night Miss Helen came to dinner. His plan had gone spectacularly well. Not only had Miss Helen seemed more at ease, but Beth had eaten her dinner, used her utensils, and remained in her chair throughout the entire meal. Such success demanded he continue the pattern, unheard of as dining with one's children was.

If he had any hope of taming his daughter's wild ways, including her lack of manners when eating, it lay in the beautiful woman beside him.

Once they were seated and had been served by the staff, their usual conversation began. He began by inquiring after their day. "Were you in Camelot again this afternoon? Or was it—"

"Sherwood Forest," Beth interrupted with a mouthful of food. Across the table from her, Miss Helen pressed her fingers to her lips and shook her head.

Beth closed her mouth and swallowed before saying more. "We were in Sherwood Forest, fighting Prince John."

Samuel had been pleased to discover that nearly all of the adventures Miss Helen's imagination conjured were based in literature. Without her even realizing it, Beth's education had begun.

"And why were we fighting Prince John?" Miss Helen asked.

"He took everyone's money," Beth said. "And they were going to starve."

"Unfair taxation," Miss Helen clarified.

"He was bad." Beth reached for her glass and tipped it sideways.

Samuel caught it before her drink could spill, then helped her bring the glass safely from the table to her lips. "Let me guess," he said. "You were Maid Marian."

Beth scrunched up her nose and frowned. She set her drink at the edge of the table. "I was Robin Hood. Watch me shoot an arrow." She jumped up, knocking the glass on its side as she thrust her left arm forward. Her right arm drew back, fork still clutched tight in her fist.

"No, Beth!" Samuel and Miss Helen exclaimed at the same time.

"Whish," Beth shouted. Her right hand punched forward, fingers straight, mimicking an arrow, and the fork flew from it, across the table. Miss Helen ducked, but not quite fast enough, and the potato-laden fork stuck fast in the curls topping her head. Beth clapped a hand over her mouth, and her eyes grew large.

"Beth!" Samuel reprimanded sharply. He stood, then reached for her as she turned from him. He leaned forward, hand outstretched to grab her, but again she was too fast, and he found himself with only a sleeve dipped in gravy for his efforts as she ran from the room, crying.

"Please see to it that she gets safely to the nursery," Samuel instructed the servant closest to the door. With a nod the man was off, and Samuel and Miss Helen were left alone, each appearing somewhat worse for the experience.

As he returned to his seat, he watched her work to dislodge the fork from her hair.

"I'm sorry," she began, but he held his hand up before she could say more.

"Do not apologize for my daughter's behavior."

"But it was I who told her of Robin Hood, who gave her the idea."

"You suggested she throw her silverware at you during dinner?" Samuel asked, unable to keep the amusement from his voice.

"No." Miss Helen succeeded in extracting the fork, though a sizeable dab of potatoes remained.

He looked away, but not before a burst of laughter sprang from his lips. He brought a fist quickly to his mouth, attempting to cover his mirth, but it was no use. She looked so utterly ridiculous.

Instead of seeming affronted by his behavior, Miss Helen's shoulders sagged with evident relief, and her mouth turned up in a smile as well. "You are a fine one to laugh, with your sleeve dripping gravy on the tablecloth."

"So I am," Samuel said, holding up his arm and laughing harder. "We're quite a pair."

Miss Helen's smile faltered.

"I know I should not be amused," Samuel said, believing she did not find the situation humorous after all. "Beth's behavior was atrocious; I am a terrible father."

"You are a wonderful father." She reached out, placing her hand on his arm. "Beth is a very fortunate little girl. She loves you dearly, and she will grow out of these behaviors."

Samuel looked down at Miss Helen's hand on his arm and constrained himself from placing his hand over it. During the past weeks, he'd learned that she did not like to be touched, especially unexpectedly. That she had voluntarily reached out to him said much—both about the changes she'd made since her arrival, and about the level of friendship they had attained. He dared not jeopardize that by reciprocating her warmth.

"Thank you." He lifted his gaze to hers and was pleased when she did not look away. An entirely pleasant, comfortable feeling settled in his chest. "Beth and I are both fortunate to have found a friend in you, Miss Helen." The truth of his statement tempered his laughter. They were most fortunate. He did not wish Miss Helen to find a position elsewhere. He wished, somehow, that she might continue on here.

CHAPTER

Samuel attached the miniature fireplace to the dollhouse wall while Miss Helen hung the last of the curtains on the windows. Between the two of them, over the past few weeks, the house had transformed into a masterpiece. He had built the furniture; she'd painted it. He'd finished the stairs; she'd laid carpet. He'd shingled the roof; she'd papered the inside. He'd added a rail to the porch; she'd worked a miracle with her needle and thread, covering the tiny beds with quilts and the tables with cloths. He could hardly wait for Beth to see their creation.

With the last piece in place, he backed up, turning his head at the same moment Miss Helen did.

"Oh!" she exclaimed at their faces so close, noses nearly touching.

Samuel laughed, then grabbed her elbow to steady her as she reeled back. "If we'd been racing to see who finished first, we'd have to declare it a tie."

"Are we finished, then?" she asked, blushing prettily as she extracted her arm and stepped back, putting more distance between them.

He almost wished she wouldn't, then mentally scolded himself for the thought. Miss Helen was much younger than her sister, and he had no business thinking of her as other than a friend. Something he would do well to remember if he did not wish to scare her off.

Though Miss Helen's shyness around him had improved, particularly during the hours they'd worked on the dollhouse, a part of her was still very reserved—cautious. She'd admitted to not fearing him, and he believed her, yet she continued to hold back, as if she was afraid of his becoming too familiar. Once, not so many weeks ago, he would have thought Miss Helen had plenty of time ahead of her to get used to him, particularly if he married Grace and Miss Helen became his sister-in-law.

But now . . . Samuel attempted to push the growing realizations to the back of his mind. Now, it did not seem likely that Grace would choose him over Nicholas. *Not surprising.* What was unexpected were his feelings—or lack thereof—on the matter. Samuel cared about Grace. He still believed that they might be happy together. But it was her sister he'd found occupying his thoughts of late. Worse than Grace's potential rejection, it appeared that Miss Helen would not be his guest much longer. Just yesterday, Christopher had returned with news of their inheritance. And while it boded well for the Thatcher family, Samuel could not bring himself to feel very happy about it. Beth would be devastated when Miss Helen left, and he would miss her company as well.

It is because of Beth that I am so upset about her leaving. Since becoming a parent, his thoughts always had to be first and foremost, for Beth's welfare. *She will be sad when Miss Helen leaves, and so I will be sad with her.*

"I think we have completed everything. I declare the dollhouse finished," Samuel said, feeling more than a twinge of regret. The cold December evenings had passed pleasantly in Miss Helen's company, during a time he might otherwise have felt desolate. In addition to missing Elizabeth more at this festive time of year, he'd lost Grace's companionship as well. She hadn't come to see him at the fence for quite some time, not since the day he'd seen her on the road with Nicholas.

Samuel stepped back beside Miss Helen, and together they admired their work.

"I think I should like to live there," she said quietly.

There was a wistfulness in her tone that caught him off-guard. He was unsure how to respond and finally came up with, "It is a splendid house." He wondered if Helen had dreams and aspirations for her future. Did she aspire to marry someone like Lord Sutherland? Had her time spent with her grandfather roused a desire for a fine home and a titled husband?

"Splendid," she said. "Excepting the fact that the inhabitants shall have to climb up the outside wall to reach the attic nursery."

"Bah." Samuel chuckled and waved his hand dismissively. "A petty detail. And a good way to add some adventure to one's day. Beth will not be bothered by it."

Miss Helen's lips twitched. "I would not be so certain if I were you." She reached in, adjusting the furniture in the kitchen once more. "Beth is very intelligent and is quite specific in her opinions."

"Well, she shall have to request another father if she does not absolutely *adore* this dollhouse." His gaze and tone turned serious. "I thank you both." He looked from Miss Helen to her maid, who was busily sewing in the opposite corner. "It would have been very plain without your talents."

"I am so glad we finished in time," Miss Helen said.

"As am I." Samuel glanced at her as an acute and strange awareness concerning time passed over him. The past three Decembers had been nothing but misery. Of course giving Beth presents had always made for joy on Christmas morning, but the month leading up to the holiday had seemed to crawl by, a time during which the constant loneliness that was his only companion hurt more keenly. But this December had been different. It has passed quickly—too quickly—filled with delightful evenings spent at Miss Helen's side, as together they created this treasure for Beth.

"Christmas Eve will not see us up late working," Samuel said, half wishing it would have. The invitation to Nicholas's Christmas Eve ball still lay in his coat pocket, where it had for several days, ever since he'd received it. The time for a proper response had long passed, and Samuel was not yet certain whether he wished to attend—*to see for myself the path Grace has chosen, and to discover that my hope has been in vain.*

Had the dollhouse not been completed, his decision would have been easy. Making Christmas ready for Beth would have come first.

"You are finished?" Harrison asked, entering the room, snow still clinging to his boots. "And just in the nick of time." He pulled a letter from his pocket and directed his gaze at Miss Helen. "This arrived from your father. It appears he's had it for some time and didn't send it on. It had already been opened."

Miss Helen took the letter and read it quickly, her fingers trembling. "It is from Lord Sutherland," she said, glancing about the room at the three of them. "He has requested my company, and Christopher's—and yours—" she glanced up at Miranda and then Harrison—"for the duration of the Christmas season."

Samuel watched as a myriad of emotions crossed Miss Helen's face. Her first thought, he would have bet, had been elation at the thought of seeing Grace. And her second thought seemed to be one of disappointment and perhaps sadness, making him wonder if she was thinking of Beth and how she would miss their daily adventures.

Will she miss me? Or does she think of me simply as Beth's father? It was entirely probable that she did, older as he was.

Regardless of Miss Helen's feelings, they would miss her. Over the past few weeks it seemed she had spent more time with Beth than her nanny did. Several times, Samuel had been on the verge of asking Miss Helen if she would consider a position as Beth's governess, something that would make Beth immensely happy and bring him a great deal of relief. He would worry about Miss Helen were she to become a governess elsewhere. And besides, her quiet, reserved manner was the very antithesis of Beth's rambunctious one. They were a good balance for each other. But now that the matter of the inheritance had been settled favorably, Miss Helen would not need to be employed. Neither did she need to stay any longer, now that she had been summoned to Sutherland Hall.

"You must go," Samuel forced himself to say. "Your sister should not be without you at Christmas." Grace had been away from her family long enough. Whatever was to happen between her and Nicholas would happen, and it would not be affected by proximity to her family now.

"But Lord Sutherland—" Miss Helen set the letter aside and dropped into a chair.

"Do not be frightened of Nicholas," Samuel said. "I believe your sister has tamed him considerably, else he would have run me over the day I spied them kissing at the crossroad."

"What?" Miss Helen stood abruptly. "They were kissing—on the road?"

"*He* was kissing *her*. Let's leave it at that," Samuel said, wishing he hadn't brought it up. Miss Helen's wide eyes and open mouth clearly showed how appalled she was. And her maid's lips had turned down so low as to almost reach her chin. Harrison eyed the door with a look that seemed to suggest he was about to charge through it, straight over to Sutherland Hall to defend Grace's honor.

"Suffice it to say," Samuel added hastily, "that I have reason to believe they have come to care deeply for each other. If not, Lord Sutherland would not have invited you for so much as tea."

"What is this about tea?" Christopher asked, carrying an armload of wood into the house.

"You are to let me do that," Harrison scolded.

"I know you're more than capable," Christopher said. "But I enjoy the work."

Restless, that one, Samuel thought. He hoped Christopher would use their recently awarded inheritance wisely and find a profession that suited him. At twenty, he still had time to learn a trade. And it looked probable that he would have enough funds to receive some schooling, at least, if that was his desire, as it seemed likely that at least one of his sisters would not be in need of support. Kindly, he had agreed to hold off sharing his good news until after Christmas.

At the least I would like to be the one to present Grace with the option for freedom she has longed for.

"I'll begin packing at once." Miranda brushed past them and hurried toward the stairs.

Samuel guessed she was eager to see Grace. He knew it had been difficult for her to be separated from her charge.

"Where are you going?" Christopher asked. "Has something happened I ought to be made aware of?"

"Yes. Your sister has been caught kissing at the crossroad," Harrison muttered irritably, his eyes still fixed upon the door.

"Truly?" Christopher's brows rose as he turned his gaze on Helen.

"Not I!" Her mouth hung open, as if appalled at the thought.

Of kissing in public, or just of kissing? Samuel wondered. "Your other sister," he clarified for Christopher. "I caught Lord Sutherland kissing her while they were out driving."

A grin spread across Christopher's face. "About time, I'd say. Jolly good news, that."

Helen shook her head and started toward the door. "I must tell Beth goodbye." She took her cloak from the hook and threw it around her shoulders. Samuel watched her leave, imagining how she must feel.

Her sister. My daughter. Is there not a way for Miss Helen to have both? He intended to find out, to put Grace to a decision, though he'd already guessed what her answer was likely to be.

But if Grace were here with me, then Helen could remain. Beth would be happy. I could be too. And if Grace marries Nicholas, could Helen not stay with her sister and visit here daily?

So simple, Samuel feared it to be impossible.

CHAPTER 9

The doors to Sutherland Hall opened, and a rather stern-looking butler stood back to admit them.

"Where is she? What have you done with her?" Harrison demanded, leading the march across the vast foyer, in search of Grace, with Christopher and Miranda close on his heel. "I've a need to see her with my own eyes before I'm about any other tasks."

Helen lingered behind. Her gaze flitted about, taking in the dark wood and somewhat somber appearance of the entrance hall. Compared to the light of Mr. Preston's house, Lord Sutherland's seemed practically medieval, though with a touch of festiveness, at least. Holly adorned all of the banisters.

How has Grace survived here? Eager to see her, though somewhat frightened of what else she might find, Helen hurried forward, arriving at the drawing room doors at the same time as the others. Together they entered, with Lord Sutherland's butler, looking rather concerned, close behind.

"It is quite all right," the man who had to be Lord Sutherland called over their heads as they rushed toward Grace. Helen spied her as she sprang from the bottom step of a ladder near an enormous evergreen tree, the scent of which filled the room.

"Helen!" Grace gathered her in a fierce hug and held her tight for a long minute, then pulled away, staring at her as if making certain she was real.

"Oh, Grace." Helen squeezed her hands as tears blurred her vision.

"And have you no thought for me?" Christopher asked glibly.

"Of course I do." Grace extended one arm and pulled him close as well. The three of them huddled together, heads bent close, each speaking and laughing at once.

"You are well?" Helen asked. She looked closely at her sister, wearing a pretty gown and with a smile that most definitely reached her eyes.

"Very," Grace said merrily. "And you?"

Helen nodded. "But I've missed you so." *There is much I want to tell you.*

"And me? No one cares for me?" Christopher said. "I might have stubbed my toe on the way here or be half starved, as I've not eaten since this morning, and the two of you wouldn't notice."

Grace ruffled his hair as if he were still a little boy. "We will always notice you." She studied him critically. "And I daresay it will not be long before other females do as well."

"None of that for me, thank you," Christopher said, and they all laughed.

Helen felt as if her heart might burst. The three of them together like this, with a fragrant Christmas tree behind them, in such a grand house . . . it was almost like being at Grandfather's again.

"I must introduce you to Lord Sutherland," Grace said, stepping from their embrace.

She turned her head, looking around the room. Helen followed her gaze and watched as it landed on the man who had spoken earlier and now leaned casually against the doorframe.

Something unspoken seemed to pass between them before Grace whispered, "Thank you."

Lord Sutherland shrugged, as if inviting Grace's family and servants here were nothing. He returned Grace's smile in a way that left no doubt as to his feelings.

He is in love with her too. Poor Mr. Preston.

"It took you all long enough," Lord Sutherland said in a loud voice. They all turned towards him. "It has been nearly a month since I requested your company. Why did you not come sooner?"

Harrison and Miranda exchanged uneasy glances, and Helen cringed. *Is he angry?* Grace had written Lord Sutherland's moods were volatile, but a change this quick was almost unbelievable. A moment ago, he'd seemed pleased to see them.

Grace put a protective arm around Helen and smiled encouragingly. Harrison stepped forward, hat in hand. "Mr. Thatcher did not deliver your dispatch for some time. Believe me, your lordship, we would have come sooner had we known."

"Well, your timing today is perfect," Lord Sutherland said, his tone considerably lighter. "This tree is in need of decorating—and Miss Thatcher seems determined to break her neck in the process of doing it. Perhaps you can assist in keeping her safe. It is proving almost too great a task for one man." He gave Grace a slow wink before turning his attention to Miranda.

"There is to be a ball here tomorrow night. I trust you can help your lady accomplish something appropriate with her hair." Once more his gaze slid to Grace, who blushed furiously as she felt her hair, much of which had fallen from its pins.

He does like it, Helen realized as she watched his perusal.

"Of course, milord," Miranda said stiffly.

"Very good." Lord Sutherland bowed slightly. "I will leave you to your reunion." With a last, fond look at Grace, he left them.

"You have *much* to tell me," Helen said, searching her sister's face. But Grace was not paying attention to her. Instead, her eyes, filled with adoration, followed Lord Sutherland until he disappeared from view.

CHAPTER

Helen stepped back from the bed and considered the two gowns laid out before her. Neither had ever been worn before, having been made nearly two years previously for her coming-out season, which had been both disastrous and short lived. The gowns had come with her to Mr. Preston's, as had every article of clothing she owned. Her father would have gambled away anything of value left in his care.

The first dress, a delicate pink silk with rosettes on the sleeves, collar, and hem, was demure and lovely. The second, a white muslin with intricate garnet beading and a crimson sash, was secretly her favorite, though Helen already knew she could not wear it this evening. The red details on the dress were bold and noticeable—a most daring, new fashion two years ago and still on the fringes now, she guessed—whereas the pink would allow her to blend in more easily and remain *unnoticed*—precisely what she planned to do.

Still . . . She stepped closer, her fingers tracing the beading along the high waistline of the white gown. Resolute in her decision, she picked it up and turned toward the armoire, intending to replace it before the maid arrived to help her. But as Helen passed before the mirror, with the dress held up in front of her, she couldn't seem to keep herself from stopping to look.

The crimson offered a stunning contrast against her pale skin and light hair. She imagined the latter swept up in layers of curls, held in place with the ruby combs Grandfather had given her and the matching necklace at her throat. *If only I were brave enough.*

But a dress like this invited a man to ask a girl to dance—the very activity Helen wished *not* to participate in this evening. Instead, she planned to blend into the scenery, preferably on a comfortable chair located behind a good-sized potted plant, from where she might see the goings-on of the ball without being seen herself.

With a sigh that was part sorrow, but more disappointment with herself, Helen returned the gown to the armoire. This evening was about Grace. It was about seeing her enjoy some long-overdue and much-deserved happiness. About seeing more of the Lord Sutherland whom Grace had described in her letters. About witnessing true love. Helen knew she had best enjoy it. Now that she had left Mr. Preston's estate, her own situation seemed more hopeless than ever.

Watching Grace is likely as close to having my own love affair as I will ever get.

Helen knocked at Grace's door. She could have come earlier, could have dressed alongside her sister and had Miranda help them both with their hair, but Grace had spent three months without her lady's maid, so it was only fair that Grace enjoy their maid by herself for one night, at least.

The door opened, and Helen entered the room. Miranda was still helping Grace, who appeared almost regal in an emerald gown. *She is not shy of wearing bold color tonight.* Lord Sutherland's mother had commissioned the gown, and it was at once apparent that she had exquisite taste. Billowing sleeves and a newly-fashionable v-shaped waistline showed off Grace's figure.

"Oh, but you look lovely," Helen said.

"I was thinking the same of you," Grace said. "How are you feeling? Have you sufficiently recovered from Lord Sutherland's greeting?"

Helen felt her cheeks warm. She nodded. "I believe so. You do not think he will ask me to dance tonight, do you?"

"I should think he will," Grace said. "You are his guest, after all." She sounded almost wistful, though Helen could not discern why.

"There." Miranda finished fussing with Grace's hem and stood, a satisfied smile on her face. "Your grandfather would be proud—of both of you," she added, turning to Helen.

Grace came toward her, looping her arm through Helen's. "Let us go down together, shall we?" She steered Helen toward the door, which Miranda hurried to open.

"I must warn you of something," Grace whispered as they walked. "Hanging above the ballroom entrance there is a ball . . ." Her voice trailed off, and her brow furrowed as she studied Helen's face, as if deciding how best to deliver bad news.

"A ball at a ball?" Helen remarked. "How odd." But then, Lord Sutherland's entire residence seemed rather strange. She did not see how he chose to decorate would matter to her. Grace seemed to tolerate the gloom and even be thriving in it. "Is this ball some ancient weapon or—"

"It is a kissing ball," Grace said. "If a lady is found beneath it, she cannot refuse a kiss."

Helen gasped. "Mistletoe! I did not think people really

believed such things. Perhaps I shall change my mind and stay in my room." She gripped Grace's arm and looked at her plaintively.

"It is only superstition," Grace said. "No gentleman will force you to kiss him. But Lady Sutherland said that if a couple in love exchanges a kiss under the mistletoe, it is a promise to marry and a prediction of happiness."

"Well, I am not in love with anyone," Helen declared as Mr. Preston came to mind.

"Then you needn't worry," Grace said. "I only told you so you would not linger in the doorway, as you are wont to do at such occasions."

"I am wont to stay in my room," Helen said.

"Too late for that." Grace kept a tight grip on her arm, urging her forward. "Lord Sutherland has seen us. To turn back now would offend him."

Helen looked down and saw Lord Sutherland staring directly at her and frowning.

"If he escorts us to the ballroom, we shall have to pass beneath the kissing ball *with* him," Helen whispered.

"Then take care to turn your cheek," Grace said, teasing in her voice.

"Easy enough for you to say. You've come to like the man quite well." For herself, Helen could scarcely imagine a more frightening proposition than having to marry the formidable Lord Sutherland.

"He is more than likeable," Grace said, a dreamy quality to her voice. She guided her sister down the stairs. "It is all right, Helen. Do not fear. He cannot marry both of us. I think we shall be safe enough until later in the evening."

They reached the bottom, and Grace flashed an apologetic smile at Lord Sutherland. "Helen did not realize there would be so many guests. She is a little anxious."

"Do you need to sit?" he asked, coming around to her other side and taking her free arm.

"Yes, thank you," Grace said. "I think that would be best. If we can get her inside the ballroom and find a chair..."

They walked quickly across the foyer and down the hall, Helen feeling as if they were half-dragging her. If they would only let her go, she could walk by herself—which would be far better than suffering Lord Sutherland's touch.

Just before the entrance to the ballroom, he paused and glanced up at the kissing ball, then over at Grace.

I am between them, Helen realized, supposing she had upset his plans.

They entered the ballroom together, and Lord Sutherland steered them toward the nearest grouping of straight-backed chairs in the long, high-ceilinged hall. Chandeliers shone down on dark paper covering the upper half of the walls and the many guests clustered about the room. Festive garlands matching that on the stair railing sectioned off a dais in the far corner, where the musicians sat tuning their instruments.

Helen sank gratefully into a chair as Lady Sutherland—who looked almost as frightening as her son, with every hair exactly in place, a gown that looked as if it cost more than Helen's entire wardrobe, and a dour look upon her face—began making her way toward them. Having already made the dowager's acquaintance the previous day and having been subjected to her presence and a steady line of questioning at breakfast that morning, Helen was not eager for her company.

"Will you do me the honor, Miss Thatcher?" Lord Sutherland asked as he turned to Grace.

Grace bit her lip and glanced at Helen.

Helen smiled encouragingly. "Oh please do dance, Grace. I should love to watch you."

Lady Sutherland arrived.

Ensuring that I will not be alone, Helen thought,

resigning herself to the fact that she was not likely to be allowed to spend the evening with only a potted plant for company.

"I'll be back shortly," Grace promised, taking Lord Sutherland's arm and allowing him to lead her to the middle of the ballroom.

Though no other couples had taken the floor, the violinists started up the moment Grace and Lord Sutherland faced each other.

Helen watched curiously as they engaged in conversation but did not yet dance.

"He has something special planned." The dowager spoke through the side of her mouth in a conspiratorial whisper, as if sharing a great secret.

"Oh?" Helen asked, showing the interest she imagined Lady Sutherland hoped for.

"He is going to lead her in a *waltz*." The dowager whispered the word, as if it were too scandalous to speak aloud.

It *was* scandalous. Helen barely contained a horrified gasp. "Does Grace know about this?" she asked, not quite believing her sister would be a willing participant. Grandfather had not approved of such intimate dances, and Grace had always tried very hard to please him.

"I daresay she does now," Lady Sutherland said as her son and Grace joined hands and began gliding about the room.

Helen leaned forward in her seat to better watch. It seemed that every person in the room had their eyes riveted on the handsome couple as well. Together they were breathtaking and beautiful, and in less than a minute, Helen had forgotten to feel scandalized and was instead lost in the looks of adoration passing between Lord Sutherland and her sister.

"When Nicholas first proposed this scheme, I was not in agreement," Lady Sutherland said. "After all . . . the scandal." Her gaze slid to Helen. "But then, thanks to your sister, the Sutherland name has already been embroiled in nearly the worst sort of scandal to be had."

Helen's fists clenched. She scooted to the edge of her chair, determined to rise in defense of Grace, when Lady Sutherland's tone changed quite suddenly.

"But I've come to realize—also thanks to your sister— that Nicholas is happier than I ever imagined he could be. He has traded his bitterness for love, and it has transformed him entirely. That is what he wished to show everyone tonight— how dear your sister has become to him, how precious we both find her to be."

Helen leaned back in her chair and placed her hands demurely in her lap, feeling immensely grateful that she'd held her tongue and not ruined the moment for Lady Sutherland, and especially for her sister and Lord Sutherland.

"Grace loves him," she said in response to the dowager's revelation. The truth had to be obvious to anyone watching them. Helen felt a pang of envy. *To be looked at like that, to be held close as Grace is, to have a man love me so much that he would declare it in front of everyone.*

She realized that it did not matter that she had failed to gain Mr. Preston's interest. It would not matter—for Grace, at least—if they never received a penny of their inheritance. She had found herself both a husband and a home and would be well cared for.

Helen knew it was probable that she and Christopher could live at Sutherland Hall as well. She wished Christopher had stayed this evening, but, detesting balls and dancing, he'd already excused himself, to return to Mr. Preston's to help move Beth's dollhouse to the Christmas tree in the main house.

As for herself . . .

Helen sighed inwardly. Grace might be happy here, but Helen was certain she could never be. She could never feel comfortable around someone as stern as Lord Sutherland, and she would feel an intruder in his home. *Even if it is Grace's home too.* Something—*many* things, likely—had changed since Grace had come to Sutherland Hall. For the first time in her life, Helen realized that she and Christopher were not the center of her sister's focus. Certainly Grace still loved them both, but Lord Sutherland now occupied her mind and heart. *As he should.*

Helen felt happy for Grace, yet she could not deny that a part of her felt sad at this change and knowing that their life together would never be as it was before. *I cannot stay here. This is not my place.*

But what was?

Her heart yearned for the warm hearth of the house that sat but a mile or so up the road. She wished she were there with Christopher and Mr. Preston now and that she could be there tomorrow morning to witness Beth's delight when she first saw the dollhouse, to share Christmas with the little girl she had come to love. *And her father.*

It seemed that Grace was not the only one who had changed.

CHAPTER 11

"Well done," Lady Sutherland said, clapping as Lord Sutherland and Grace returned to the side of the hall following their waltz.

"It was lovely," Helen agreed. "Though I could never dance like that."

"Nor should you," Grace said, with a sideways glance at Lord Sutherland.

He answered with a wicked grin. "If you will excuse me a moment, ladies, I must greet our latest arrivals." He bowed and turned away just as Mr. Preston entered the ballroom.

Helen's heart leaped at the sight of him. *He came! Has it been but one day since we parted?* It seemed much longer than that; Lord Sutherland's estate seemed so far away from the cozy world she'd inhabited.

She watched as Mr. Preston scanned the room and stopped when he'd spotted her. *Or Grace?* Without hesitation, he began making his way over to them. For a moment Helen worried that he did not know the extent of Grace's affection for Lord Sutherland. Then she remembered that it was Mr. Preston who had spied them kissing at the crossroad. *Surely he must know of their feelings for one another.* Helen felt a surge of hope as Mr. Preston continued walking toward her.

Instead of going to greet other guests Lord Sutherland stayed at Grace's side. He moved closer and placed his hand at her elbow. "Are you thirsty after our dance? Would you like some refreshment?"

"Mr. Preston!" Helen exclaimed as he arrived at their group. She rose to greet him.

"Good evening, Miss Helen." Mr. Preston bowed, then turned to Grace.

"Hello, Grace."

"Miss Thatcher to you," Lord Sutherland snarled, stepping forward.

Mr. Preston called her by her Christian name. Helen felt as if she'd been struck.

Beside her, Grace held a restraining hand upon Lord Sutherland's arm as she sent a pleading look to Mr. Preston.

"My apologies," Mr. Preston said. "Miss Thatcher, Lord Sutherland. Lady Sutherland."

Lady Sutherland did not return his greeting, and Helen felt the sting of rebuke as if it had been directed at her.

"It was good of you to invite me," Mr. Preston said to Lord Sutherland. "It is good to be here again." He glanced round the room before returning his look to them. "Miss Thatcher, may I request the pleasure of your company for the next set?"

Yes. Helen smiled timidly, still frightened by the prospect of actually dancing, but at the same time thrilled that he had asked.

But it was to Grace that Mr. Preston held out his hand, stepping in front of Lord Sutherland to reach her.

"I—of course," Grace said, taking his hand and allowing him to lead her away.

Lord Sutherland watched them go, looking as stunned and stung as Helen felt. "Would you care to dance?" he asked her in somber tone.

Helen shrank, neither wishing to offend nor to dance with him.

"I do not bite, you know," he said.

"No, thank you, sir—milord," Helen corrected. "I am not a very good dancer."

Lord Sutherland gave a curt nod. "Excuse me, Mother," he said, and left them, presumably in search of a more willing lady.

Helen watched as Mr. Preston led Grace to the center of the floor. Lord Sutherland found a partner and joined their set, and the dance was begun. In contrast to the waltz, the mood of this dance was fraught with tension. Anyone with half an eye on the participants could not help but notice the stares and mutterings passing between the couples as they completed the steps. Grace seemed caught in a balancing act between two men—the forbidding Lord Sutherland and hopeful Mr. Preston, whose expressions seemed as gentle as Lord Sutherland's were harsh.

The dance was not yet halfway over when Helen decided she could take no more. She swayed on her feet, feeling ill. Her heart was breaking—for herself and for Mr. Preston, who perhaps really had no idea of the depth of Grace's feelings for his neighbor.

"Are you all right?" Lady Sutherland asked, not unkindly. "You look a little pale." She patted Helen's arm as if offering condolences. "Don't pine for Mr. Preston, my dear. You wouldn't want him. It is his fault that my daughter is dead."

Helen shook her head and backed away from Lady Sutherland. "It isn't," she said, defending Mr. Preston against such cruel gossip. "You don't know him as I do. He would never have hurt Elizabeth. He did everything he could to save her. He loved his wife. He adores her still."

And he adores Grace.

Turning from Lady Sutherland, Helen fled the ballroom, tears clouding her vision as she ran past the dreaded kissing ball. She had no need to fear it. The only man she might ever have considered kissing was in love with her sister.

CHAPTER

Helen trudged through the garden on her return trip to Sutherland Hall after visiting with Beth. At noon, Harrison had driven her to Mr. Preston's estate, where, for a few brief, blissful hours, she and Beth had played in the nursery with her new dollhouse. Time with Beth had been like balm to Helen's soul. For, while last night Mr. Preston had made it abundantly clear that the time they'd spent together meant little to him—including the last months' worth of meals taken together and the many hours they had worked, side by side, on Beth's dollhouse—Beth, at least, remained loyal in her affection and her desire to have Helen as her friend.

Both her greeting and parting hugs had gone on long enough that one would have thought the two of them had not seen each other in ages or were about to part for years. Beth had elicited a promise from Helen that they would continue their playtime, a promise Helen felt only too grateful to make. Beth's love was constant, something Helen needed as much as the motherless little girl seemed to need her.

Determined to keep that promise by visiting every day, Helen plodded across Lord Sutherland's snowy yard, intent on finding a faster way to reach Mr. Preston's home so she'd be free to come and go as she pleased. Mr. Preston had once mentioned a connecting gate between the two properties, and Helen hoped to discover it sooner, rather than later, if she was to keep her toes from being frostbitten.

Stomping her feet to keep them from going numb, Helen continued, following the fence toward ominous Sutherland Hall looming in the distance and—*Mr. Preston and Grace!* They stood facing one another, just a short distance from the wall. Beside them, the gate Helen had hoped to find was ajar.

They were the last people Helen had expected to see together today. She ducked behind the closest bush, then watched as Mr. Preston knelt in the snow before her sister and spoke words that she, herself, would have loved to hear from his lips.

"I will spend the remainder of my life in the pursuit of your happiness," Mr. Preston promised.

Hardly daring to breathe, Helen waited for Grace to answer. *How can she refuse?* Yet Helen did not know how her sister could accept, either, given her obvious attachment to Lord Sutherland.

Helen watched, her heart breaking as Grace fell into Mr. Preston's arms, crying even as she rejected his proposal of marriage—a proposal more beautiful than anything Helen could have ever conceived.

Yet Grace had thrown it away, dismissed it along with the near-perfect man who had offered up his heart.

"Why torture me so—and yourself, too?" Grace demanded of Mr. Preston when he confessed that he'd believed she would refuse his suit.

What do you know of torture? Helen thought, trying to keep her bitterness at bay. She loved Grace, adored her with sisterly affection. Grace had practically been a mother to her. Helen wished for her sister to be happy, and she knew from watching Mr. Preston all these weeks that Grace could be happy. With him.

A slushy dollop of snow fell from the bare branches of a tree, landing on the bridge of Helen's nose and over her right eye. She gasped and quickly swiped the wet snow from her face. Squinting against temporary blindness, she ducked lower behind the bushes and waited tensely, expecting either Grace or Mr. Preston or both to turn her direction.

When neither did, Helen felt irritation rather than surprise. She could probably throw a snowball at them, or stand and wave her hands, and they still would not take notice of her. No one ever did.

Why, just a few days ago, she and Mr. Preston had been close enough that he might have kissed her, and instead of taking notice, he'd laughed the incident off as if it had been nothing. It had not been *nothing* to Helen, but one of many agonizing moments spent in his presence when she felt that exhilarating, yet distressing, feeling that set her on edge.

She supposed she should have felt pleased that Grace had rejected him. *I will not have to endure having Mr. Preston as my brother-in-law.* It was small comfort at first and then no comfort at all as Helen watched Mr. Preston produce a sheaf of papers from his coat.

"I asked Christopher to wait until today and to let me tell you the good news."

Our inheritance. Helen's heartbeat quickened. *We will leave now. We'll move far away, and I will never see Mr. Preston or Beth again.*

Dear Beth. Tears filled Helen's eyes as she thought of the tiny hands clasped around her, holding so tight. *I promised Beth I would continue to visit, but now . . .*

"You may go wherever you like," Mr. Preston said. "Whenever you like. I have already spoken with several landlords about properties available for rent. I know of some that are far enough from here..."

The rest of his words were lost to her as Helen turned and ran toward the main path. Not wanting to chance Grace finding her—and demanding an explanation for her tears—Helen left the brick walk and ran through the garden, heedless of the mud ruining her slippers or the hem of her dress dragging through the snow.

She knew only that she must be alone, and quickly, where she might cry in private for her heart that had just been broken for the second time in one day.

CHAPTER 13

"Spine straight. Don't slouch," Lady Sutherland barked. She walked around Helen, who stood perched on a chair while the dressmaker pinned the hem of the gown she was to wear to Grace's wedding. The same day Mr. Preston had proposed to Grace, Lord Sutherland had proposed as well, and his offer she had accepted. In the week since the announcement of their decision to marry, Lady Sutherland had taken on the personality of a general preparing for war, determined to have everything and *everyone* exactly as she wished—or so it seemed to Helen. She'd born the particular brunt of Lady Sutherland's rebukes, though Grace had endured her share as well.

"Do you want your gown to drag on the ground so that you trip and fall on it?" the dowager demanded. She stood with arms crossed in front of her, cheeks sucked in and lips puckered. "If you do not improve your posture, that is exactly what shall happen, and I shall be shamed in front of everyone who has come to see my son wed."

"I'm sorry," Helen murmured, ducking her head, then lifting it at once after realizing what she'd done.

If only Lady Sutherland understood that her criticisms make me want to shrink even more.

Helen wasn't certain how Grace managed to tolerate her future mother-in-law with such . . . grace. But not only did her sister seem unfazed by Lady Sutherland's remarks, she seemed to be developing an affection for the woman.

Remarkable, what love can do.

Apparently pleased with the dressmaker's progress—or simply too put out to endure their company any longer—the dowager took her leave, snapping orders to the servants trailing behind her.

The door closed behind Lady Sutherland, and Helen shuddered, grateful to have escaped this latest confrontation with only a mild scolding.

"You'll have to excuse her," Grace called from across the room where she, too, stood on a stool as her gown was adjusted. "This is the last wedding she will ever plan, and doing so means a great deal to her."

Helen merely nodded in response, not daring to say anything in front of the other women in the room.

Someone knocked once loudly. The door opened, and Christopher's head appeared. "Still up here?"

"We're getting close to being finished," Grace said. "Another half hour, I'd think."

Christopher pushed the door open the rest of the way and stepped into the room. He looked from Grace to Helen as a grin spread across his face. "You two look quite fetching. I'm feeling rather grateful that you're both attached, so I'll not have to be watching out for you anymore. A brother does get tired of beating off the gentlemen who are after his sisters."

"What do you mean we are *both* attached?" Grace asked, brows raised as she looked pointedly at Helen.

Helen shrugged. The only person she'd become attached to was little Beth. *And that has hardly resolved my difficulties regarding men.*

"Lord Sutherland has just returned from London," Christopher said, changing the subject, much to Helen's relief.

"At last!" Grace exclaimed, as if the three and a half days he'd been gone had been thirty. She clasped her hands in front of her chin, only partially hiding a delighted smile that both warmed and wounded Helen.

I am glad she is so happy. I will miss her so much. The past few days had been enough for Helen to realize she could not become a permanent resident at Sutherland Hall. It was too dark and dreary here, and she feared its other inhabitants too much.

"Tell him to come up—oh, wait. He cannot. My dress—" Grace looked down at the layers of lace flowing about her.

"Mademoiselle, hold still please," the dressmaker admonished. Grace straightened and lowered her hands to her sides once more.

"He wishes to see all three of us, in his study," Christopher said.

"Now?" Grace asked. She turned away from them as the dressmaker began work on the other side of her skirts.

"Ten minutes ago, actually," Christopher said. "He made it sound rather urgent."

"Is he in a mood?" Grace asked, her tone unconcerned.

"Perhaps," Christopher said. "He's serious, certainly."

When is Lord Sutherland not in a mood? Helen wondered. The only time she'd ever witnessed his smile was when he danced or conversed with Grace.

"He did not seem particularly jolly," Christopher said. "But I'll go down to meet him now. Come along when you can."

"We will. And thank you," Grace called.

"You should go, too," Helen said, fearful that a slow response from Grace might kindle whatever foul mood Lord Sutherland happened to be in. "Allow both seamstresses to finish your hem, and they can help me after you've gone."

"Are you certain?" Grace asked, craning her neck, attempting to view Helen over her shoulder without moving too much. "You must be as tired of standing as I am."

More, Helen thought. It wasn't her wedding or gown to be excited over. "I'll be fine. Hurry now. Finish up and see your betrothed."

"All right. Will you explain for me?" Grace asked.

Helen addressed the seamstresses. "S'il vous plaît, faites sa robe avant la mienne."

Grace nodded her consent and sent Helen a look of gratitude.

"I could still teach you French, you know," Helen offered, as the woman attending her moved across the room to do her bidding.

"I should probably let you." Grace sighed wistfully. "My inability to communicate with Lady Sutherland's seamstresses is yet one more fault she finds in me."

Privately, Helen thought Lady Sutherland required much more than French lessons to improve *her* communication. Lessons in civility would be more fitting.

But to Grace she simply said, "You learned all you needed to at Grandfather's. An earl has fallen in love with you, after all."

"So he has . . ." Grace said, the same dreamy look upon her face that Helen had seen so frequently the past week. She tried, unsuccessfully, to keep her envy at bay.

French, music, painting, needlework . . . All the skills she possessed that Grace did not were not important to affairs of the heart. Yet Helen was happy for her sister and could think of no person more deserving of joy than Grace.

Helen waited patiently while the women finished the hem of Grace's gown and helped her change.

"Merci," Grace said when she was at last free of the delicate layers and dressed in her morning gown once more. "Thank you for waiting, sister," she said to Helen as she practically ran from the room.

"You're welcome," Helen called. To the dressmakers she added, "Ne pressez vous pas avec ma robe." She hoped they would take a very long time to finish her gown. In contrast to Grace, she was in no rush to leave the protection of this room. The past three days with Lord Sutherland away had been somewhat less stressful. Like his mother, he made Helen nervous, and she still wasn't quite certain how to act around him. Grace seemed to suffer none of these concerns. *But then, she brings out the best in him.*

Harrison would be here with the carriage soon, and Helen looked forward to a delightful afternoon with Beth. She sighed inwardly, longing for the peaceful, happy weeks she'd enjoyed as Mr. Preston's guest.

She wondered how he was faring, as she had not seen him in the days since Grace had refused him. Even during visits with Beth, he had been conspicuously absent. Helen wished she could inquire after Mr. Preston's well-being without arousing suspicion. She should not have been privy to that intimate and heart-wrenching conversation between the two of them. Indeed, she wished she had not. She could not seem to forget the hurt she'd felt both for Mr. Preston and herself.

All too soon, her gown was finished, and she was being helped from it. When her own dress was back in place, Helen lingered, anxious about going downstairs. She stood at the window, staring off into the distance, imagining that she sat at her window in the guesthouse, overlooking Mr. Preston's glorious gardens. She remembered the day they'd taken flowers to his wife's grave and the tender words he'd spoken. *How would it be to be loved so very much?*

Could Lord Sutherland possibly love Grace as much as Mr. Preston had loved Elizabeth? Strangely, Helen believed he did. The way he'd waltzed with Grace at his ball, the affectionate looks she caught passing between the two of them at dinner, and even the way his gruff manner seemed to soften when he was around her, all indicated the depth of his caring.

He loves her. And more than anything, I am glad of that.

Raised voices in the hallway pulled Helen from her reminiscing. The door banged open, and Grace rushed in, followed closely by Miranda.

"Oh, Helen." Grace ran toward her, meeting her halfway across the room. "He is sending me away." Tears burst forth as she buried her head on Helen's shoulder.

"What? What's this?" Helen held Grace close. "You must be mistaken. Calm yourself, and tell me what happened." She patted her back and spoke soothingly as she had with Beth the day she'd fallen and skinned her knee playing in the garden.

Miranda wagged her finger at the door, as if someone stood there. "No good, that man," she said, being uncharacteristically vocal. "Knew it the first time I saw him."

Grace momentarily composed herself. "Do not speak ill of Lord Sutherland. He *is* a good man. And I love him so." Self-control spent, she burst into tears once more. "First Grandfather's inheritance. And now Father is dead."

"What?" Helen leaned back, holding Grace away from her. "Father—our father is—"

Grace nodded. "Dead, Helen. He shall trouble us no more. And worse, Nicholas knows of our inheritance."

"Of course he does," Helen said. "You wrote to me some weeks ago that you had told him. He agreed to help us, remember?" She wondered suddenly if Lord Sutherland's assistance was what had finally swayed the court in their favor.

After weeks of unsuccessful attempts to obtain their inheritance, Christopher had quite suddenly and unexpectedly been awarded the full amount Grandfather had bequeathed.

"But what has any of that to do with you—with your wedding?" *Father is dead.*

"There is to be *no* wedding," Grace said, her breath coming in quick, short gasps. "Nic—Lord Sutherland wishes to free me from our betrothal. He thinks it *best* if I leave."

CHAPTER 14

January 1828

Christopher stood before the fireplace in Samuel's drawing room. "I blame myself. I should not have answered Lord Sutherland's questions. I should have—"

"Been less than honest?" Samuel suggested. He brought a hand to his mouth as he considered Grace's brother and the current problem. Nicholas had cried off, ending his betrothal to Grace, causing her to do little *but* cry for the past day and a half. Samuel could not have been more surprised when the five of them—Christopher, Grace, and Helen, along with Miranda and Harrison—had shown up on his doorstep yesterday afternoon, seeking refuge.

For lack of a better term, Samuel thought bitterly. It had taken a hefty dose of self-control to refrain from marching over to Sutherland Hall, grabbing Nicholas by the front of his coat, and shaking some sense into him. It required even greater restraint now to not walk into his own guest house, gather Grace in his arms, and offer comfort as well as renew the proposal he'd given her just two weeks earlier.

"She still won't see me?" Samuel asked Helen.

"No." Helen gave a slight shake of her head but did not look up from her task—sewing something tiny and intricate, it appeared. "She wishes to leave Yorkshire as soon as possible and asks continually about the properties you found for us."

"She needs time, is all," Samuel said, as much to himself as to the others.

"She needs *him*." Christopher turned from the fire to look at them. "All the time in the world will not stop her from loving Nicholas Sutherland."

"Love he doesn't deserve," Samuel muttered.

"Perhaps, but it isn't really the point," Christopher continued. "What matters is that I fix this. Grace deserves to be happy, and Lord Sutherland is who she would be happy with. We must find a way to reunite them."

Samuel scoffed. "You obviously have no idea the kind of grudges Nicholas is capable of. Once he develops prejudice against something—or some*one*—his mind is not easily changed."

"He isn't angry with Grace." Christopher strode to the cabinet and helped himself to a drink. "Rather, I believe he feels hurt—by the discovery of her meetings with you all those weeks—and now he distrusts her. He feels that, had she been given another choice first, she would not have chosen him."

"She *was* given another choice," Samuel said. "Two, even—myself or a remote life in the country—and she refused both." He ran a hand through his hair, exasperated with both his former brother-in-law and now—perhaps—his brother-in-law to be as well.

If only I could get a moment alone with Grace. He'd offer her comfort—and marriage. *I know I could make her happy.*

"Lord Sutherland does not realize that you proposed before he did," Christopher said. "Neither did I, or I should have made it very clear to him that she had refused."

"Forgive me for not wanting to make public news of my rejection." Samuel rose from his chair and began pacing the room.

"I do not blame you," Christopher said, returning to stand before the fire. "But Lord Sutherland will, and so we must remove you from the landscape if we are to reunite the unhappy couple."

"And how do you hope to accomplish that?" Samuel asked. "Am I to return to London for a season? Or is that not far enough to appease my stubborn neighbor? Perhaps I should be forced to the continent." He sounded almost as bitter as Nicholas.

"The problem has little to do with your whereabouts," Christopher said.

"How else do you plan to *remove* me then?" Samuel asked. "Ought I to be fearful for my life?" He gave a short, harsh laugh. "What outrageous plan have you for my demise?"

Christopher folded his arms in front of him. His eyes narrowed, and his mouth twisted in thought as he appraised Samuel. "Marriage."

"Most amusing." Samuel decided he was definitely upset with Christopher.

"It is not amusing at all," Helen said, surprising Samuel. "That was most unkind."

He turned to look at her, having almost forgotten she was in the room, and found her glaring at her brother.

Good, he thought. *Someone needs to set the whelp straight.*

As if attempting to fend them off, Christopher held up his hands. "Hear me out," he pled. "I only meant that we must make it appear to Lord Sutherland that your"—he looked pointedly at Samuel—"*interests* lie elsewhere. We both know the lengths the man will go to preserve his pride and hold on to his anger. But he loves Grace; I know he does," Christopher said. "I've heard as much from his own lips. However, he *believes* that she cares for *you*. And he feels he has been played a fool."

"Are you proposing . . ." Samuel waited, not really wanting to hear the young Mr. Thatcher's suggestion but half suspecting he might be on the right path.

One that will reunite Grace and Nicholas. What is right *about that?*

"I have in mind a simple deception," Christopher said. "We must convince Lord Sutherland that you are betrothed to another young lady. Then—and only then—will he consider trusting Grace again."

Samuel rolled his eyes. The scheme was as preposterous as he'd feared. "And where do I find such a young lady? It's not as if I can put an advertisement in the paper for a temporary fiancée."

"No," Christopher agreed. "That would not be good, and it wouldn't work besides. The ploy must be believable, so the young lady should be one you have known for some time."

Samuel pinched the bridge of his nose, sensing a headache coming on. "I could ask one of the Middleton girls. The oldest, Beatrice, has had her eye on me for quite some time. Then again, she has also been after every unattached male within the parish."

"That *could* work." Christopher nodded his head slowly.

Samuel scowled. "I was jesting. I've no desire to marry a Middleton, or any other woman around here, which is *exactly* what would happen were I to pretend betrothal to one. I won't do it. I care for Grace deeply, and I wish her happiness, but there are limits to my help. I cannot involve myself with another woman on *any* pretext, if for no other reason than the little girl asleep in the nursery upstairs. I cannot risk anything that might hurt Beth."

"Well said," Helen agreed quietly.

"I see what you mean." Christopher turned toward the fire once more, bracing his hands on the mantel. "You cannot risk your daughter becoming attached to a woman she does not know. We must take care not to hurt Beth or disrupt her life. And . . . you need a woman willing to play along. One who would not reveal Beth's identity. Which leaves us only one choice." He pushed off the mantel and strode purposely to the corner of the room. "Helen will have to do it."

Several seconds of stunned silence followed this suggestion, as if both parties concerned were so horrified that their voices had failed them.

"No," Samuel and Helen finally said, both speaking at once.

"I cannot," Helen said. "How could you, Christopher?" Her fingers clenched the sewing in her lap.

"She cannot," Samuel agreed. "Why would you make such an absurd suggestion?" One more stupidity like that, and the young Mr. Thatcher would find himself out on his ear.

"What is absurd about it?" Christopher spoke in a calm, level voice. "You and Helen have known each other for some time now. She has resided on your property these three months, during the last of which you took nearly every meal together and spent a great deal of time in each other's company. Were the two of you to develop a sudden affection for each other, it would seem both natural and believable."

"Perhaps if Miss Helen were older," Samuel said, returning to the formality they had used up until the weeks before Christmas, when they *had* spent so much time together. He glanced her way and was not surprised to find her sitting very still, with her head bent.

She is afraid of men, he might have added. And she certainly was not ready for marriage—not ready even to pretend it.

"I am nearly eighteen and six months." She spoke to her lap. "Though you see me as only your daughter's playmate, many women my age are already married."

Christopher's mouth quirked in a smile. "You see?" He placed a hand on Helen's shoulder and squeezed gently.

"I mean no offense, Miss Helen," Samuel hastened to say, feeling somehow that he had already offended her, "but realistically, would you be able to pull such a thing off? You do not seem to care for being close to other people. You and I are somewhat comfortable around each other now, but that has taken months, and we are yet nowhere near the ease of a betrothed couple. Could you pretend an engagement if that required being touched by or in close proximity to me frequently and around other people? "

The clock ticked quietly as he waited for her reply. Christopher looked as if he wished to speak, but Samuel shook his head and mouthed "wait" while nodding to Helen.

Another minute passed before she lifted her head; she did so not looking at either man, but instead at the vase of roses on the table in the center of the room. "I regret that you have noticed my difficulty, Mr. Preston. I assure you it is not personal, but I apologize all the same. I have enjoyed your company on every occasion. But you bring up a good point. I am not like other young ladies my age. I prefer staying home to going out. I prefer sewing doll clothes for Beth—" she held up the miniature gown she was working on—"over spending my evenings in a crowded salon or attending a ball. Marriage does not seem to be my path. Rather, my path seems to be that of a governess, as you once suggested." She rose from her chair.

"If you gentlemen will excuse me, I will take my leave. Harrison can escort me to the guest house."

"Wait," Christopher said, his hand on her arm. "Could you do this—*would* you, *will* you . . . for Grace?"

Helen closed her eyes, a strained look upon her face.

"That's not fair," Samuel said. "You can't place such a burden on your sister. Grace's happiness is not her responsibility."

"Isn't it?" Helen asked, her voice full of emotion. She opened her eyes, and he saw in them a change, a resolute determination of purpose. "Grace made *my* happiness, my entire well-being, her responsibility for many years. Why should I not do the same for her?"

Because . . . Samuel could find no argument against her self-sacrificing logic. This was not the first time he'd witnessed such unfailing love from this trio of siblings. Had Grace not purposely ruined her reputation so she, and particularly Helen, would not be forced into marriage? The irony of their current situation was not lost on him. Christopher and Helen were set on doing all they could so Grace *would* marry after all. And part of making that happen required Helen pretending to marry as well.

"Together we can reunite Grace and Lord Sutherland." Christopher turned Helen toward Samuel, guiding her across the room, his hand at her back.

"And what is your part to be in this scheme?" Samuel asked shrewdly, staring hard at Christopher. "Aside from concocting it, that is?"

"*I* will see that Lord Sutherland learns of your betrothal and has opportunities to witness your affection firsthand."

Helen winced.

Is it the thought of Nicholas or the idea of affection which causes her more distress? Either way Samuel did not like to see her so discomfited.

"Now," Christopher said. "Let us agree to keep our secret, and keep it well. We shall all have to be at our best if our plan is to succeed." Christopher thrust his hand forward, palm down. "To Grace's happiness."

"To Grace's happiness." Reluctantly, Samuel placed his hand on Christopher's. He could not quite believe he was agreeing to do this, to help unite Grace and Nicholas—a *second* time.

"To Grace's happiness," Helen said in a voice somewhat stronger than her normally soft one. She placed her hand over Samuel's.

Her touch was surprisingly warm. Their eyes met, and for just a second Samuel glimpsed a tenderness there that he had not seen before.

CHAPTER 15

After bidding Mr. Preston—*Samuel*, she must try to call him now—good evening, Christopher and Helen stepped into the frosty night on their walk to the guesthouse. Samuel had offered to have them driven, but Helen had declined, believing a little cold air might help clear her head and cool her simmering temper.

She hurried onto the snowy lane, walking ahead, without waiting for Christopher to offer his arm. Her hands clenched into fists at her sides, she marched briskly, arms swinging to and fro.

I cannot do this. This is a disaster, or it will be soon enough. Just thinking of what she had agreed to—what they were to pretend—made her stomach churn. Not because she couldn't imagine herself betrothed to Samuel. But precisely because she *could* imagine such a scenario all too well.

Since that day in October when she'd first seen him pining for his wife, and then later, when she'd discovered his interest in Grace, Helen had worked very hard to entertain *no* thoughts concerning Samuel other than as Beth's father.

And now I am expected to pretend the opposite?

"You are unusually quiet this evening," Christopher remarked.

Helen glanced at him sideways. "I am always quiet, and you know it."

"But there is a certain—tension—to this silence," Christopher said.

"*Now* your perception sets in," Helen muttered. "Little good that does me after I have made a bargain with the devil."

"You think Samuel Preston the devil?" Christopher jumped in front of her, stopping them both. A smile played at the corners of his mouth, and Helen longed to strike it from his face. Never, in her entire life, could she recall ever being this angry at her brother.

"I was not referring to Mr. Preston as the devil, but to *you!*"

The smile broke free into a broad, toothy grin. "Why, gentle sister, I am surprised. Such words from the mouth of an angel. Or, perhaps you are not so angelic after all?"

"At the moment, no, I am not. I would cheerfully murder you right now, were a weapon provided."

Christopher threw his head back and laughed wholeheartedly, sending puffs of white into the chilly air. Then, linking his arm through Helen's, he pulled her toward the guesthouse once more. "Such thanks I get for my kindness. *Tsk, tsk.* And here I expected gratitude." He sighed heavily. "Oh well, I suppose that will have to wait."

Helen tugged her arm from his and turned to face him. "Gratitude? For forcing me to pretend engagement to Samuel? Do not expect it, Christopher—ever. You have no idea what you've done." Whirling away from him, she renewed her stomping down the lane.

He took a running step to catch up and nearly slid on a patch of ice. "That's where you would be wrong." He jogged alongside her, then in front of her again, turning so he walked backward as he continued their conversation. "I am well aware of your feelings for Samuel."

Helen stopped so quickly that it took a few seconds for Christopher to react and stop as well.

"What do you mean?" she whispered. "What are you talking about?"

"I know you love him."

She met Christopher's gaze, which was smug and full of confidence, while hers, no doubt, appeared stricken and overly bright for the tears building behind her eyes.

"I do not." *I've tried so hard to avoid the very thing.*

Christopher lowered his head and gave her a sober look. "There is no shame in it. Samuel Preston is a good man—the perfect man for you, really."

"He still loves his wife," Helen protested. "And now he also loves Grace."

"He will always love his wife," Christopher said. "And from what you've told me, I daresay you've made peace with that already. As for Grace . . ." He moved alongside Helen, linking arms again, and they started strolling once more. "He cares for her, but it is not love. Not yet."

"But it could be," Helen said. "That is what he wishes. You saw him tonight. He *wants* to love her if she would only have him."

"No. Samuel is in love with the *idea* of being in love again," Christopher said with rather more wisdom than Helen had supposed him to have concerning matters of the heart. "Grace has helped him to see that possibility, after a very long time when he did not think there could be another woman he might care for as much as he did for Elizabeth."

"How is any of this favorable for me?" Helen asked, feeling colder and more disconsolate by the minute. *If Christopher was able to discern my true feelings, has Samuel also? Is that why he was so averse to our pretending engagement?*

Instead of answering her question, Christopher asked another. "Do you know how it was that Samuel became enamored of Grace?"

Helen shook her head. "Not really. She said only that he'd seen you both at the theatre with Grandfather."

"He did," Christopher said. "And he was touched by the care Grace showed Grandfather. When Samuel learned that Grandfather had died, he imagined he might find in Grace someone who understood the loss of a loved one, someone who had also experienced sorrow. And so he sought her out."

"You think he may find the same in me?" Helen had no idea how Christopher saw this situation as something she ought to be thanking him for.

"In you he has discovered something different, a woman who loves his daughter," Christopher said. "He has witnessed your compassion and caring, much as he observed those things in Grace at the theatre. Only with you, he has seen much, much more."

"Yet that has not caused him to love me," Helen said.

Compassion and caring are not enough.

"He doesn't dare because he believes that you fear him." Christopher nudged her shoulder with his as if chiding her for a fault. "You are correct in believing he sees you as someone to care for his daughter. Now you must show that you care for *him* as well."

"And I suppose you are going to tell me how to go about that," Helen said, elbowing Christopher in return. "I thought this plan of yours was about helping *Grace*."

"It is," he assured her. "But other opportunities may present themselves."

Helen sighed heavily. "There has been ample opportunity these past months for Samuel to show interest in me, but never once—" She paused, recalling those few occasions when she'd sensed a connection between them, when it had seemed they were on the verge of crossing some invisible barrier. *But we never did.* "—not once has he shown interest in me as anything other than a playmate for Beth."

"Hmm," Christopher said, sounding rather disinterested. "That, dear sister, is in the past. What you must do now is play your role as his fiancée convincingly. Which, I believe, you will do best if you are not play-acting at all."

"That is what I fear," Helen admitted. "I will be showing my true feelings, and though the end of your scheme may see Grace happy, it is I who shall fall to pieces with a broken heart, which will have no hope of mending."

"Courage," Christopher said, putting his arm around her shoulders. "Allow yourself to care for Samuel, and when you fear you cannot, think of Grace. Do this for her—and for yourself."

"What of Samuel?" Helen asked. "How does he fit into your schemes? Isn't being rejected by Grace punishment enough for his kindnesses to our family? Would you use him ill?"

"I will do nothing of the sort; I promise you," Christopher said. "I have considered all parties involved, and I pray and predict a favorable outcome for all."

They'd nearly reached the guesthouse, and though Helen was not entirely satisfied with the conversation, she felt no need to continue it. Christopher knew of her feelings; it appeared that Samuel did not. Christopher believed there was yet hope for all of them—Grace and Lord Sutherland . . . *Samuel and me.*

Do I trust Christopher, the man who has always said he wanted nothing to do with marriage?

"What do you know of all this?" Helen asked, turning to him suddenly. "In fact, *how* do you know of this? You've hardly been around of late. For a self-proclaimed eternal bachelor, you seem suddenly keen on matters of the heart."

"You do not give me enough credit," Christopher said with a sly smile.

"Perhaps not," Helen said, mistrust in her voice. She tapped a finger against her lips. "Could it be that you are more intelligent than you appear?"

"I am positively *brilliant*." Christopher puffed his chest proudly. "When this is all done with, you will agree. Though I must confess that Miranda may have put a word or two in my ear."

"*Miranda?*" Helen glanced up at her maid's window. "You cannot mean that *she* put you up to this." If Christopher was the least likely male to be involved in a romantic scheme of any sort, Miranda was easily his female counterpart.

"Don't misjudge her," Christopher said. "Miranda was once young, and she had a love affair of her own. She is not entirely unfamiliar with the yearnings of a young woman."

Helen felt her mouth open in surprise. The cold rushed in, stealing her breath almost as much as Christopher's announcement had. "Miranda—was in love?"

"Harrison told me." Christopher ran up the porch steps ahead of her.

"Do share," Helen said, running after him.

Christopher looked around furtively, as if he feared Miranda might be lurking. "It was Harrison's brother," Christopher whispered. "They were to be married, but then he was killed in battle during the Napoleonic wars. Afterward Harrison helped her get a position as a maid in Grandfather's house."

"How long ago was this?" Helen asked.

"Nearly twenty-five years. Long ago, but not so long that she has forgotten what it feels like to love someone. It was she who first alerted me to the possibility of a match between you and Samuel."

Helen leaned against the rail and tried to picture a young Miranda in love with a dashing young soldier who looked much like Harrison. "I never knew, never imagined."

"It's probably best to act as if you still don't," Christopher advised.

"Just one more thing for me to pretend," Helen said, brought back to the present and her own ill-fated affair.

Christopher shook his head. "No other pretending is necessary, remember?" He grabbed the doorknob, then looked back at her. "I should mention one more thing."

"Yes?" *What else?* She probably didn't want to know.

"Try being angry more often," Christopher suggested. "It brings out a rather attractive side of you."

He pulled open the door and ran into the house before the scoop of snow she'd gathered from the rail could hit him.

CHAPTER

Samuel stomped snow from his boots and knocked briskly on the door of the guesthouse. He'd barely removed his hand when it swung open. Grace stood before him, an expectant, hopeful look on her face. Her eyes landed upon him, and Samuel watched as the hope gave way to disappointment and telltale sorrow. A few weeks earlier, he would have teased her for this reaction, would have feigned that his feelings were hurt—though at the time, there would have been some truth to that.

But now...

The wound caused by her rejection was healing. Somehow, even over the course of their autumn of friendship, and in spite of the hope he'd felt, he'd realized deep within himself that they were not destined to be more than friends. If he was to be honest with himself, he had to admit he'd known since the moment at his ball when Nicholas had appeared beside her.

I likely realized it before Nicholas. And, as it appeared

that his former brother-in-law still didn't realize what he'd had, once again it was up to Samuel to show him.

Grace's lip quivered slightly before she forced it into a smile. "Hello, Samuel."

He doffed his hat and gave a slight bow. "Good morning, Grace." He took her hand and kissed the back of it lightly.

Her smile brightened to one more genuine. "Have you come to cheer me up? Because I am not sure that will work if we are not standing with a fence between us."

"I daresay you are right," Samuel said with only the slightest hint of melancholy. He'd had that day of hope when Nicholas sent her away, the fleeting thought that Grace might yet be his, but in seeing her tearstained face and hearing her weep out her heartache the past few days, Samuel realized that was not to be. And so he tried to put aside the notion once and for all. Grace had given her heart to another. Now Samuel must do all in his power to reunite her with Nicholas.

She stepped back and motioned for him to come inside.

Samuel entered the cozy foyer, feeling warmth from the adjoining sitting room fire already.

Grace closed the door behind him. "Have you found more properties for us to consider?"

"No. Only the three, I'm afraid. The others—" He twirled his hat and sighed. "They are either too close to those who know your past, or—"

"Or the landlords will not have us because my reputation precedes me," Grace finished.

"I am afraid so," Samuel said.

"No matter." She patted his hand lightly. "After all, that is what I had planned for all along. What was it the poet George Herbert said? " She brought her hand to her chin, considering. "'I have made my bed, and now must lie in it.' Or something of that sort." She frowned. "Though, in this instance, that is a rather bad pun, considering the bed I ended up in."

Samuel noted the lack of humor in her voice. "I'm glad to see you're up to quoting literature again, at least—a sure sign of improvement. I think a different line of Herbert's is more fitting: 'He that hath love in his breast, hath spurs in his sides.'"

"And everywhere else," Grace muttered. She wrung her hands suddenly. "Oh, Samuel, what am I to do? I never thought I could live with Nicholas, and now it seems I cannot live without him." She folded her arms across her middle, as if attempting to hold in her pain.

He took a step closer to her. "Do not despair." Simple, empty words—words he'd heard often enough from others in the weeks following Elizabeth's death. "Time—" He could not bring himself to say that time would heal her wound. He knew well enough it likely would not. Instead, he needed to focus on setting the situation right.

"I am afraid books are my only solace," Grace said. "And even they cannot seem to transport me from sorrow as they once did." She sighed heavily. "But enough of that. Here you stand, yet I've not even invited you for tea."

"I cannot stay." Samuel glanced about the foyer. "You are not alone, are you?" Surely her siblings and servants both understood the need for Grace to have company at all times right now. When Elizabeth died he had borne his grief alone. And it had not been good. "Are Miranda and Harrison not here?"

"Harrison is meeting with Christopher to prepare for our journey. We mean to make a decision quickly and be gone as soon as possible."

"There is no rush. You are no trouble here," Samuel hurried to assure her, though he guessed her real reason for wanting to leave. Being so close to Nicholas, yet not being with him, had to be difficult.

"Thank you, Samuel," Grace said. "Your generosity knows no bounds. But being here now troubles *me*. It will be better when we are all settled elsewhere and can begin anew."

That wouldn't do. How could they possibly hope to reunite Nicholas and Grace if she left the province? Samuel chose his words with care. "You do realize that no matter how far away you go, your heart—or part of it—will remain here." He glanced out the window in the direction of Sutherland Hall. "Or rather, there. Troubles of the heart follow anywhere you go."

Her eyes narrowed, "Who said that?"

"I did." Samuel shrugged. *I am starting to sound rather wise—somewhat like Helen.* "No doubt I read something similar in a book once. But I speak from experience." Instead of reaching out to take her hands to offer comfort as he had so many times before, he shoved his hands deep in his coat pockets. "After Beth was born, I went to London and thought to never return. I believed that by staying away from the place that held Elizabeth's memories, life would be easier. I didn't wish to smell her roses or hear her pianoforte or see her horse in the stables. I told myself it would be easiest to pretend that my life with her had not happened."

"But you had your daughter," Grace said.

"Yes. Beth was so like her mother from the time she was an infant. But she was not what brought me back. Instead of feeling less grief in London, I felt more. I had to return here to make peace with the past. If I was to go on with my life, I had to confront my memories—good and bad."

"You are still confronting some of them," Grace said.

"Yes," Samuel agreed, remembering the day he'd told her how Elizabeth had died in childbirth, and how—as a physician—he still felt responsible. "But I do know *some* peace. And it is because I dared to face the past."

"It is different for me." Grace turned away. "The man I love is not dead. It is not a grave I dread visiting, but seeing the very man himself. I do not think I could bear it. So I must leave."

"I will be sorry to see you go," Samuel said.

They stood silently for a minute, Samuel staring at her back and wondering at the charade he had come here to begin. Was it even worth attempting? Was there any possibility it could work? He didn't see how, if Grace was determined to leave so soon.

Movement at the top of the stairs caught his eye; a flash of blue skirted out of sight. *Helen.* Had she overheard any of his conversation with Grace? If so, what did she think? He supposed, at the least, he ought to proceed with their plan for this morning.

Samuel cleared his throat. "Is Helen here?"

Grace turned to face him, brushing hastily at her wet cheeks.

He checked the impulse to step forward and offer comfort. *Would this entire thing not be easier settled were I to seek out Nicholas and perhaps knock some sense into him?* Unlike his former brother-in-law, Samuel was not usually given to violence. But seeing Grace's tear-filled eyes made him keenly desire the opportunity for a solid punch to Nicholas's jaw.

"You are here to see Helen?" Grace said, bringing him back to the room and the task at hand. "Yes, of course." Her brow furrowed slightly as she gave him a peculiar look. "Is she expecting you?"

"I hope so," Samuel said, forcing a smile. *Though it may be easier if she is not—if, over the course of the last two days, she has decided she wants no part of this ridiculous scheme.*

Grace moved toward the stairs at the same moment Helen appeared at the top. Head bowed as she customarily held it, she began her descent, a sapphire-blue cloak swishing about her ankles. She reached the bottom, paused, then looked up at the two of them, wearing a dazzling smile.

"Good morning, Grace. Hello, Mr. Preston."

Samuel took her gloved hand and kissed the back of it, lingering a few seconds longer than necessary, enough to enjoy the sweet scent of whatever perfume she wore.

"You look quite lovely this morning," he said, finding it very true. Complimenting her on her appearance was easy. Helen *was* a beautiful young woman, perhaps never more so than this morning. Her golden curls were swept back from her face and held with a set of glittering sapphire combs that matched her cloak, the gown beneath it, and especially her eyes—eyes that seemed to sparkle with a joy he hadn't before seen in them.

He was impressed with her acting already.

"Are you two going somewhere?" Grace asked, looking from one to the other uncertainly.

"I have been invited to play," Helen said, laughter in her voice. "By Beth. It has been our habit for some time now."

"And I have come to escort Helen across the snowy lane," Samuel said.

"Aren't you dressed a bit—formally—for play?" Grace asked, a hint of suspicion in her voice.

"Beth is quite particular about her playmates," Samuel cut in. "She insists upon best dress and manners in the nursery." He winked at Helen and watched a blush steal across her face. "Shall we be off?" With a twinge of guilt, he held his arm out to her. It didn't feel right to be so jolly—or to be pretending at being so jolly—in front of Grace right now. As Helen placed her hand upon his arm, he reminded himself of their worthy cause.

"I'll be back in a few hours," Helen said, waving to her sister.

Samuel nodded. "Good day, Grace. I hope you find some peace in it."

"Perhaps I shall," she said, a curious expression on her

face as Samuel turned from her and guided Helen to the front door.

He replaced his hat, and outside they walked in silence beyond the narrow drive and out of view of the guesthouse windows. Still Helen kept her hand on his arm. She had not acted uncomfortable with their closeness, and he wondered at this, given her skittishness on previous occasions. He considered telling her that she needn't continue holding onto him but then thought better of it. If they were to convince others of their betrothal she needed to get used to touching him. Besides, he did not wish her to fall on the slippery ground. He hadn't come to fetch her to play with Beth before, but he should have. He frowned, feeling rather appalled by his apparent lack of concern for a lady who had been in his care. The idea that he had neglected his guest so did not sit well.

Using his free hand, Samuel withdrew a folded piece of paper from his pocket, then shook it open. "Christopher suggested we begin with this list of things that we should know about each other. It seems he doesn't have much confidence in my courting abilities."

"It isn't you he's worried about," Helen said. "I've never done any courting before—or rather, no one has ever courted me." Her voice quieted with the admission.

"At your choosing, however. Is that not so?" Samuel asked, glancing at her. "I thought that you did not like attending balls, or even being out in public at all."

"It is partially my choosing," Helen said.

"Only partially?" His brows rose. "You do like going out? Or perhaps . . . Was there was someone you *wished* to be courted by?"

"Perhaps once." She waved her hand dismissively—

What? His curiosity was piqued. Was she so disbelieving of the idea that someone might find her attractive? That she felt so little confidence in herself bothered him.

"I was not speaking of simply a desire to be courted. What I meant was that it is not of my choosing to be—afraid of men." She kept her gaze straight ahead as she spoke, as if focused intently on the path.

"You wish that you were not shy?" Samuel asked.

"I am not shy—truly," she added. He leaned closer to better see her, a questioning, skeptical look upon his face.

"Ask Grace and Christopher or Miranda and Harrison," she said. "Ask your daughter."

"Those are all people you know well," Samuel said. "It is one thing to be comfortable with family and friends, but you are shy with all else—even with me, somewhat, and I have known you more than three months."

"You are a man."

He barked a short laugh, then tried to cover it with a cough. "I am glad you've noticed. We shall call this lesson one in courtship: the lady must take note of a man."

Samuel was beginning to see the wisdom of Christopher's list. *Best to follow his advice. He knows his sisters much better than I.*

"You are mocking me." Helen stopped walking and faced him, her hand slipping from his arm.

"No—yes," he admitted. "Perhaps a little." He winced at the admission as she moved beyond his reach.

"I did not intend to tease," he said. "It was the way you said *man*. As if I were a disease."

A hint of a smile formed on Helen's pretty mouth. "In my defense, most of the men I've met *are*."

Samuel laughed again, and this time she joined him. It was a lovely sound, and hearing it made his heart feel surprisingly light.

"My dear Helen." He scratched the side of his head. "It

would seem that you have not become acquainted with the right sort of men. A few of us are decent fellows."

"I know." Her quick response had him glancing at her again and noting her rosy cheeks. He wondered if they were attributable only to the cold.

He reached for her hand, and she allowed him to take it. He tucked it into the crook of his arm as they started off on the path once more. "We shall work to overcome your concerns then, shall we?" Perhaps this exercise would benefit both sisters.

"We shall work to reunite Grace and Lord Sutherland," Helen corrected in a tone that suggested she did not wish to speak of herself any longer.

"Agreed," Samuel said. "But look, we are halfway to the house and haven't discussed a single item on Christopher's list. It would seem I am as hopeless as your brother believes me to be." Samuel glanced at the paper again. "Ready to begin?"

Helen nodded and looked at him expectantly.

Samuel cleared his throat and attempted seriousness, though he found the paper and questions on it an annoyance. Surely he and Helen could carry on a conversation based on more important things than the trivial subjects before him. "What is your favorite color?"

She hesitated a moment, then spoke quietly. "Red."

"That is somewhat surprising," he said. "I would not have guessed."

"I realize it is not an appropriate color for a lady to favor," Helen said.

"You may prefer whichever color you like," Samuel hurried to assure her. "Red is simply bold. I would have guessed that you prefer something calm, perhaps pink, like the gown you wore to the Christmas ball."

"You remember what I wore that night?" Her fingers fluttered on his arm.

"Why does that so astonish you?" Samuel asked. "I guarantee that every man, excepting perhaps the near-blind Mr. Phillips, took notice of you. You were easily the most beautiful woman in attendance."

She stopped walking but did not release his arm, so he was forced to stop too. "Remember, we are not pretending to each other, only to my sister and Lord Sutherland." She looked at him reproachfully. "You cannot tell me I was the prettiest girl there when you had eyes only for Grace." She pulled away from him and took a step back.

True enough. He'd been focused on forcing Grace—and Nicholas—to a decision that night. Until now it had never occurred to him that in doing so he might have hurt Helen. "I spoke the truth about your beauty. But I am also guilty with regard to your sister." Samuel held his hands out, palms up. "I did allow myself to care for Grace—more than I should have," he admitted. "In my defense, I had other motives that night as well. Nicholas had made his feelings for Grace abundantly clear with their waltz, but I wanted him to act on those feelings and to come to a decision about his future with Grace. I believed that if I presented myself as competing for her affection he might finally take action. And they *were* engaged—in a manner beyond the betrothal forced upon them—the very next afternoon."

"Only after Grace refused *your* proposal," Helen said, her brow wrinkling as if trying to puzzle it all out. "Were you not sincere in your offer, then?"

"Very much so," Samuel said, feeling again the sting of the moments following Grace's rejection. "I care for your sister, and I'm sure we could have been quite happy together. But before I asked the question, I knew what her answer would be. No one who saw Nicholas and Grace dancing could have mistaken the feelings of either. Whether she was ready to admit it to herself or not, she was already in love with him. My proposal forced her to examine her feelings and make a choice."

"I think you are proving to be very good at this game we are playing," Helen said. "You've already been manipulating the circumstances for months. This is merely a continuation."

Samuel frowned. "*Manipulate* is a rather harsh word. I have never forced anyone to do anything, nor do I intend to now. I merely helped provide conditions where two people, whom I believed would be a good match, might have the opportunity to get to know each other and fall in love."

"I am rather stunned at the trouble you went to for my sister," Helen said. She searched his eyes. "Why? And why continue helping us now? We were complete strangers to you."

"And what a pity that was." Samuel found himself wanting to reach for her and hold her hands as he had held Grace's so many times in a gesture of friendship, but he was not at all certain Helen would be comfortable with such a touch. Instead, he clasped his hands behind his back. "I watched your family at the theatre—your sister and brother, your grandfather . . ."

Samuel realized that he hadn't seen Helen on those occasions. In truth, she'd never been a part of their outings. *By choice?* He both hoped so and hoped it was not so. Did she dread going out so much that's she'd voluntarily missed out on the opportunities her grandfather had been able to provide? What other explanation could there be? Surely they had not excluded her deliberately.

"I'd never seen a trio more loving or concerned for one another," he said. "I had determined to attempt to meet your family, but they quite suddenly stopped coming to the theatre. Shortly thereafter, I learned of your grandfather's death, followed by word of your father's intention to marry off your sister. So I made my interest known."

"He intended to see *me* married," Helen said, her voice quiet again. She looked down. "Grace persuaded Father that she was not too old to marry, and he sent her in my place. Once again, she saved me."

"And so we shall save her now," Samuel said. He looked at Helen a long moment, her golden curls hanging on both sides of her face as she studied the ground. Had Grace stepped in and protected her, sheltered her so many times that this extreme shyness and lack of confidence was the result? The idea bothered him. Helen needn't be this way, needn't miss the joys of life, whether that meant not attending the theatre or a ball, or being able to have a conversation with a man.

Or realizing her worth.

"I was in earnest about your being the most beautiful woman at Lord Sutherland's ball." He nodded slowly as she at last looked up at him. "In the short time I was there, I heard both ladies and gentlemen commenting on your beauty. The latter were quite smitten with you, while several ladies sounded as if they wished to *smite* you." He grinned. "Envy never lies."

"And beauty is not always a blessing," Helen said.

"True," Samuel said, guessing that she referred to difficulties with other women being envious. He doubted her sister was among those. "Grace is beautiful too, though her features are not as striking as yours. Her personality was what I found myself attracted to. She exudes confidence, speaks her mind, and is always up to some mischief. Life around her will never be boring—one reason why she is so good for Nicholas. He tends toward the boring and serious."

"Grace and I are complete opposites in that regard," Helen said with a sigh of dejection.

"I wouldn't say that." Samuel held his arm out, and she placed her hand upon it. "You've agreed to this *conspiracy* of Christopher's—something very Grace-like of you to do. Plus, your favorite color is red." Samuel silently congratulated himself on directing the conversation back to the list. He was beginning to suspect that before this exercise ended, he would grow quite appreciative of Christopher's paper and the safe topics it suggested.

"Is there a particular reason you prefer red?" he asked.

"Because of a dress I had—a long time ago, when I was seven."

"Did your father buy it for you?" Knowing what he did of the deceased Mr. Thatcher, Samuel found that possibility highly doubtful but could think of no other reason why a dress would be so long remembered.

"Has Grace not told you of our father?" Helen asked, turning her head to look at him. "He never bought us anything. If it had been up to him to clothe us, we would have been—cold."

Samuel worked to hide a smile. But their circumstance growing up was nothing to smile about. He cleared his throat again, something he feared he'd do a lot around her as he tried to avoid hurting her feelings. Conversing with Grace was much easier; he'd always felt like he could tell her anything and be anything around her, rather like family. He missed that freedom. "Where did you get the dress, then? If it has determined something so very important as your favorite color, there must be a good story behind it."

"Yes," Helen said, a wistful smile on her lips.

"Will you not share it?" Samuel asked, wishing he needn't pry words from her. *Patience*, he thought, giving himself the same advice he'd given Grace. He could not expect Helen to confide in him the very first day of their pretended relationship.

"You wish to hear it?" She glanced at him, wariness apparent in the lines creasing her forehead.

"I do." They were nearly to the house and would soon part company for a few hours, at least. If their plan was to work, they would of necessity spend much of their time together in the coming days.

"All right. I will attempt to explain." Helen bit her lip and appeared to consider a moment before beginning her tale. "Grace never let me help with the wash. Have you noticed her hands?"

"I have," he said solemnly. "Her scars speak of years of love and sacrifice."

"They do," Helen said, her eyes bright. "And she did not want me to have similar scars. So I was never allowed to wash clothes. I hung them, folded them, and, when I was seven, she taught me to iron. By then, Christopher helped with deliveries and did other odd work to earn money."

"Go on," Samuel said, still uncertain how any of this related to a red dress.

"One day I was ironing what I thought to be a beautiful red gown." Her face flushed as if embarrassed. "You may well guess that some of the customers we had were not of the type that polite society associates with."

Or at least they don't admit it, Samuel thought ruefully, remembering how it had been suggested by a few well-meaning, but off-the-mark acquaintances that his feelings of loneliness might be abated with a visit or two with women of loose morals. "I understand," he said. "Continue your story."

Helen's eyes reflected appreciation for his lack of censure. "The red gown had several layers. Each had to be pressed, then carefully hung over the side of the board so as not to wrinkle while the next section was ironed."

"Sounds like tedious work."

"It was. I hated it. I complained to Grace. I thought her job more fun—after all, she got to play in the water, or so I thought."

Samuel smiled. "Exactly something like Beth would think. No wonder the two of you are such great friends."

"Beth is adorable," Helen said. "Do not ever let her get near an iron or a laundry tub."

"I intend to keep her safe from all such dangers," Samuel said in mock seriousness.

"Good." Helen offered him a tiny smile. "My hands haven't the scars of Grace's, but many a time, I suffered burns from the iron."

"Were you burned while ironing the red gown?" Samuel guessed.

Helen nodded. "Worse, I burned a hole in the dress. One corner of one of the outer layers caught on the board. I didn't notice, so I ironed it with the other layers, over and over. When I shook the gown out at the end, there was a hole, right in the front. Oh, how I cried."

"Was Grace very upset with you?" Samuel asked, even more perplexed as to how red could possibly be Helen's favorite color when it had to do with such disaster.

"She never scolded me. She just looked at the dress and said, 'Oh, Helen.' Then she took Christopher with her and left to make the deliveries. They brought the gown with them, and they were gone for hours. I fretted, worried that something terrible had become of Grace, that she was being punished for my mistake, that no one would pay her to do laundry anymore. And if that happened, I didn't know what would become of us." Helen's forehead and nose bunched with worry as she recounted the anxiety of that afternoon.

Samuel could imagine the scene all too well. He'd seen how many ladies of the upper class mistreated their servants and could imagine that those working in a brothel might treat a young wash girl even worse—and that when she *hadn't* made a disastrous mistake.

"It was dark when they finally returned. Grace had a basket with new laundry to be washed, and Christopher carried a large bag of potatoes. We hid them all over the house—never more than two in the same location, lest

Father find them. Grace said they were what we had to eat for the next month, so we had to be careful to make them last."

"Did they last?" Samuel asked, imagining the three children near starvation. Grace would have been only thirteen at the time, and Christopher nine. And at seven, Helen would have been far too young to be charged with the task of ironing women's gowns. They'd all had to grow up so quickly.

"The potatoes almost lasted the month," Helen said. "We went only a day or two without, and that happened most months anyway."

"And you love the color red because it reminds you of this dreadful time?"

Helen laughed. "Of course not. I love red because of what came next." Her eyes sparkled. "That Christmas was the one year I received a present—a beautiful red dress Grace had made from the ruined gown. The woman it had belonged to had been furious and demanded that Grace pay for it. Of course, we couldn't begin to do that, but Grace had given the woman an entire week's worth of pay—except what Christopher had taken to buy the potatoes—and agreed to pay her most of the rest of our earnings for the month, as well as doing her laundry for free for several months beyond that. In doing so, Grace was able to keep the gown—and kept it hidden from me. When I slept at night, she stayed up, sewing the dress for me from the very gown that had caused so much trouble." Helen smiled, a faraway look on her face. "I'd never had any new clothes before, or even anything that wasn't mostly rags. I felt like a princess when I put that red dress on."

"If you were half as beautiful as you are now, I am sure you looked like one too." Samuel imagined a younger, smaller Helen twirling about in the made-over gown.

"Grace sewed Christopher a pair of fancy knee pants

from one of the layers, though he never seemed to care for them quite as much as I cared for the dress."

"I should think not," Samuel said. "Most nine-year-old boys wouldn't wear such breeches, preferring to be—as you said before—cold."

Helen pressed her lips together and attempted a stern look, though he suspected she wished to laugh, however inappropriate the topic was.

"Grace used every scrap of that fabric," Helen continued. "She tied strips of it onto a string, which she wound all around the house for Christmas. We thought it very festive. And we had sweet potatoes—instead of regular—for Christmas supper. Father wasn't home, so we stayed up late and danced and played. It was glorious. How I loved that dress—and Grace."

Samuel loved the look of rapture Helen wore as she finished the story. He could sense the depth of her love for her sister and was beginning to understand why Helen had agreed to pretending a relationship with him if it meant Grace's happiness. His affection and admiration for the Thatcher family swelled at hearing the story of the red dress, and he thought that red might be his favorite color now too.

"Whatever became of the dress?" he asked.

"I outgrew it," Helen said sadly. "Twice Grace altered it and then lengthened it as much as possible. Still, I loved it and kept it hidden safely away, beneath our mattress, so Father couldn't gamble it away."

"Where is it now?" Samuel asked. Perhaps Helen still had the gown, or maybe it had been left behind when the siblings fled their grandfather's house.

"I don't know where it is, exactly." Her wistful smile returned. "I was eleven when Grace began taking me on deliveries. Some of the places we passed were worse than our own little hovel, and one day I saw a girl wearing only a large shirt with a rope tied around the waist."

"You gave your red dress away." *Of course.* What else would generous, kindhearted Helen do? He recalled the way she had jumped in to help with Beth that first morning at breakfast and the many hours she'd spent making things for his daughter's Christmas present. He remembered her kind words at Elizabeth's grave and the empathy she had shown him whenever he had bad days.

"It made the girl so happy that *I* became happy doing it," Helen said. "Peculiar how that works, isn't it?"

"One of life's more curious phenomena," he agreed. "You are fortunate to have experienced it when you were so young. You've more wisdom than many people twice your age."

"I am not *so* young now," Helen insisted, her annoyance apparent from the way her curls shook as she tossed her head. "But I *am* fortunate to have Grace as a sister. She deserves to be happy."

"And she shall be," Samuel predicted. "We will succeed. Nicholas *will* want her back, and he will know that nothing is in his way."

"I hope you're right," Helen said. "I have never seen Grace so miserable, and that is saying something."

He was certain it was, given their upbringing—or lack of one.

They reached the house, and the butler appeared to open the front doors as if he'd been there waiting for their arrival.

"I'm so glad you're here!" Beth launched herself at Helen the moment she'd crossed the threshold. Samuel caught them both from careening back out the doors.

"Beth, that is no way to treat a guest," he scolded, but only half-heartedly. He loved seeing his daughter so happy, though he knew he needed to curb her wild ways. Strong-willed though Elizabeth had been, she was a lady in every sense of the word. Each morning on his walk, he mulled the problem over.

"Miss Helen isn't a guest," Beth declared, laying claim to Helen's hand and towing her toward the staircase. "She's my friend."

"Thank you for walking with me," Helen called to Samuel over her shoulder.

"My pleasure," he said, for the benefit of any servants who might be watching—and also because it was true. The story of Helen's red dress had touched him. He wouldn't have guessed that a simple question about one's favorite color would reveal so much about a person. He suspected, however, that Christopher knew otherwise.

"No small victory," Samuel murmured as he reflected on their walk and watched Helen ascend the stairs. She'd spoken more the past twenty minutes than during all of their previous conversations. Perhaps, as she'd declared, she really wasn't as shy as he'd believed.

"Let's play Going to a Ball." Beth gathered her dolls from the various rooms of the dollhouse. She held up the two girls, clothed in the finery Helen had sewn for them. "I'll be these." She thrust the boy doll at Helen. "And you be him."

"Very well." Helen leaned forward to accept the assigned doll. "But I really don't know much about balls. I haven't been to very many." She sat the doll in front of her on the rug.

"You went to the Christmas Eve ball with Papa," Beth said.

Not with *him, though that would have been lovely.* "And like your father, I did not stay long."

"Did you dance?" Beth lay on her stomach, chin propped on her hands.

"I did not," Helen said.

"Not even with Papa?"

"Not even with him," Helen said, wistfully. "I wanted to," she admitted, remembering the awful moment when Samuel had asked Grace to dance instead of her. "But I didn't."

"Why not?" Beth asked.

"Well . . ." Helen considered how to best explain. Beth was the sort of child who proceeded to go after whatever she wanted. Helen smiled as she imagined Beth all grown up and marching across a ballroom to request a dance from the gentleman she favored. Perhaps by then, if there were enough grown-up girls with Beth's temperament, such a thing would be in vogue. "When a lady attends a ball, she must wait for a gentleman to ask her to dance. If he does not, then she does not get to dance with him."

"That isn't fair." Beth stood one of the girl dolls on the carpet in front of her. "This lady is going to ask the gentleman with the brown hair to dance with her." She pushed the doll toward Helen's. "I would like you to dance with me, sir."

Helen stifled a laugh as she stood the requested "gentleman" on the floor beside Beth's "lady."

"I would be honored," Helen said. She bent the doll forward in a bow. "Now the lady must curtsy," she whispered.

"Why?" Beth asked.

"Because it is proper and polite." Samuel's voice above them startled Helen.

She tilted her head back to look up at him. Never once, during all of her weeks of playing with Beth, had he appeared in the nursery. She had never considered that he might, hadn't ever worried that anyone besides Beth would be privy to their conversation or observe their play. Helen felt foolish sitting on the floor, making dolls converse. And how much of their conversation had he heard?

"Miss Helen and I will show you how a gentleman and lady greet each other before dancing." Samuel held his hand out to her, and nervously, Helen accepted. He pulled her up, and they stood—far too close—facing each other.

"How long have you been here watching us?" she asked, not daring to meet his gaze.

"Long enough to realize that I should have asked you to dance at Nicholas's ball."

Heat flooded her cheeks.

"I did not think you cared for dancing," Samuel said.

I would care with you as my partner. But of course she could not say that, so she said nothing and simply looked past him, toward the nursery door.

"Come, let's show Beth how to dance properly," he coaxed. Still holding her hand, he tugged her from the rug to the wood floor and the large, open space before the window seat. "It appears my daughter is greatly lacking in social skills. I am beginning to fear I have done her wrong in allowing such free reign. It is good you are here to show her what is proper."

"Beth has plenty of time to learn to be proper." Helen raised her eyes to his and found that they twinkled with merriment. "Right now you wouldn't wish her to be any other way."

"You're right. I wouldn't. Even so, at some point, she must learn what is expected of her." He sent a pointed look in Beth's direction, though she likely did not notice, bent over and attempting to stand on her head as she was.

Samuel gave a weary sigh. "The older she grows, the more I lose hope that she will ever conform to those expectations. She has too much of her mother in her." His smile left no doubt as to the direction of his thoughts, and Helen felt a moment of longing. *If only the thought of me might make him smile like that.* But he was attracted to women like Elizabeth and Grace, who were vivacious and full of life. Not to shy ones who struggled to put two sentences together when in his presence.

"Watch closely, Beth," Samuel instructed. He released Helen's hand and walked a few paces away, then returned and stood to face her again. "Miss Helen, would you do me the honor of being my partner for this next dance?"

After a slight hesitation, she played along, telling herself it would be no different from making the dolls talk to one another. "I would be delighted, Mr. Preston." She held the sides of her skirt and dipped into a curtsy as he sketched a bow. He held his arm out, and she placed her hand upon it. They promenaded around the room—and a giggling Beth—before returning to the same spot.

He stopped and turned to face Helen. "Ready?"

"For what?" she asked warily.

"The dance I owe you. I think a waltz will do. If my titled neighbor can get away with such a thing, I ought to be able to as well."

Helen shook her head and took a step backward. "Grace said I mustn't dance the waltz."

Mr. Preston stepped forward, so that they were close again. "Do you always do what your sister tells you to?" he asked with a rather wicked glint in his eye. "After all, it was she who set the example and waltzed first." He captured Helen's hand before she could move again and placed his other at her waist.

"We have no music," she protested, feeling a little shocked and breathless already at being so near Samuel and feeling his hand at her waist. "I don't know the waltz."

"We shall count it out, and I'll teach you," he said. "Beth, pay attention. I have no doubt that by the time you're of age, this dance will be acceptable everywhere."

"You would wish your daughter to dance this closely to a man?" Helen asked.

He appeared to consider a moment. "The right man, yes. But the wrong one—" His expression darkened. "I think it is a good thing that many years yet separate Beth from courtship." He looked steadily at Helen. "Place your hand on my shoulder."

She did, hoping he would not notice her fingers trembling.

"This dance is counted in threes. Follow my lead. We will move in a circle about the room. Ready?"

Feeling anything but ready, she nodded.

"Count with me, Beth," Samuel called. "One—" He stepped forward, and Helen moved back. "—two, three." He guided her sideways next, forming a square.

"One, two, three," Beth shouted far too quickly for them to follow. Helen glanced behind her and saw Beth bouncing up and down on her toes. "One-two-three."

"That's it," Samuel said, guiding Helen to one step for each of Beth's three shouted beats. "You're a natural."

"Grandfather saw that we all had dancing lessons," Helen confessed, "though he never allowed us to learn the waltz."

"It is not so different—nor as scandalous—as all that." Samuel led her so that their circle widened. They glided past Beth, who clapped happily and continued her counting—still far too fast.

But Helen hardly noticed. Somehow she heard the music in her head. As they began their third circle around the room, her hand relaxed on Samuel's shoulder, and she smiled.

We are dancing. It did not matter that they were not at a ball. It was better this way, just the two of them, the only onlooker a precocious three-year-old.

"Aha!" Samuel said, startling her so that she nearly missed a step. "I saw that smile. You are enjoying yourself."

Helen did not try to deny it. "Because you are an

excellent partner," she said. "Much as I suspected you would be."

"You did?" His brows arched as if he did not believe her. "I had no idea you'd thought on the matter at all, or I most certainly would have asked you to dance at Nicholas's ball."

"It is probably better that you did not," Helen said. "I would likely have been flustered in front of all those people."

"No reason for you to have been," Samuel said. "You have everything they have—and more. You are a beautiful, sweet young lady. Any man would be fortunate to have you as his dance partner—or more."

Any man but you? Oh, Samuel.

He led them nearer the window, where the sunlight poured in from outside. "Christopher is of the opinion that we ought to spend a week in London."

"Why?" Helen asked, unable to suppress a shudder. She would be perfectly happy never to visit the city again.

"If we are seen together in public at a few select events—the right events—rumors will be likely to reach Nicholas, which will validate our claim to a relationship."

"Why must it be London?" Helen asked, as the familiar fear gripped her. "Can we not find a country dance or some other outing to attend here?"

"Nothing of the sort would carry the weight of our presence in London," Samuel said gently. "The Sutherlands are well connected there. I have heard that Lady Sutherland has returned to the city already. Apparently she and Nicholas quarreled after Grace left. For one who seemed so set against the match, Lady Sutherland has become quite enamored of your sister."

"If Grace gained her affection, it was hard won," Helen said, recalling Grace's many angst-filled letters where she was certain that all in the Sutherland household detested her.

"Nevertheless, she has it. And if Lady Sutherland is to discover—or perhaps even witness herself—that my interests lie elsewhere, she is likely to take that news directly to her son." Samuel guided them to a stop near the window seat. He released Helen's waist but kept her hand as they sat. "What is it about London that you dread so much?"

"The people," Helen said. "There are so many. And I don't fit in there, in anywhere. Not with the lower classes or with the ton. I never will. And I don't want to."

"Then we are a good pair," Samuel said. "I will never meet the ton's expectations, but that has not stopped me from enjoying a good musicale or taking a stroll around the park."

Helen bit her lip in indecision. "Must we attend any balls?"

"I don't know," Samuel said. "But as we haven't any invitations currently, I think it is quite possible we will not. Wouldn't you like to visit the theatre?" He leaned closer and appeared so earnest in his concern that, for a moment, Helen allowed herself to imagine he really did care for her.

"I would like that." How many times Grace had returned from the theatre and regaled Helen with the stories and songs she'd seen and heard. Always they had tried to coax Helen into attending, but no matter how she wished it, her fear of going out in public had always made her physically ill right before it was time to leave. She didn't dare hope that her nerves would be any better now.

"It's settled then," Samuel said, pulling her to her feet once more. "We shall leave tomorrow."

Helen gasped. "*Tomorrow?*"

"Time is of the essence. Grace seems determined to leave Yorkshire, and once she does, it will be all the more difficult to reunite her and Nicholas. We must establish our relationship—quickly."

Tomorrow. Helen brought her free hand to her chest, covering her rapidly beating heart. It was one thing to pretend a relationship with Samuel here, but could she go out in public and do the same?

"I want a turn." Beth ran toward them and slipped her hand into Helen's free one. "I want to dance."

"And so you shall," Samuel said. "We will invent a new waltz—for three." He took Beth's other hand, then stood and pulled Helen to her feet. The three began turning a circle. "One, two, three. One, two, three."

Beth leaned her head back and giggled. Helen felt a rush of affection for the little girl *and her father.*

The world was changing. Grace would marry Lord Sutherland. Somehow the two would get together, and all would work out. Then, before long, Christopher would strike out on his own. He longed to be gone already. Helen had noted his restlessness for some time. Once he left, she would be alone—their perfect trio changed and separated, never to be put back quite the same way. And as much as Helen feared being near people, the idea of being all alone frightened her even more.

But here I could be happy.

"Faster," Beth demanded, and Samuel counted even quicker, the numbers blurring into one another, as did the pattern on the walls as they ran in a circle.

Beth laughed, and Helen did too. Her head spun, and her stomach felt fluttery—not just from their spinning. At last Beth collapsed, and Helen and Samuel rushed forward to catch her. They did, holding Beth safely between them in the cradle of their joined hands.

Helen looked up and found Samuel close—closer even than he had been during their dance lesson. They locked eyes for a moment above Beth's tousled head.

"Thank you," he said. "For making her so happy."

"You're welcome." *If only I could make you happy too.*

CHAPTER

"I am going to be ill," Helen said for at least the fifth time since their carriage ride had commenced.

Samuel did not respond. He'd already shown sympathy, offering every remedy he could think of, including stopping the carriage so she might get out for a bit. Christopher had a different approach for dealing with his sister's nerves, and while Samuel didn't necessarily agree with it, he couldn't argue with it either. Christopher's methods had gotten them this far.

"Please," Helen begged. "Let us turn back."

"If you must be ill, do so before we arrive, and be sure to lean over *his* shoes." Christopher jerked his head Samuel's direction. "As your affianced, he is sure to have more patience for it than your brother."

"When did you become so dreadful?" Helen asked, turning from them both to stare out the window.

Samuel felt torn between offering comfort and laughing out loud. It was apparent that she was not acting; her fear was a nearly palpable thing. Her fingers curled around the seat, clenching and unclenching. Tears hovered in her eyes, and in the dim light, he could see that she'd grown very pale.

Christopher, in spite of his callous words, did not appear to be doing so well himself. Whenever Helen was not looking, he studied her carefully, as if to judge how near the edge his sister really was. Cruelty toward her—toward anyone, likely—was not in his nature. Samuel could see that it was straining him.

The carriage began slowing. Samuel pushed the curtain aside and glanced out the window. He felt a thrill of excitement at seeing the familiar street and buildings. He preferred the country over London in most everything, but he could not deny his love of the theatre. The evening promised to be especially exciting. Sir Walter Scott's work was always outstanding, but even more than that, Samuel felt privileged to be escorting Helen for her first time. He found himself almost more eager to see her reactions to the play than for the play itself.

But first they had to get her inside.

He turned to her and spoke quietly. "We are almost there."

"I cannot do it." She gave him a look of such abject misery that he was at once in agreement. Her face had gone from pale to ghostly, and she was shaking.

"You *must*," Christopher said. "Quit thinking of yourself, and think about Grace as we left her yesterday—still so sad that she would not accompany us. Do you want her to be happy? Then you must go through with this. Lady Sutherland will be in attendance tonight, and her box is not far from Samuel's. If she sees you together"—he looked from Helen to Samuel—"she will tell Nicholas. He will begin to question whether or not, and indeed to strongly suspect—if your acting is good enough tonight—that there is nothing between Samuel and Grace."

Surprisingly, his speech had the desired effect. Helen straightened her back, removed her clenched hands from the seat, and took several deep breaths. "For Grace. Think only of Grace," she muttered as the carriage rolled to a stop.

The door opened, and Christopher exited first. Samuel moved aside and held his hand out to Helen to help her down. She took it briefly, then descended the steps. He followed her into the brisk night air. The carriage had not been particularly warm, but the cold outside was still a shock, one he hoped might do her some good and restore a bit of color before they entered the building.

He offered his arm, which she took, smiling up at him as she did. He looked down at her as they passed beneath a streetlamp—and felt his breath catch for reasons entirely unrelated to the cold. Helen gazed back with a look of adoration and love such as he hadn't seen or felt from a woman since Elizabeth. It startled him and set his heart to racing so that he was the one feeling off kilter as they passed through the doors.

Thinking of Grace had certainly motivated Helen to action. Samuel doubted he'd see a better performance on the stage tonight than the one she'd just given. He had best mind *his* reactions. *Remember, she is only pretending.* For a moment he allowed himself to wonder what it would be like if she were not. *If she truly did care for me...*

Once inside the Adelphi Theatre, Helen's attention wandered elsewhere. He noted the pressure on his arm increasing, but otherwise, she showed no signs of distress. Instead she appeared to be taking everything in, her gaze frequently lifting to the walls and their large paintings or the ornate woodwork and chandeliers hanging from the ceiling. He guessed she was both admiring the artwork and craftsmanship as well as using them to avert her attention from the throng of people milling about.

They climbed the stairs to his box, and Samuel felt a

moment of satisfaction and pride as he ushered her inside. He'd waited patiently for this box to become available and had then paid dearly for the privilege of calling it his. Yet since Elizabeth's death, he had been to the theatre only twice—both times alone—and he had oft considered letting his seats go. But just now, he felt immensely glad that he still had them and that Helen was here to enjoy the play with him.

He seated her first, then took the chair beside her. Christopher sat behind them, on the pretense of giving them privacy.

"Your grandfather's box was over there," Samuel said, pointing to the box at their left.

"You don't suppose the new duke inherited Grandfather's box as well and might be here tonight, do you?" she asked with worry in her voice.

"It's possible," Samuel answered honestly. "But you are with me. You needn't worry about him."

He could tell that not worrying was difficult for her, though the opulence of their surroundings appeared to be making the task easier. As patrons below took their seats, the hum of voices filled the theatre. The orchestra began warming up. The velvet curtains still covered the stage, waiting for the moment of reveal.

Helen turned to him, a smile in place. "You did not tell me that everything would be so *red*."

He laughed. Of all the things he'd anticipated her enjoying tonight, the color of the seats and curtains had not occurred to him. "Ordered especially for you, milady."

"It is grander than I had imagined."

"Just wait until you experience the splendor of the play," he said and again felt a thrill of excitement on her behalf. How enjoyable the evening promised to be. "Have you read many of Sir Walter Scott's works?" Samuel asked, hoping to keep her mind occupied until the show began.

"I have not. What is this one about?"

"It is a romanticism of the Jacobite cause and rebellion—a theme common in so many of his novels."

Helen frowned. "It is a play about *war*?"

"And love," Samuel corrected. "*Waverly* was a most moving novel. I trust that the theatrical version will capture those moments adequately."

"What is this gentleman saying to you?" Christopher asked, leaning forward between them. "If he becomes too friendly, Helen, jab him with your elbow. I'll take note and push him forward over the edge. We'll have him dispatched in no time."

"That is quite the picture you paint," Samuel said, with a wry grin. "Perhaps that was your plan—to remove me all along. Some thanks I get for sharing my box with the lot of you."

"I mean only to appear as a proper chaperone," Christopher said.

"You may rest assured that I will treat your sister with utmost respect," Samuel assured him.

"Good." Christopher leaned back in his chair. "Just don't treat her *too* properly. You ought to at least hold her hand or something. And Helen, react appropriately when he does."

Helen's mouth opened in an appalled *O* a second before Samuel shot Christopher a look, letting him know he'd gone too far.

"We are managing our own courtship just fine, are we not?" Samuel asked her.

"Quite," she said, turning from both of them and sitting straight-forward in her seat. "After all, we have already danced a waltz."

Helen's reactions to the acting and the music were

everything Samuel had hoped for. He found himself watching her more than the stage, though both the acting and story were as moving as the novel. But tonight, Helen commanded his attention. He did not mind in the least.

When the curtain opened during the second act, the look of absolute rapture that appeared on her face made him quite certain that the cost of maintaining his box had been worth it. Her eyes were riveted on the stage, and he watched as she became caught up in the story, gasping at some moments, sighing with others. When it seemed that the hero would be victorious, Helen brought her clasped hands to her heart. Samuel watched her delicate features then crumple with despair when the hero instead was vanquished. And when the girl he loved rejected him, a tear slid down Helen's face.

Instinct urged Samuel to comfort her, so he reached for her hand, taking it securely into his own. Her mouth curved upward, and she looked over at him with such a loving expression that he again felt as if his breath had been stolen. He wished she would quit doing that. No doubt the display was convincing to any who saw it, but it almost convinced him, too. He didn't want to entertain any feelings that, when this was all over—when Grace and Nicholas were reunited and all was well—would not be reciprocated. Grace had rejected him already. He had no need to feel the same sting from her sister as well.

He returned his attention to the play and tried to put Helen's look of adoration from his mind. Unfortunately, her hand, still nestled in his, made that impossible. He'd expected for her to have pulled away by now. Instead, she appeared to be settled comfortably in her chair, enjoying the show as well as their closeness. Out of curiosity, he gave her hand a gentle squeeze during a particularly frightening scene—when it appeared the hero would be killed. Helen squeezed back, and Samuel felt her touch as if it had spread all the way up his arm.

Curious and more curious. Absently, he stroked the back of her hand with his thumb, thinking how very long it had been since he'd sat this close to a woman and held her hand. It was decidedly pleasant, and he realized he would do well to take care with experiences like this. Helen was too young for him—too young, too good, too beautiful to be saddled with an untitled widower who had proposed marriage to her sister first. She deserved better than that.

Better than me. And he intended to see to it that she realized as much. His duty, aside from helping Grace and Nicholas to reunite, was to coax Helen from her shyness, precisely by partaking in evenings like this. He had no doubt that after tonight, she would be able to overcome her fears and again attend the theatre. The thought pleased him, even more than holding her hand, so he focused on what else needed to be done to launch her properly into society, where she might someday make a suitable and happy match.

The play ended, and it was with some reluctance that Samuel released Helen's hand so she could stand and clap enthusiastically.

"I take it you enjoyed the performance," he said, rising to join her.

"Oh, yes." She turned to him, eyes bright with excitement. "It was absolutely wonderful. How can I ever thank you, Samuel?"

"You already have," he assured her.

Her excitement reminded him of Beth on Christmas morning when she'd first seen her dollhouse. *The dollhouse Helen did a great deal of work on.* Had he ever thanked her properly for that? He wasn't certain, and the thought that he could have been so remiss bothered him.

It seemed there was a great deal concerning Helen that

he had either neglected or ignored. But it was as if he hadn't really seen her until these past few days. *Because she had not wanted to be noticed?* He suddenly wondered if that was the truth or merely his own perception.

The curtain closed for the last time, and she took his arm almost before he'd offered it. They left the box, Christopher, on her other side, looking particularly cheerful.

"Splendid performance, was it not?" Helen asked him, no less enthusiastic.

"Brilliant," Christopher said. "Best I've ever seen."

"Now I shall have to read all of Sir Walter Scott's novels. Do you have them?" she asked, looking up at Samuel.

He opened his mouth to answer at the same instant her expression changed from one of joyous enchantment to terror. Samuel followed her gaze and found a man openly staring at Helen in a most inappropriate manner.

"I know you," the man said, pushing through the crowd. It was not a question but an assumption, one that somehow seemed to carry a threat.

"Get her out of here," Christopher told Samuel, stepping in front of Helen and blocking her from the man's view. He addressed the stranger. "We have met before. I was too young then to give you this." Christopher's fist shot forward, connecting squarely with the man's jaw in a bone-crunching move that sent the man sprawling backward. Helen screamed, as did several other ladies. Samuel grabbed her hand and pulled her toward the stairs.

"Christopher, no!" She looked back over her shoulder. "Sir Crayton will kill him. He's a pirate."

"Your brother seems able to handle himself," Samuel said, praying he was right. They ran down the stairs and hurried through the foyer and the crush of people and out to the cold street below. Helen hadn't yet put on her wrap, but he took only a second to throw it across her shoulders before raising his hand and shouting for a cab.

He spied a hackney down the street and pulled her toward it.

"What of your carriage?" Helen asked.

"Christopher will get it." Samuel shouted the address to the driver, then opened the door and practically shoved Helen inside. He hesitated on the step a moment, torn between returning to aid Christopher and escorting Helen home. Knowing he could not send her on alone, but feeling as if he was abandoning Christopher, he climbed into the carriage, shut the door, and pounded on the roof.

Helen sat huddled in the far corner, shivering from either cold or fear—or both. Samuel gathered her in his arms and held her close. "It's all right. You are safe now." He brushed her hair aside and felt her cheek, wet with tears.

What just happened? He longed to ask but sensed that he shouldn't—not now, at least, while the trauma was still so fresh. What had she said the man's name was . . . Crayton? Samuel tried to recall where he'd heard the name before but could not. *He is a pirate.* What connection might Helen have with that sort?

Her silent tears turned to sobs, and Samuel tightened his arm around her. "I won't let him hurt you," he vowed. He silently promised to discover the problem when Christopher returned.

Helen clung to him the entire way back to the townhouse, never once rejecting his nearness, and Samuel felt grateful that he was at least able to comfort her. Whatever had frightened her had been bad enough that being in *his* arms no longer proved quite so difficult. He had not missed her hesitation about dancing with him a few days past, nor the stiff way she held herself as far from him as possible. He would never have predicted that three days hence, the same woman would willingly allow him to have his arms around her and to hold her close.

He meant to protect her no matter the cost. Though not knowing from what or whom, that he was to protect her troubled him. Had Christopher put them all in danger? Could his actions lead to Beth being in danger?

"It is not me I am crying for, but Christopher," Helen said when they were almost home and she had calmed herself enough to speak. "Crayton is the vilest of men. If he does not harm Christopher this night, he will make certain to hunt him down and finish the job later."

"Let us wait to see what has happened before we rush to any conclusions," Samuel advised, though he, too, felt concern for her brother.

Why had Christopher acted so rashly, and what action had this Crayton taken before to merit such an attack?

The coach pulled to a stop in front of the townhouse. Samuel stepped out and paid the driver before helping Helen down the steps. They made it inside, where Miranda waited up for Helen.

"How was—what happened?" she asked, question changing mid-sentence. Miranda glared at Samuel accusingly. "She looks as though she's seen a ghost."

"Only a man named Crayton, though it has affected her quite as badly."

Miranda's lips pressed together in a tight line. "I'll take her from here." She put an arm around Helen and guided her toward the stairs.

"Wait." Helen turned to Samuel once more. "Thank you for a wonderful evening. I shall always remember it. Everything about it was perfect until . . ."

"It was perfect for me too," Samuel said.

And now he would be perfectly discontent until he discovered what it was that had ruined it.

CHAPTER 18

Almost a full hour passed before Christopher arrived, walking through the door, his cheeks and nose bright with cold but otherwise appearing untouched.

"I was going out to look for you," Samuel said, removing his coat as the butler helped Christopher take his off. "I'd waited about as long as I could."

"Sorry. I left the theatre on foot and took several side streets because I didn't want to risk being followed. But all the cabs must have been in the district, so I had to walk for some time before finding one."

"You didn't come home in our carriage?"

"No." Christopher shook his head. "Didn't you?"

"No." Samuel motioned to the butler to bring back the coats they'd just handed him. "I wasn't sure of the extent of the trouble, and I didn't want to wait around to find out. You said to get Helen out of there, so I did. We took the first cab I could find."

Christopher took his coat then cringed as he put his hand through the sleeve. "Let's go. I'll tell you about it on the way."

"You're hurt." Samuel stepped forward, his physician's instinct and training kicking in. "Let me see that hand."

"It's nothing." But Christopher held his hand out. Samuel probed it gently, noting when Christopher grimaced and flinched.

"I think you may have broken the middle phalanx of your index finger."

"So long as I broke something on Crayton's face as well," Christopher muttered.

"A distinct possibility," Samuel said. "We need to get this splinted."

"Let's get the carriage first," Christopher said, pulling his hand back, but cradling it carefully in front of him. "The harm has been done. An hour or so more isn't going to matter."

It could, Samuel thought. *If the break is a bad one.* But Christopher appeared to have enough range of motion that the delay probably wouldn't make anything worse. "All right," Samuel said, after a moment's hesitation. "Keep it still though. I suppose the cold may do it good." He turned to the butler. "Lock the doors, and do not admit anyone other than the two of us tonight," Samuel instructed him, then he donned his hat and turned up his collar as he followed Christopher out into the cold, dark night. There were no cabs about, so he shoved his hands deep into his pockets and prepared for a long walk—a good thing, because he had rather a lot of questions to ask Christopher.

"Who is Crayton?" Samuel's breath hung in the air—a miniature, translucent cloud viewed only by the light of the gas streetlamps.

"He is Sir Edmund Crayton, knighted for *his service* to the crown—pressing men from merchant ships into the

Royal Navy and claiming the cargo of those ships as his own."

"What has any of that to do with Helen?" Samuel asked, already disliking the man. Two years earlier, he'd lost a valuable cargo in a similar scheme. Who knew but that it might have been carried out by the very same man?

"Some years ago, before Grandfather found us, Father was in particularly dire straits and well into his cups one night when he met Crayton at a tavern. Crayton convinced Father that every man had something of value, and one only had to search to discover what it was. That was the night Father first had the idea to get his own daughters married to get money for himself."

"Crayton planted the idea," Samuel said.

"Yes, though I've no doubt Father would have come to the same conclusion on his own eventually. Grace and Helen are both blessed—or cursed, depending upon how you look at it—with beauty." Christopher adjusted his scarf, wrapping one end of it carefully around his exposed hand.

The night had grown bitter; a cab would have been preferable, but strangely Samuel found he did not overly mind the cold. Anger was keeping him warm.

"Your father arranged a marriage between Crayton and Helen?" he guessed.

"Crayton and Grace," Christopher corrected. "Helen was only twelve then, but at eighteen, Grace was old enough to marry. If it had not been for Grandfather, she would have been forced into it."

"Thank goodness for your grandfather."

Christopher nodded. "To the end of his life, he berated himself for not finding us earlier, for not making amends with our mother. But he *did* find us, and at a critical time—the very day the solicitor appeared at our door, inquiring after our welfare, we went to live with Grandfather. Father was furious. He insisted that Grace meet her *obligation* to marry. I'm uncertain what agreement he'd arranged, but I do know that Grandfather paid a rather large sum for Crayton to go away. He was most displeased, as was Father."

"I imagine he would have been with his main support and his *assets* removed," Samuel said, thoroughly disgusted by Christopher's story. He felt somewhat ill, recalling that he had once entertained George Thatcher in his home, had in fact worked with the man to force Nicholas into a betrothal to Grace.

"Unfortunately, he retrieved those assets last year," Christopher said.

"And Crayton became involved again?" Samuel asked.

"Yes and no," Christopher said. "During his initial betrothal to Grace, he visited the house, but Grace was not home. Helen was—alone. I'd found work and was gone most days, and Grace had left to collect and deliver laundry. Sometimes Helen went with her, but more often than not, she stayed home to finish the ironing and cook supper."

Samuel didn't like the picture Christopher was painting. During their meetings at the fence, Grace had described the meager home they'd grown up in well enough that now, he could picture Helen there—alone.

"So Crayton discovered that she was by herself," Samuel prompted, his jaw set hard. He felt both ill and angry and wished he'd been the one to smash Crayton's face at the theatre.

Christopher gave a curt nod. "I swear I heard her screaming half a mile away. I ran as fast as I could and burst through the door in time to find her pushed up against the wall, Crayton towering over her, doing his best to convince her to do his bidding. Her face was bloody, her dress torn..."

"Little wonder she thinks men are a disease," Samuel muttered.

"That was not the end of it," Christopher said. "Father

arrived just after I did. He made a show of taking Crayton to task for trying to 'sample' the wrong girl. But after he had left, Father unleashed his anger on Helen, shouting at her and hitting her more, telling her how he expected her to behave better next time—that if a man wanted her attention and was willing to pay for it, she'd best be prepared to give him what he wanted."

"Dear God," Samuel exclaimed. "Her own father."

"He was never a father to any of us," Christopher said. "We shed no tears at his passing."

"I can see why not," Samuel said.

"When he sent Grace off to be purchased by the highest bidder . . ."

Samuel inwardly winced at Christopher's choice of words. *I was one of those bidders.* At the time, he hadn't realized the extent of her father's wickedness—or Grace's reluctance to marry.

"We believed Helen to be temporarily safe. But Father had other plans. He'd contacted Crayton again to let him know that his younger daughter was all grown up—and available."

"How did you manage to escape a second time?" *With no grandfather to come to your rescue and no funds or other relatives to turn to.*

"It was your letter," Christopher said. "Your invitation to stay came at our most desperate hour."

Samuel considered this as they passed by several shops and neared the theatre district. Grace had not asked him to send for her siblings, but the idea to do just that had come to him, nonetheless. And he had acted on it immediately. *Thank heavens.* His heart lurched as he imagined what might have been Helen's fate, had he not extended the invitation when he did.

"We had been planning to leave," Christopher continued his story. "Though truly, we'd no idea where to go.

I think Helen was perhaps reconsidering marriage to the duke, though she would not have been happy with him."

"And here I have been telling her how beautiful she is," Samuel said. "How men will vie for her attention—while she is no doubt well aware and only too eager to avoid that very thing. I am amazed we convinced her to come to London at all."

"She would do anything for Grace," Christopher said. "Helen blames herself for our necessitated return to our father's house after Grandfather's death. The duke would have gladly allowed her to stay—and likely Grace and me as well—had Helen agreed to be his wife."

"Is he not a good man?" Samuel asked.

Christopher shook his head. "In the little time I knew him it appeared he was short of temper and rather cruel. I do not believe him to be as bad as Crayton, but I saw little to recommend his character."

At last they turned to the street beside the theatre, and Samuel saw his carriage, sitting alone, the driver struggling to stay awake.

"We are fortunate that nothing has befallen him," he said as they hurried over.

"My apologies," Samuel called to the driver, who sat up quickly as they approached. "The lady was ill, and we left in a hurry much earlier."

The driver nodded, then made to jump down to get the door for them, but Samuel waved him away. "No need. Just get us home quickly."

They bundled inside, Christopher still taking care to protect his injured hand. The air inside felt even colder than it had seemed during their brisk walk.

"You don't think Crayton was looking for Helen tonight, do you?" Samuel asked when they were settled and the coach was moving.

"I don't see how he could have been," Christopher said. "Though I worry he'll do that very thing now."

"We are scheduled to dine with the Fredericks tomorrow evening. Shall we return home instead?"

Christopher did not answer immediately but stared out the window, appearing to consider. "I do not see how Crayton could be at the Fredericks—or even learn of our presence there. But neither do I see that staying in London will accomplish what we had hoped. I did not see Lady Sutherland in her box tonight, so attending the theatre did not achieve our goal."

But we did. Helen enjoyed herself. Samuel could not regret the evening. He would always remember Helen's sense of wonder, her appreciation, and the pleasure she'd taken from the performance. *The pleasure I experienced being there with her.*

As much as he felt fear on her behalf, he also felt anger. How dare Crayton or anyone else keep Helen from living and enjoying life? The man had no claim on her; she ought to be free to attend the theatre or a ball as she pleased.

"I admit that I am worried," Christopher said.

"For yourself or for your sister?" Samuel asked. "When we left, she was convinced that Crayton would murder you—if not tonight, then at some future time."

"That is not an unfounded concern," Samuel said. "Though I think Helen has more cause to worry."

"What do you mean?"

"I hit Crayton tonight partly because I've wanted to—and he has deserved it for a long time—but more to create a distraction so she could get away quickly. I've no proof, but I believe that before Father died, he might have accepted money from Crayton in trade for Helen."

"And he died before he could deliver her," Samuel said.

"Or perhaps Father died *because* he didn't deliver."

Christopher's words hung in the air between them, throwing the chaise into an even deeper chill.

"We're going home tomorrow," Samuel said. The prickle of fear he'd felt at the theatre when Crayton's eyes had landed upon Helen took root. "I see now why a cut from your sister would not have sufficed to dismiss Crayton. You have my profound gratitude for your quick thinking and actions tonight."

"You are most welcome," Christopher said. The coach grew quiet. Though the hour was late, Samuel found he was not tired. Instead his mind churned with possibilities and the magnitude of their problem.

Crayton was not likely to go away. Suddenly the cause of reuniting Grace and Nicholas seemed insignificant. Samuel's new worry—one he felt pressed to find a solution for immediately—was keeping Helen safe from Crayton and any other man who would ill use her.

"One thing good has come of this," Samuel remarked sometime later, when they had reached the townhouse and were ascending the steps. "I understand your sister better now. She is far braver than I had realized."

CHAPTER

The country dance Helen had requested to attend in place of a city ball became a reality with the delivery of an invitation the week after they arrived home.

"Grace says Mrs. Ellis is the biggest gossip in the shire," Helen told both Christopher and Samuel after her sister had gone to bed. "Even if the Sutherlands are not in attendance, they are sure to hear about it. We *must* go. It is the perfect opportunity to prove to Lord Sutherland that you are otherwise attached."

Both men seemed surprised by her request.

"Are you sure you are feeling up to it?" Samuel asked, genuine concern in both his voice and eyes. He'd been treating her this way—as if she were some sort of fragile doll—since the incident at the theatre. And while Helen could not say she disliked his concern, she did find it somewhat annoying. If she'd learned anything that night, it was that she had been missing a great deal that life had to offer. Crayton's appearance had frightened her, to be certain, but not so much that it overshadowed the beauty of the evening.

The music, the stage, the acting, and dancing—even the people in attendance—had all been mesmerizing. She hadn't known where to look first, only that she must *not* look at Samuel, which had been all she wanted to do after he had begun to hold her hand.

"I am perfectly well, thank you. We are not in London. Sir Crayton has no idea we are here, and even if he did, Christopher has another hand which he may break on my behalf."

Christopher flashed her a grin and growled good naturedly as he held up his bandaged fingers. "Any time, sister."

"I believe that honor will be mine, if there is a next time," Samuel said. "Had I known of Crayton's past dealings with your family, I should have beat Christopher to the punch—or at the least joined him. Perhaps we could have finished Crayton off once and for all."

"He will not so easily be done away with," Helen predicted. She bit her lip as the old worry resurfaced. "But we shall deal with him later. We must focus on the matter at hand. Grace intends to leave tomorrow."

"Harrison, Miranda, and I are going with her," Christopher confirmed. "We'll see her safely settled while you two see to turning Nicholas's heart around."

"I don't see how we can if Grace is gone," Samuel said.

Helen searched for any sign of melancholy from Samuel over Grace's imminent departure. "He will have to come to her."

"He won't," Samuel said. "You don't know how stubborn Nicholas is."

"He only needs the right motivation," Helen said, more determined than ever for their plan to work. "Don't worry.

This will all come together splendidly. Now, if you gentlemen will excuse me, I'm off to bed. If I'm to be up dancing half the night next week, I need my sleep."

"Something has changed with her," Samuel mused after Helen had gone upstairs.

"She feels a little confidence I'd say, thanks to you." Christopher stood and stretched. "I'm off to bed too. This hand hurts like the deuce, so it takes a while for me to fall asleep. And I've got a seven-hour ride to face tomorrow."

"About that—I'm sorry," Samuel said. "A house for your family was not as easy to come by as I'd hoped. Grace was quite thorough in ruining her reputation."

Christopher waved off his concern. "Don't trouble yourself over it. I wish we were closer to Helen, but, God willing, we won't be there too long."

"God willing," Samuel agreed.

Christopher paused in the doorway and looked back. "Take care of Helen for me."

"I intend to," Samuel promised.

"I know," Christopher said. "I just needed to hear you say it."

Samuel decided for certain that his new favorite color was red when Helen descended the stairs the evening of the Ellises' ball. With the departure of her siblings and servants, he had insisted that Helen move her things to the main house. Knowing what he did of Crayton now, he did not wish her to be at the guest house without at least Harrison and Christopher present. Samuel had made his servants aware of the situation with Crayton, and all were on alert to watch out for him or any other stranger who ventured on his property.

LOVING HELEN

Helen's farewell to her siblings had not been as tear-filled as Samuel had expected, but then, for the past week, Helen had not been quite what he'd expected. How was it that the incident he'd feared would have made her more apprehensive had somehow freed her to move forward?

He'd never seen her happier—more radiant or talkative. And he'd never seen her lovelier than the moment she appeared on the stairs, in a white gown accented with intricate garnet beading and a crimson sash that fastened just above her small waist. Blonde curls fell perfectly around her face as she descended to meet him.

She paused on the bottom step, fingers toying with the rubies resting at the base of her slender neck. He swallowed, keenly aware of her presence as long-forgotten feelings of attraction stole over him. His gaze strayed from Helen's curls, to her eyes, and then her lips, which were turned up in a smile. They looked invitingly soft and welcoming.

What am I thinking? He reined his thoughts in abruptly, took her gloved hand, and kissed the back of it. *And that is to be all the kissing there is.* He mentally scolded himself. Helen was like a younger sister. He wanted to see her properly launched, free to choose her own path to happiness and whatever gentleman claimed her heart. He would do well not to damage that heart in the meantime; elsewise he might be no better than Crayton and whatever other lecherous men her father had subjected his daughters to.

He helped her with her wrap, and they stepped out into the snowy evening. With the day's heavy snowfall, the carriage had been traded for a sleigh. Samuel wondered briefly how the others were getting on and if they'd been forced to stop their journey to make similar accommodations. He tried to muster some concern but couldn't seem to keep his mind on Christopher and Grace, or even on Grace and Nicholas and their troubles. The woman sitting close beside him on the seat commanded all his attention, yet she hadn't uttered a single word.

"I hope you'll be warm enough," Samuel said, placing the heavy robes over their laps. "It isn't often we have an evening like this, and I thought you might like—"

"I love it," Helen exclaimed. "The trees are simply gorgeous, and the moon is full. The night is stunning."

As are you. He kept his thoughts to himself, knowing as he did now what grief her beauty had brought her in the past. He valued Helen for much more than her appearance, and he wished her to realize that. "It is perfect, because I am in the best company."

Her only response was a smile. Samuel nodded to the driver, and they were off, gliding down the snowy lane as the bells on the horses' harnesses jingled merrily and the lanterns swayed in front of them.

Neither Samuel nor Helen spoke; there was no need to. The silence was comfortable, the night beautiful, with the tree branches silhouetted in white and delicate snowflakes falling around them in the silent, snowy wood.

They passed Sutherland Hall, which looked as foreboding as ever. Light shone from Nicholas's study, and Samuel wondered if Nicholas spent his days—and nights—busy in work as an attempt to forget Grace. Samuel felt a moment's pity for his neighbor and former brother-in-law, no matter that there was bad history between them. *I am doing what I can for Nicholas,* Samuel thought then promptly returned his attention to Helen. For the moment, all was right and magical in *his* world, and he wished to enjoy it.

Too soon they reached the Ellis residence. He lifted the blankets and climbed down, then held a hand out to Helen. She took it and did not let go even after reaching the ground.

"Are you ready for this?" Samuel asked.

"That depends," she said. "Are you going to attempt a waltz with me in public?"

"Never," he said. "At least not at the Ellises'. Mrs. Ellis is so proper as to not entertain anything scandalous. In fact, I am rather surprised she has invited me at all, as I have no . . ."

"Title. Yes, I believe you've mentioned that a few times," Helen said, a smile in her voice. "Were you aware that I am also lacking in that department?"

"We had best get your sister to patch things up with Lord Sutherland, then, and soon, too," Samuel said. "At least then you'd have some claim to nobility."

She laughed. "That is *exactly* the reason we are doing this."

"Helen." He caught her arm, stopping her before she could begin the walk to the house. "You look beautiful tonight. I know that such words don't please you, but—"

"It pleases me that *you* think so." Her eyes darkened, and he glimpsed the serious side of her for a brief second. Just as quickly, the look was gone, and her earlier merriment returned. "You are not bad-looking yourself, for a man without a title." She tossed her curls and walked ahead of him on the snowy path.

Is she flirting with me? He hurried after her.

She left her wrap, and he his coat, with the butler and followed the line of guests into the ballroom. It was a bigger assembly than Samuel had expected, and he worried that Helen might be overwhelmed. She kept her hand on his arm even after they entered the ballroom, and he wasted no time asking her to dance.

"May I have the honor?" he asked, inclining his head toward the dance floor.

She merely smiled and allowed him to lead her to the center of the room and into formation for a quadrille. The last time he'd danced one had been just a few weeks ago, on Christmas Eve, when he'd partnered with Grace. It wasn't a particularly enjoyable dance—Grace had been rather preoccupied, and Nicholas had looked wont to murder him.

Samuel hoped this dance tonight would be a vast improvement. He considered all that had happened since the last and felt somewhat uncomfortable in realizing that his feelings had changed so much. It was not that he didn't care for Grace any longer—he always would—but the manner of his love had changed, had transformed to that of a friend . . . which told him the depth of his feelings had not been what he had proclaimed them to be.

Though they might have been. He and Grace could have been happy together.

Just as Helen and I could be happy together. He pushed the absurd thought aside. He had promised her brother that he would take care of her, and Samuel very much doubted that *taking care* included indulging in his own, developing feelings. Doing his best to keep that in mind, he bowed, and the dance began.

They were among the first couples to take their turn, and as they promenaded around the circle, Samuel noted the attention of the other men straying from their partners to Helen. She'd also caught the eye of several others—men and women—around the room. Little wonder, striking as she was in white and crimson and with her halo of golden curls. He only hoped that the attention she garnered would be the right kind.

If his servants were to be believed, ever since Nicholas's ball, the gossip had changed from berating Grace to speaking of what a good match she had made and how remarkable it was that she'd gained Lady Sutherland's favor and tamed her son. Samuel hoped the same good favor might transfer to Grace's sister tonight.

Silently he assessed each man present, considering them as possible suitors for Helen. Mr. Penhale was too old and stodgy; Helen would be bored in an instant—for while Samuel had at first believed her incapable of stimulating conversation, of late he'd discovered in her an animated intellect, a young lady most enjoyable to talk with, though their silence on the ride over tonight had been every bit as pleasant and comfortable as their recent conversations.

They took their places in the circle and waited for the next pairs to begin.

Sir Vacher—too much a rake. Lord Ainsworth—a braggart. Certainly none among their circle would make a good match for her. Samuel felt a bit like Nicholas as he wove in and out of the set, sending a message with his eyes to the men. *Leave Helen alone. She is not for you.*

The dance went on far too long with too much switching of partners. He found himself thinking of their waltz in the nursery and how the three of them had collapsed with laughter at the end. He wondered that he had not appreciated that morning—and Helen—more.

How is it she has been under my roof these many months, yet I've scarcely paid her any attention?

"Are you quite well?" she asked when they stood beside each other again. "You look a bit lost this evening."

He did feel that way, truth be told. "I am well enough," he said. "Just assessing who is here and making sure you are safe."

"Of course I am. I'm with you." She smiled and stepped away again to form the star at center.

At length the dance ended, and Samuel was left feeling as if he'd been cheated somehow. He vowed to wait until later in the evening, when the dances lengthened and the tempos slowed, before asking her for another dance. At least then he might have a chance at holding her in his arms for more than a second or two at a time.

After all, we are here to convince the neighbors that I am courting her.

Samuel had scarcely escorted her to the side of the

ballroom when an unfamiliar gentleman came to claim her hand. Samuel caught a fleeting look of uncertainty as she accepted and left the protection of his side. He attempted not to scowl as the man led her away, then thought the better of it and scowled openly. It was exactly the sort of thing Nicholas would have done—and had done—in proclaiming his intent toward Grace. Though somehow, Samuel doubted he looked as foreboding.

"Are you feeling well this evening, Mr. Preston?" Lady Ellis stood before him, waving her fan as she spoke. "Are you overheated? It is rather warm in here. I must instruct Mr. Ellis to have the servants open some windows."

"The temperature is not bothering me," Samuel assured her, prying his eyes from Helen to look at his hostess. "Your ballroom is lovely, as are you." He bent, kissing the back of her hand.

"Not as lovely as the young lady you've brought with you this evening." Mrs. Ellis leaned closer, holding her fan up in front of her face, as if that would hide their conversation from anyone who might be watching. "Tell me—is she the sister of the girl Lord Sutherland disgraced?"

"She is the sister of Lord Sutherland's fiancée," Samuel corrected, grateful thus far that Nicholas had had the good sense to keep his mouth shut about the broken engagement.

"And did she accompany you to the theatre recently?" Mrs. Ellis asked, poorly feigning a look of innocent curiosity.

Samuel narrowed his eyes and pretended shrewdness as he looked at Mrs. Ellis. "Guilty as charged. It appears we have been caught." *Perfect.* "Though I hope you realize that Miss Helen's brother was also seated in our box. She was properly chaperoned throughout the night." *Excepting our hasty carriage ride.*

"Of course." The fan flapped rapidly. "And tonight? Did he accompany you in your carriage?"

Drat. He'd been remiss as to endanger Helen's reputation by driving with her alone. He pasted on a smile. "Unfortunately, her brother is away at the moment. We took the open-top sleigh, so as to be in sight of the driver and others at all times."

Mrs. Ellis, with her love of gossip and fever for scandal, would realize this was still a significant breach of etiquette.

"And I suppose you would enjoy having others admire her at your side," she said. "Quite a beauty, isn't she?" Mrs. Ellis watched Helen dancing. "A good thing if she is in want of a husband. I hear their father died in shame, leaving the family penniless."

Their father lived in shame. "Helen and her siblings have been estranged from their father for some time. Previously they lived with their grandfather, the late Duke of Salisbury. As to being penniless, that is not at all true. He left them an inheritance."

"Oh, I see." Mrs. Ellis snapped her fan shut.

Samuel could tell that he had deflated her enthusiasm.

"Will they be staying at your guesthouse much longer?" she asked.

Nosy, nosy. Samuel searched the dance floor for Helen and her partner, then chose his words carefully. "That depends. Grace, of course, will not stay much longer—only until the wedding. And Christopher is eager to be out on his own. Whether Helen goes with him remains to be seen." The violins lingered on the closing notes of the song. "If you will excuse me, Mrs. Ellis." Samuel bowed, then walked briskly across the room to intercept Helen as she bade her partner farewell.

Samuel took her elbow and guided her toward the refreshment table. "How are you?"

"Very well, excepting my toes." She looked ruefully at her slippers.

"Not everyone can dance as gracefully as I do?" he teased.

"Thank heavens for that, or every other dance partner would make me dizzy until I collapsed at the end of each piece."

"I believe I have just been insulted." He noted her rosy cheeks as he handed her a drink.

"Not at all." Helen peered at him over the top of her cup. "On the contrary, our dance in the nursery was the finest I have enjoyed."

Our dance. "We'll see if you feel that way at the end of the evening." He looked past her to see two men approaching. "Drink that quickly. I think your respite is about to end."

Helen swallowed, then lowered her cup as she turned to face the newcomers, Baron Edwards and Mr. Barlow. Samuel assessed them as they made their introductions. Barlow seemed a decent sort of fellow. He owned property a few miles up the road. Samuel had never known him to be any trouble. But he hadn't known him to be anything extraordinary, either.

And Helen deserves extraordinary.

Edwards, on the other hand, had obvious flaws. His dress and manner were flamboyant to the point of distraction. Samuel found himself looking away so as to avoid a headache from the bright purple vest. He hoped very much that the baron would not ask Helen to dance, as the color clashed terribly with her gown.

He could tell each was on the verge of asking her for the next set, and he wondered what was delaying them and whether there was some game between them. The thought both annoyed and alarmed him, and before Samuel had quite realized what he was doing, he'd taken Helen's cup and set it aside.

He held out his arm to her. "You promised the next dance, remember?"

If she was astonished, she hid it well and placed her hand upon his arm. "It was a pleasure to make your acquaintance, gentlemen."

Samuel led her away, though not before overhearing Baron Edwards say to Mr. Barlow, "But they have already danced."

"At least it is not another quadrille," Samuel said, guiding her to the end of the set that had formed in the center of the ballroom.

"What have you against the quadrille?" she asked.

"Nothing, when I am dancing with a young lady whose company I do not enjoy." They faced each other.

"Am I to assume that you enjoy my company, then?" Helen asked.

"Very much." Samuel felt his heart plummet as he realized the truth of his answer.

We are only acting. She is but acting. And doing far too fine a job of it.

He studied her face for any sign of concern or tiredness. "How are you feeling—truly?"

"Disappointed," Helen confessed.

Not what he'd expected to hear. "I don't understand."

"All this time, I was too frightened to attend the theatre or a ball or party because I was afraid of men like Sir Crayton and my father. And though I did see Crayton at the theatre, and it *was* awful, his presence did not ruin the night for me. The performance was so much more than I had imagined—the whole evening felt magical." She smiled as she remembered.

"I suppose I expected a ball to be just as glorious as the theatre," Helen said. "But so far, I have only walked around a circle with you, had my toes stepped on, and my eyes offended."

Samuel followed her gaze to the baron's overly bright ensemble.

"You do not care for the quadrille either," he said, amused at her confession. "As for the other, I am afraid you are learning the sad realities of a ball. I am sorry that it is a disappointment. Perhaps if we attended a larger gathering in London."

She shook her head. "I don't believe so. Lord Sutherland's ball was more what I had imagined, and it was not so very large."

"What was it about his ball that pleased you?" Samuel asked. "I understood that you did not stay long."

"I did not." She looked away, and he was reminded of the woman she'd been just a short while ago. "Before I left, I enjoyed watching Grace and Lord Sutherland dance the waltz. The way they looked at each other was so . . ."

"Ghastly?" he suggested. At the time, he'd found Nicholas's blatant display of affection overbearing. However, since then his opinion had changed somewhat. *If given the same opportunity would I not dance a waltz with Helen?*

"It was personal." A smile touched her lips.

"Ah," Samuel said, beginning to think he might understand. "And you believed all balls to be as intimate as that waltz?"

"No. I think I realized that was unique, but a woman does dream and imagine . . ."

A few weeks ago, he would not have believed that she ever dreamed or imagined about anything to do with balls or men.

She only needed to realize that not all of us are a disease.

The music began, and they met at the center. Recalling Nicholas's actions at the ball where Samuel had first met Grace, he took every opportunity to be close to Helen. His hand lingered on her waist as they turned. He caught her eye each time they passed. He touched her hand, then squeezed it gently each time before letting go. The dance had a large set, and the longer they danced, the more her face became flushed. When at last it was their turn to promenade beneath the bridge, he whispered to her.

"I am the envy of every man here with you as my partner."

Her cheeks reddened so much that they nearly matched the beading on her dress. He winked at her just before the bridge ended and they parted.

"Mr. Preston," she scolded when they met once more. "You are being quite—*personal* tonight. I am not certain what to make of your behavior."

"That's all right," Samuel said. "Mrs. Ellis knows *exactly* what to make of it, and she is spreading her opinion of us far and wide."

Helen followed his gaze to their hostess, who was ensconced behind her fan on the far side of the room. "Oh dear."

"Do not worry. She will be talking of *us*, not of you." He'd assured that by asking Helen to dance again so soon. "We have satisfied her curiosity in inviting us this evening by giving her much to speculate about."

"Let's hope that gossip reaches Lord Sutherland."

"Indeed," Samuel agreed, sobered by the reminder of what they were about.

The dance, though long, ended too soon, as far as he was concerned. Reluctantly, he allowed another neighbor to claim her hand, then stood brooding, knowing it would be some time before he could dance with her again. He supposed he ought to dance with some of the other women, but the idea held no appeal.

The evening passed slowly for him as he stood on the edge of the room, watching Helen. In the past while attending such events, he stayed only a short while, leaving after a dance with one or two ladies. After that, the reminder of all he was missing, plus an overwhelming longing to have Elizabeth at his side, inevitably sent him home early to an evening spent staring at her portrait and feeling his loss anew. Balls had become a sort of self-torture, which he avoided as much as possible.

Not until his harvest ball last September had he hosted any sort of party after Elizabeth's passing. He hadn't had the heart or stomach for it earlier. Only with his interest in Grace and her imminent arrival had he decided to hold a ball. It had been a dismal failure almost from the very start. Nicholas's untimely arrival and then abrupt departure—with a very ill Grace in his arms—had sent most of his guests home early, feeling subdued. And after allowing Nicholas to take Grace with him, Samuel had felt more alone than ever. He'd had his few years of being happily married. He was blessed to have a daughter. And he still had a lifetime of empty evenings and sleeping alone to look forward to.

The familiar melancholy stole over him as he watched Helen glide about the floor. Silently, he found fault with every one of her partners, though were he to have given voice to his complaints, they would have rung hollow. Many were good fellows and would make a fine match for Helen. If she married someone here, she would remain close to Grace as well—assuming their ruse worked and Nicholas and Grace ended up married.

Samuel sighed and removed the watch from his vest to check the time. Another hour to go at least. He wasn't certain he could endure that long.

Helen approached him after the end of a dance. "You look rather like your grumpy neighbor Lord Sutherland tonight," she said, coming to stand beside him. "I do not think you care for balls very much."

"I used to," Samuel said, trying to remember that time. "Going home alone is always a painful reminder of the past."

She placed her hand on his arm. "Tonight you are not going home alone. And there is no need to stay for the entire evening. We have accomplished what we came to do."

"Almost," Samuel said as he heard the strains of violins begin. "One dance more, and then we will leave. He took her hand in his. "This is the closest thing we will get to your personal waltz in Mrs. Ellis's ballroom."

He held her hand and led her easily through the dance steps as they twirled about the ballroom in the midst of the other couples. Helen's smile never faltered, but she did not seem to be looking at him as she had earlier.

"What is wrong?" he asked on their third turn about the room.

"I am thinking of your wife," she confessed. "And feeling so sad." Her eyes shone bright with unshed tears.

"Don't be sad for me," he commanded rather urgently. "Aside from the fact that Mrs. Ellis will tell everyone that I am a brute who made you cry in public . . ." This solicited a tiny smile. "You must not worry over me. I have Beth. We are quite happy."

"I know." Helen sniffed loudly but did not elaborate on what else might be troubling her.

Samuel held her as close as was decently possible and tried to offer comfort. When next he attended a ball—if he ever chose to again, which was doubtful—he would not have her at his side. But he would remember this evening and the enchantment that first Grace, and now Helen—*especially Helen*—had cast upon him. How blessed he felt to have known them each, if only for a short time. How grateful he felt to have been the one privileged enough to help them on their ways to happiness.

The dance ended, and Samuel tucked Helen's hand into the fold of his arm. They left the ballroom and claimed their wraps without so much as a word between them. When they climbed into the sleigh for the ride home and still had not spoken, it seemed that their night was to end as silently as it had begun.

The horses were off, the sleigh gliding through the snow. Their breath frosted in the cold air, and Helen snuggled closer. It seemed the most natural thing in the world when Samuel put his arm around her and pulled her near. She leaned her head against his shoulder and sighed.

"A sigh of contentment, I hope?" he said.

"As close to contentment as I am likely to ever get." She tilted her head to look up at him. "Thank you for a lovely, *personal* evening, Samuel. Thank you for showing me what I have been missing. And thank you for helping Grace."

For a minute, he had hoped—before she'd mentioned her sister—that Helen would say something else. But that was his foolishness for imagining things that were not there. "You are most welcome."

She rested her head again on his shoulder. He willed the sleigh to move slowly through the night and tried to be grateful for the evening they'd had and a memory he would cherish forever.

CHAPTER

It was with reluctance that Helen took Samuel's hand and stepped from the sleigh. The ride home from the Ellises' had been far better than the ball itself; she had enjoyed every minute seated close to Samuel and was sad to see their evening come to an end.

They went into the house, and the butler took her cloak. She brushed snow from her hair and waited as Samuel was helped from his coat as well. He offered her his arm, and together they started up the stairs, her steps dragging with reluctance. At the top they would part ways, she to the east wing and her waiting lady's maid, he to the west, where his rooms and Beth's lay.

"Good night, Samuel," she said as they paused in the hall. "Thank you for a lovely evening." Helen relinquished her hold on his arm.

"Wait—please." He caught her hand, brought it to his lips and held it there.

She gazed at him curiously, breathlessly.

Samuel lifted his head but did not release her. He stepped closer. "May I—would you—"

Yes? Anticipation thrummed through her. *Something wonderful is about to happen.*

He closed his eyes briefly, his lips turned down and brow wrinkled as if he was caught in some sort of inner debate. After several seconds his features smoothed and he looked at her once more, though in not quite the same way.

Somehow she felt keenly disappointed at the change.

"Will you come to the nursery with me to check on Beth?" he asked. "She is quite the different child when she is asleep. You really should see her."

"I am rather enamored of the awake version," Helen said, trying to keep the disappointment from her voice. "But all right." He still kept her hand, and she followed him down the hallway and felt somewhat scandalous for behaving thusly, so late at night.

Nonsense. I spend time in the nursery every day.

Beth's door was closed, but Samuel turned the knob with his free hand and slowly pushed it open. "I check on Beth every night and have yet to waken her nanny. I believe she sleeps rather soundly."

Evidence of such came in the form of muffled snoring from the room adjoining the nursery. Helen and Samuel exchanged guilty smiles at hearing Nanny Mary's snores. Ignoring these and the continued thought that she should not be here, Helen entered the room behind Samuel.

Moonlight poured in from the bay window, bathing the nursery in a soft glow. Helen pulled her hand free of Samuel's and crossed to the bed where Beth lay, curled up with one of her dolls clutched tightly in her fingers.

Samuel was right. She appeared different in sleep—serene and a little bit older. *More innocent than during the day, when she is almost always up to some mischief.* For some reason Beth's changed appearance made Helen sad. Carefully she sat on the edge of the bed and touched Beth's cheek. "She is growing up."

"She will be four soon," Samuel whispered. "Has she told you how many days must pass before her birthday?"

"Every day—several times a day," Helen said, smiling.

"And to think she did not know much of numbers or counting until you taught her," he remarked.

"She is very intelligent," Helen said, stroking Beth's hair.

"So is her tutor."

Helen turned to him and caught him gazing at her with a look of such tender affection that at first she thought it must be for Beth.

But no. He is looking at me. Their eyes locked, and Helen again felt the same anticipation and hope she'd had moments earlier, at the top of the stairs.

"The night is not quite over," Samuel said. "There is time yet for one last dance, a waltz I think."

This time Helen did not hesitate but rose and accepted his hand. He led her to the moonlit circle before the window, and they faced one another. As before, he placed his other hand at her waist, and she laid hers on his shoulder. This time they did not count out loud. There was no need. They simply looked at one another, and their dance was begun.

Instead of swirling her about the room, Samuel led them in a tight circle, slowly and quietly. They did not speak, but the silence felt comfortable as it had on their sleigh rides to and from the ball. His brown eyes had grown serious, as if considering a weighty matter. But Helen felt only light, a buoyant kind of happiness lifting her soul as Samuel held her close.

Outside the snow had begun to fall again, tiny flakes floating down on an already laid carpet of white. The fire in the grate burned low, yet the room felt perfectly warm. *She* felt perfectly warm whenever Samuel held her close.

The imagined song came to an end far too quickly, as

Samuel slowed their already leisurely pace until they were stopped in front of the window and stood facing one another.

Helen's breathing seemed much too shallow and quick for the little exertion their dance had required, and she worried the ruby necklace rising and falling would give her away, in spite of her best effort to calm herself.

But this is not fear. I am not afraid. Her eyes met Samuel's, and his appeared as searching and inquisitive as hers.

What are you thinking? There were too many possibilities that could crush her fragile hope, so she dared not ask. To hear him mention his wife at this moment would be her undoing, when all Helen could think of was how far past pretending she had strayed.

Care for me. Just a little.

It seemed he might, for when her hand slid from his shoulder he caught it and held it over his heart, beating every bit as quickly as her own.

"Helen—"

A great snort came from the adjoining room, and Helen and Samuel sprang apart, staring at the door apprehensively. The noise came again, and she brought a hand to her mouth to stifle laughter. Samuel was not so successful, and a sort of choking guffaw escaped.

New sounds—feet on the floor and a match being struck—came from the nanny's chamber. Light flared beneath the doorway as Helen began backing her way out of the room.

"Who's there?" Nanny Mary's voice sounded frightened.

"Only me," Samuel said, composed once more and sounding defeated. "I came to check on Beth. My apologies for disturbing you."

Helen continued her retreat and made it safely to the

hall. Samuel had not followed but still stood as she had left him, alone in a circle of moonlight.

"Goodnight," she called to him softly.

He looked at her a long moment, then nodded and turned away, his expression appearing almost as troubled as it had been that first morning in the garden. She waited, expecting Samuel to say something or come over to her, but he remained where he was, staring out the window. Helen took a step forward, longing to go to him, to put her arms around him and lay her cheek against his back and offer comfort. But something held her back.

If he wanted my comfort he would ask for it.

Instead, Helen felt as if she had been dismissed. She stood at the threshold of the nursery, longing to go in and be a part of the family on the other side. But she had not been invited and was not really part of it at all.

I have only been imagining. It has all been pretend.

CHAPTER 21

February

"I've been thinking," Samuel began at dinner the following week. *Far too much about you.* "And I feel we must not continue on this way. Reuniting Grace and Nicholas is taking too long."

Helen, about to take a bite, stopped her fork halfway to her mouth. "Too long?" There was no mistaking the hurt in her voice.

Do not look at me that way. Samuel cleared his throat uncomfortably. "What I mean to say is that we are not accomplishing what we set out to do. The longer Nicholas is apart from Grace, the more difficult it will be to make him see the necessity of taking her back."

"What do you suggest?" Helen set her fork down, bite uneaten, though she appeared to swallow with difficulty anyway.

"We must present the evidence to Nicholas in person." Samuel took a deep breath, committing himself to the course he'd been considering for the past few days. "We must invite him here."

"Will he come?" She sounded skeptical rather than nervous, and once again Samuel found himself in awe of the transformation he'd witnessed in her the past month. If nothing else, their charade had helped her. *And hurt me.* Now, it seemed, he had not only Beth's feelings to worry over if Helen left, but his as well.

"I do not believe that he will accept my invitation," Samuel said, "unless we provide a compelling reason for him to do so."

"A reason?"

As her brow furrowed, her nose wrinkled, as he'd noticed it did when she was concerned. He wished to kiss the wrinkle away and tell her not to worry. He wished he could spend the indefinite future easing her worries. *I am a fool to imagine it.*

"I shall send him a message telling him that I have decided to marry again and would like his blessing."

"*Marry?*" She sounded a little breathless.

Does the idea still frighten her so much? Samuel ignored her wide, bright eyes and forged on before she could voice an objection. "We shall send word for Christopher and Grace to join us for a celebratory dinner. Nicholas will be furious at my audacity, so he will come to tell me off—if not more than that—and then he shall see you and me together. He will see Grace and realize that both her feelings and his are unchanged. And everything will be as it was before. Everyone will live happily ever after." *Except me.*

Almost a minute passed before Helen spoke. She appeared to be considering the idea or composing herself—which one, he could not tell. Finally, she took a drawn-out sip of water before sharing her opinion.

"What if the invitation is not reason enough? What if he still won't come?"

"I've thought of that." Next came the part of the plan that would prove most difficult—and risky. "I have a messenger in mind who is sure to gain his favor."

This time, there was no mistaking the alarm flooding Helen's face. "Not Beth."

He nodded soberly. "She is almost four. It is time. She deserves to know her mother's family. And they deserve to know her."

"That is most gallant of you," Helen said. "But Samuel, are you quite certain?" She placed her hand over his on the table.

"No." He looked at their hands, thinking of how natural it seemed that she would comfort him, that she sat by his side every night, that she spent her days playing with his daughter.

Why didn't I realize sooner? He felt that he'd wasted all of the precious months they'd had together, especially December, when they'd spent so much time in each other's company. If he'd only realized then, if he had but examined his feelings and told her—before her brother's preposterous suggestion.

Which is not so unbelievable after all.

"I am not sure at all that I want to share Beth with Nicholas and Lady Sutherland. But I am certain that it is the right thing to do." Samuel looked at Helen, searching her eyes for any sign of her feelings—other than those they pretended for each other. "I have been remiss in many things; it is time I remedy those I can."

She smiled warmly and patted his hand once before withdrawing hers. "I will trust your judgment then. Beth is your daughter." She spoke the last quietly, as if reminding herself more than stating the fact to him.

"That may be," Samuel said, deciding it was high time he lightened their mood. "But I daresay she likes you more than she does me."

Helen's shoulders lifted in a delicate shrug, and when she looked at him again, her eyes twinkled, though somehow

Samuel felt that she was still playacting—as if she knew of his attempt at humor and was merely going along with it. "Perhaps if you would take to sewing doll clothes in addition to making swings, she would prefer your company."

He held out his hands and laughed. "I fear to imagine what creations these would come up with."

"Let us hope for now that it is your mind that has conjured something good." She leaned back in her chair and folded her arms as if settling in to listen awhile. "Tell me in detail of your new plan to reunite my sister and Lord Sutherland."

"This was not my plan." Samuel crouched behind the bushes outside of the drawing room at Sutherland Hall as rain poured down. Beth had been out in the rain but a minute or two, as she was escorted from the carriage to the front doors. But he and Helen had now spent several minutes outside getting soaked. Samuel fervently wished he'd been able to convince her to stay home. He tried once more to persuade her to leave. "Your brother will have my head if you become ill."

"Shh," Helen scolded, as if those inside might somehow overhear. Hair plastered to the sides of her face, she stood, peering above the bushes to see through the window. "Oh dear."

"What? What is it?" Samuel started to rise, but Helen pressed her palm to his head, pushing him back. He tottered a moment on the balls of his feet, arms flailing before he fell back, sitting hard in the mud.

"For some reason, Beth jumped out at Lady Sutherland, startling her so that she nearly fell," Helen explained. "But she is all right now. Lord Sutherland has joined them."

"And?" Samuel prodded, grimacing as he put a hand on the soggy ground and tried to right himself.

"He is talking to Beth," Helen said. "He appears somewhat startled—which is to be expected, of course." She glanced over where Samuel had been but found him sitting on the ground instead. "What are you doing? Come look for yourself. You know his moods and manner better than I."

Keeping an oath to himself, Samuel pushed up from the wet ground and joined her in looking through the window. The scene that met his eyes soon caused them to mist—or perhaps it was just the rain impeding his vision. Moisture aside, he could not deny that he was witness to one of Nicholas's more tender moments. When Nicholas at last nodded his promise to Beth that he would come to dinner, then took her hand in his, Samuel knew a moment of deep contentment, of a wrong begun to be right.

"She is safe," Samuel said. "Nicholas is a man of his word. He will be joining us when he brings her home this evening."

He turned from the window to find Helen taking in his muddy appearance. "You're a mess."

He grinned, his heart feeling lighter than it had for some time. "Was it not you who told me there was a price for spying? I suppose my muddy clothing is the cost. Whereas you"—he reached out with his clean hand, brushing a strand of wet hair from her cheek—"have lost only a few curls for our efforts."

She stilled beneath his touch but did not shrink from it. Her eyes closed briefly, and for a second, Samuel felt hope that his touch had affected her as it did him.

"Would that was all I had lost," she whispered, then moved suddenly.

Still bending low, she crept from the house, toward the garden and the gate they had entered. Samuel followed, perplexed by the meaning of her words and the change that had come over her. As soon as they were safely out of sight of the house, he caught her arm, stopping her.

"What were you speaking of back there?"

She shook her head and pulled away, resuming her walk at a brisker pace. They reached the garden wall and the bench Grace had stood on when conversing with him last fall. Helen glanced at the bench briefly before hurrying through the gate, which they'd left ajar. She continued onto Samuel's garden paths while he closed and fastened the gate.

When he'd finished, he ran after her as she headed toward the open lawn.

"Helen, wait!" He caught up with her near the ash tree with the swing he'd made for Beth. Remembering the day they'd first played here, that first glimpse he'd seen of the other Helen—the one who'd been so present lately—he determined to discover what was troubling her. He took her hand this time, forcing her to stop beneath the bare limbs of the great tree.

"What is wrong?" he demanded. "What have I done to upset you?"

"It's not you." She shook her head. "It's me—my fault."

Her tears mingled with the rain on her cheeks, and he realized that this conversation would take more than a minute; but they were both still getting soaked. "Come with me." He took her hand, pulling her across the lawn and toward the shelter of the gazebo. She didn't resist. Only when they'd climbed the steps and were safely out of the rain did he drop her hand and turn to her. She promptly burst into tears. More bewildered than ever, Samuel wrapped his arms around her and held her close as she cried.

Outside the gazebo the rain continued falling, and it felt as though the temperature was dropping quickly. He worried that she would catch a chill if he didn't get her inside and out of her wet cloak. But for now, whatever was troubling her seemed to be the more pressing issue, so he stood patiently until, at length, her tears stopped and she stepped from his embrace, wiping at her eyes. "I'm so sorry, Samuel."

"For crying? Don't be," he said, attempting humor. "It's good for me to offer comfort to a lady in need every so often. Keeps the gentlemanly skills in practice."

"Not for crying . . . though I've done your jacket no favors."

He glanced at his shoulder, wet from both rain and her tears. "No harm."

"But I *have* done you harm," she exclaimed, looking as if she would cry again. "I spied—on you."

"Really?" Instead of feeling put off by her admission, as it appeared she believed he would be, he felt intrigued, even flattered, perhaps. "When?"

"That morning I met you in your garden—Elizabeth's birthday—though I didn't mean to then, and I only heard you talking for a moment."

He nodded. "You admitted as much that day. I know it was quite by accident. I have appreciated your honesty—and trustworthiness about my—uh—unusual conversations."

"There's more." Helen rushed on. "That same afternoon I decided to walk in the gardens. I did not realize that the fence separating Lord Sutherland's property from yours was so close, and I came upon you and Grace. I discovered that you had affection for each other."

"I see." The feeling of lightness he'd enjoyed earlier vanished amid a renewed guilt that he'd shown and felt interest in Helen's sister. "It wasn't what you thought," he said, but he wasn't sure he could explain exactly what it *had* been. He'd cared for Grace, but now he cared for Helen.

As if she would believe that.

"At first I only wanted to hear her voice and know she was well," Helen said. "But the more I heard, the worse I felt. Because . . ."

"I'd already shared with you my intent for her to be with Lord Sutherland?"

"Ye-es," Helen said, looking as if there was something more she wished to say.

The moment passed. She wrapped her arms around her middle and began pacing. "But it is even worse." She passed him but would not stop or turn his way. "On Christmas Day, I was coming home from playing with Beth. And I came upon you and Grace *again*. This time on Lord Sutherland's side of the fence." Helen stopped, facing out of the gazebo, toward the guesthouse.

Oh no. Samuel closed his eyes briefly. *My proposal.* "How much of our conversation did you overhear?" Samuel asked.

"Enough." She still hugged her arms to herself, and her head hung as well, shoulders hunched forward, as if in defeat.

"And how did *that* alter your opinion of me?" Samuel asked. He recalled the day they had walked from the guesthouse and discussed this previously when she had accused him of being manipulative. At the time he hadn't realized that she'd been privy to the intimate details of his proposal.

"It didn't change my opinion." At last she faced him. "It broke my heart that Grace refused you. And now it is you who shall have an altered opinion of me, thinking of me as little more than a busybody."

"I think—"

"I am so sorry, Samuel." She forged ahead. "It was wrong of me, and I have suffered for it more than you will ever know. I feel so terribly wretched."

As do I. One thing in particular that she had said bothered him. *It broke my heart that Grace would refuse you . . .* If Helen had truly been saddened that he and Grace were not to marry . . .

Then it seems unlikely that Helen has developed any true feelings for me.

"*How* have you suffered?" he asked.

Her brow furrowed, as if perplexed by his question. "I regret intruding on your privacy. You were so sorrowful that morning in the garden, and I foolishly thought you might welcome my company."

"I did welcome it," he said, then recalled her awkwardness and remembered that he *hadn't* particularly wished for her to join him.

"You see?" Helen said, and Samuel realized she must have read the truth on his face. "Later, when I heard you with Grace, I was angry with her for teasing you on such a solemn day, but then I realized she was teasing you from your sorrow. That is something I could never do." Helen wrung her hands and gave him a look that spoke of misery. "And then your proposal was so beautiful, so I was sad for you again—that Grace could hurt you so. Yet after seeing her with Lord Sutherland, I knew she must refuse your offer."

Pity. Pity is all she feels for me. Disappointment enveloped Samuel. "Do not worry yourself on my account." He tried to keep the bitterness from his voice. "Any hardship in that situation I brought entirely upon myself. I encouraged Grace to care for Nicholas, so she did. I have encouraged you to consider becoming a governess, and so you have." *Still a terrible idea.* Another one—one he had not before considered—struck him.

Perhaps Helen had hoped her sister and I would marry so she might stay on as a governess for Beth. He had no doubt that Helen loved his daughter. It was Samuel's turn to look away, staring out at the rain and feeling very dismal. "It would appear that I am good at giving advice to beautiful young ladies in need."

"Is that so awful?" Helen asked.

Yes. "Of course not." He faced her once more, a falsely bright smile in place. "What would be awful is if you were to become ill from staying too long in wet clothes. I promised

Christopher that I would take care of you, and if he catches us like this, he will think little of my promise." Samuel gazed at her tenderly and knew he would always think of Helen as she was now, at this very moment, standing in his gazebo, drenched, yet looking more beautiful than he had a right to notice.

"Thank you for accompanying me to look after Beth," he said rather brusquely. "And now we had best hurry inside and prepare for our visitor this evening." He held his arm out to her from habit, and when Helen placed her hand upon it, he assumed it was from the same.

Not because she has developed any particular affection for me. Not at all.

CHAPTER

Helen waited inside the door of the "big-person dining room," as Beth had named it in December, when she'd been allowed—until the fork incident—to dine with them.

Christopher entered the room. "Lord Sutherland and Samuel have just finished their discussion about Beth," he whispered, sending Helen a look filled with meaning. The focus of their evening was about to shift drastically—to Grace.

"Time for my most convincing act ever," Helen said. *Except that it is no act.* Pretending to be in love with Samuel was not difficult at all. There was no pretending.

Lord Sutherland entered the room, his gaze drawn to them immediately. Helen smiled, and though he did not return it, he did not appear as fierce as before. Instead, a sort of haunting sadness lurked in his eyes as he searched the room, no doubt looking for Grace.

Helen felt she understood something of his sadness.

Soon enough, her time with Samuel would be over, and she would be the one unable to smile.

They took their seats. Lord Sutherland, appearing rather concerned, spoke. "Is Grace ill again?"

"I hope not." Samuel glanced at Christopher. "Was Grace well the last time you saw her?"

"It depends upon what you mean by the word *well*," Helen said.

"What Helen means," Christopher clarified, "is that Grace is healthy in body, but her spirits are quite low."

"Why is that?" Lord Sutherland leaned back as a servant poured his drink. "Why is she not here with you?"

"She would not come," Helen said. "It is too painful for her to be so near you."

"So near *me*?" He stood and threw down his napkin. "That is absurd. She lived in my home for three months and endured my company quite well."

"No small miracle," Samuel muttered. Helen shot him a quelling look.

"Whatever she has told you is not true," Lord Sutherland said. "I treated her with the utmost respect, gave her every courtesy, let her go when the blasted inheritance came through and Christopher made it clear you—" he glared at Samuel—"intended to propose."

Christopher picked up his spoon and began sipping his soup. "*Letting her go* is the offense I believe she finds most painful."

Helen and Samuel began eating, ignoring Lord Sutherland still towering above them, casting murderous glares at them all. Instead of withering beneath his anger, Helen felt surprisingly calm. *Samuel is here. I am safe.* It was a comfort she had grown far too used to.

And behind Lord Sutherland's rage, she sensed his distress. *He misses Grace. He still loves her very much.*

"If she does not wish to reside here, then why are you

not with her?" Lord Sutherland demanded, looking pointedly at Samuel. "If she were my fiancée, I would be with her instead of letting her go off alone to who knows where."

"She *was* your fiancée." Helen's words were brave, but she kept her head down as she buttered her bread. "And you did let her go off alone."

"I let her do what she'd wanted to do all along," Lord Sutherland said defensively. "What she'd dreamed of and planned for years."

"Dreams can change, milord." Helen turned to Samuel. *Mine have.* He reached for her hand, taking it in his, causing her heart to race.

"What is this?" Lord Sutherland gestured to their joined hands.

"*This*," Samuel said, "is why I asked you here tonight. Helen and I have discovered that we have feelings for each other, and I should like your blessing in courting her with the intent that she shall become my wife." His look seemed to convey all the meaning she put into hers, and Helen desperately wished to believe it—to believe that his words were true and that he did want her for his wife. She could not pull her eyes from his and felt somewhat dazed by the look of tenderness and affection he was showering upon her.

Lord Sutherland, appearing stunned himself, took up his wine glass, tilted his head, and threw the drink back quickly, draining the contents. He still had not sat down. "Helen?" he gasped when he had finished. "It is *Helen* you wish to marry. Not Grace?"

"Grace would not have him," Christopher said matter-of-factly, taking another bite of meat.

Lord Sutherland directed his questioning gaze at Helen.

"It is true," she said, distilling all but the slightest wistfulness from her voice. "As I knew it would be all along. Her letters were full of stories about you, Lord Sutherland.

We could all tell, very early on, that it was you she was falling in love with. It was why we encouraged her to stay."

Samuel nodded slowly, confirming their story. "I did care for her," he admitted. "But my affection was never returned, and my feelings for Grace were never what they are for Helen. I only wish it had not taken me so long to come to a realization of what was right in front of me—what I had near for so long yet failed to recognize or appreciate."

Could he possibly mean those words? Helen's heart beat rapidly as hope surged. He sounded so sincere.

Lord Sutherland glanced at the door as if he wished to leave—immediately. They stared at him, collectively holding their breath.

Will he believe us? I believe us—or I want to.

"Will you tell me where she is?" Lord Sutherland asked at last.

Helen bit her lip to keep from shouting for joy.

"I'll do better than that," Samuel said, unable to contain a grin. "I'll take you to her."

"Best performance ever," Christopher said when Lord Sutherland had gone home and the three of them had retired to the drawing room. "You almost had *me* convinced that you've fallen in love with each other." He raised his glass to toast them. "To Helen and Samuel and their talents working together to bring Grace happiness."

Neither Helen nor Samuel joined in his toast. Samuel raised his glass but did not drink. Helen sank lower in her favorite chair opposite Samuel's by the fire.

I have but one more evening with him.

It had been decided at dinner that she and Christopher would travel to Grace at the country house the day after tomorrow. Samuel and Lord Sutherland would follow within the week, as soon as Lady Sutherland had been notified and the necessary arrangements could be made for a hasty wedding.

Once he'd realized Grace was not in love with Samuel but was still in love with him, Lord Sutherland had become a man of action. He would have begun his journey at once, that very night, had Samuel and Christopher not persuaded him to more logical steps—meaning that Lord Sutherland would not only go to retrieve Grace as soon as possible, but that he would marry her quickly as well, putting an end, once and for all, to their separation and misery.

But just beginning mine. Helen would likely be expected to stay with Christopher at the country house after Grace wed. Miranda and Harrison were there, too, so it would not be all bad. Truthfully, it would be much as her life before.

Without Father to interfere. But without Samuel and Beth to love.

Helen pushed the thought aside, knowing it would bring tears; and she could not cry now, here, in front of Christopher and Samuel. She would have ample time for that later.

"You're quiet tonight, sister," Christopher said. Setting his glass down, he came to sit on the nearby sofa. "Already contemplating the next part of our plan?"

"*What* next part?" She had done what she said she would. It had worked. Her usefulness here was over.

"Yes," Samuel joined in, sounding rather out of sorts himself. "What next part? We are finished here. Let the poor girl rest."

I am not *a poor girl.* Helen fumed inwardly, upset that so quickly he would return to speaking of her as a child as he used to.

"You have but one task more to perform, so as to quite thoroughly convince Lord Sutherland of your affection." Christopher leaned against the back of the sofa, one leg thrown casually over the other, a sly grin on his face. "You must share a farewell kiss when we take our leave of this place."

"No!" As before, when Christopher had first introduced this preposterous scheme, they both spoke at once, but this time there was no hesitation.

"How could you, Christopher?" Helen knew he was baiting her to anger, but she could not seem to help herself from exhibiting her fury. How dare he suggest such a thing when he knew how she felt about Samuel?

I cannot kiss him. It will make our parting that much worse.

"I can because I must," Christopher said. "You have never been kissed, and surely Lord Sutherland will expect as much of a couple planning to be married."

"He will *not* expect it," Helen insisted. "He knows I am shy."

"As shy as you were tonight, when you so boldly stood up to him? Or when you openly held hands with Samuel and made eyes at each other at the table?"

"We did no such—"

"Nicholas will not be here to see us part," Samuel interrupted, saving her from embarrassing herself and lying as well. She could only imagine what she had looked like, lost in Samuel's tender display of affection as she had been earlier this evening.

That is all it was. A display.

"On the contrary," Christopher said. "Lord Sutherland most certainly will be here to see us off. I told him to come the morning we depart and that I would share with him the map outlining the best route to take."

"You might have done that another time," Helen said irritably, clasping her hands in her lap to keep from strangling him.

"I might have," Christopher said, his grin broadening. "But I did not."

Not trusting herself to keep control of her fragile and overwrought emotions, Helen stood and made to take her leave. "Good night, Samuel. I apologize for my brother's—audacity," she said, lacking a more appropriate word. She hurried past Christopher. "Thank you for ruining one of my last nights here."

He caught her wrist. "Not so fast. You'd best practice that kiss. I shall watch to see if it is convincing."

"Enough!" Samuel said, standing also. "The country has not helped your manners," he said to Christopher and came to stand beside Helen. "Your sister has done nothing to deserve such torture."

"I apologize," Christopher said, sounding only half sincere. "I did not mean to distress either of you, but this seems the last and logical conclusion to your pretend courtship. And as Helen has never been kissed—"

"I believe we have established as much," Helen snapped. She felt her face burn and wished, as she had not for the past several weeks, since before this pretense began, that she might disappear.

"I will see to it that Helen is adequately prepared," Samuel said, not meeting her astonished gaze, but staring pointedly at Christopher. "But it will not be *here*, tonight when she is not expecting it. And most certainly, her first kiss will not be in a drawing room with her brother looking on." He held out his arm to her. "Come Helen. I'll walk you upstairs."

Together they turned their backs on Christopher and exited the room, one in purpose yet again, though Helen could feel no victory in their unification against sharing a kiss. For as much as the idea terrified her, she could not deny that a kiss from Samuel was suddenly something she wanted very much.

CHAPTER 23

A *first kiss is a special thing and must be undertaken with the proper amount of preparation. Timing, location, and of course the person whom you shall kiss, are all of the utmost importance. Should you feel ready to experience your first kiss (and only if you feel ready—do not let that dunderhead brother of yours force you to it!) meet me at the gazebo at sunset.*

Yours, Samuel

Helen reread the note left beside her breakfast plate a third time, then clutched it to her, a treasure she was certain she would keep forever. *As will be the memory of my first kiss.* She had every intention of meeting Samuel that evening at sunset. And though that was a good eight hours from now, her heart beat rapidly in anticipation.

Still holding the letter close and feeling rather dreamy, she started toward the stairs.

"Miss Helen, are you ready to play?" Beth called from

above, a second before she began sliding backwards down the banister.

"Goodness," Helen exclaimed, catching her at the bottom. "This is a new trick—and not one I am certain your father will like."

"Mama used to do it." Beth beamed. "Uncle Nicholas says I am just like her."

"A high compliment indeed," Helen said, feeling slightly less happy at the reminder of Elizabeth as she tucked the note into her pocket. The last woman Samuel had kissed was his wife.

Whom he still loves dearly. And whom he imagines himself to be conversing with this very moment in the garden. Will he tell her of me?

Helen tried to imagine the one-sided conversation but could not, though she guessed it included his asking Elizabeth's pardon for a kiss he must give to a poor girl who would otherwise never experience one.

He is humoring me; that is all, Helen thought, her mood turning quite glum. *And making certain that I am prepared, lest Lord Sutherland really does appear at the moment of our departure.* No longer quite so certain that she wished to meet Samuel this evening, Helen took Beth's hand and began the climb to the nursery, resigned to, but finding less satisfaction in, resuming her role as a governess in training.

Eight hours later Helen peeked around the corner of the house. Samuel stood inside the gazebo, his silhouette highlighted in the setting sun. Pulling her cloak tighter, she took a deep breath and willed her heartbeat to steady. She had been here several minutes already, arguing with herself, trying to decide which course of action was best.

Kissing Samuel was a poor idea that would only bring more heartache. On the other hand, if she did not take advantage of this unique opportunity, might she spend the rest of her life regretting it? This was likely to be the only kiss she would ever receive, and from the only man she would ever care for.

I should allow him to kiss me. I must.

Before she could change her mind yet again, Helen stepped from the shelter of the house and into plain view. She held her head high as she walked toward the gazebo and Samuel, who still had his back to her. When she was close enough that he might hear, she called out to him.

"Good evening, Samuel."

He turned suddenly, a look that almost seemed a combination of relief and happiness lifting the corners of his mouth and deepening the brown of his eyes. "You came." He walked forward, his hand held out to her as she ascended the steps.

"I had to—I wanted to," she clarified, lest he think Christopher had forced her to it. Beneath Samuel's searching gaze, she felt her face heat.

He brushed his fingers gently across her cheek. "You are very pretty when you blush. Has anyone ever told you that?"

She shook her head. "Not until now."

"Good. The person who gives you your first kiss ought to compliment you as no one has before. For example . . ." His hand fell from her face. "You are the finest three-person waltz dancer I know." He held his hand to the side of his mouth and whispered, "Though you must not tell that to the third in our party. She would be most upset with me."

"I shall not breathe a word of your compliment, sir." Helen pressed her lips together with her finger.

He nodded his approval. "In addition to your dancing skills, you sew the loveliest doll clothes I have ever seen."

Helen arched a brow. "And you are a connoisseur of doll clothing?"

"Of course," he said in mock seriousness. "You know my Beth. She demands only the best."

"That she does," Helen agreed, feeling some of her anxiety ease with his teasing.

"Which brings me to my next compliment," Samuel said. "You have the caring and instincts of a mother. No doubt you shall be a great one someday."

Would that I might. She swallowed, suddenly uncomfortable. "That is not likely, but I thank you."

"Beth has absolutely shined beneath your tutelage."

He still finds my best to be with children.

Helen shook her head and tried to keep the building emotion at bay. "She cannot help but shine, no matter who is fortunate enough to be her companion."

"Speaking of companions," Samuel continued as if he had not noticed her discomfort. "You are an excellent partner at the theatre." His smile broadened, as if remembering that pleasant evening. "You have more courage than anyone I know." He took her hands, squeezing them lightly. "You are possessed of a fine intelligence and a quick wit. And you are not at all shy, as I was once led to believe."

"Goodness," Helen exclaimed, tugging her hands from his and bringing them to her warm cheeks. "You had best be careful. So many kind words are likely to go to my head. I believe I feel slightly dizzy already."

"Then my ploy is working," Samuel said, raising his hands in a sign of victory. "But I am not finished." His eyes narrowed as one corner of his mouth quirked up. "You have a gift for espionage, the likes of which I did not realize until you confessed them to me on this very spot."

"*That* is no compliment," Helen said glibly.

"To me, it is," Samuel said. "I admit to feeling very flattered that you watched me. That you sought me out to walk with me that morning."

"Only because Grace had told me how young ladies at balls go about catching a man's attention," Helen admitted. "I foolishly believed that if I wore my prettiest dress and curled my hair, you would take notice of me."

Samuel cocked his head to the side. "You wished me to notice you—even then?" One brow rose, as if he did not quite believe her.

Helen sighed heavily. This was not at all how she'd imagined this evening would go, but now that she'd begun speaking, she realized she needed to confess the whole of it—to finish what she'd begun to admit yesterday. She looked past him as she spoke.

"Last October, I worried that all would not go well with Grace and Lord Sutherland and that we would find ourselves outcasts once more. I knew it very likely that Father would force me to marry. So I thought that if I must marry, I should at least prefer to wed a man who had shown me kindness." She dared to glance at him. "*You* had shown me kindness."

"I see." The teasing had left Samuel's voice. "And now that your father is gone, you will not be forced to wed anyone."

"No." She turned away.

He will not kiss me now that he knows how I had thought to use him.

"May I assume, then," Samuel continued, "that if you chose to pursue a man, it would no longer be an act of desperation, but perhaps something your heart genuinely desires?"

What is he asking me? "Ye-es." Helen spoke hesitantly.

"Look at me, Helen." He so rarely asked anything of her, and never commanded, that his order took her by surprise.

She turned to him as he'd requested and found him to be standing very close. "Oh!" She startled as his arms came suddenly around her.

"I am going to kiss you now," Samuel said, looking at

her, his face so near, his lips hovering just above hers. "That is what you came for, right?"

She nodded, not daring to take her eyes off his, lest he begin before she expected it.

"What should I do with my hands?"

Samuel looked at her arms, which were pinned at her sides by his. "Put them on my shoulders."

"Why?"

He smiled. "Because I would like them there. And so you may easily push me away if you find that you do not care to be kissed after all."

"Oh." She was positive that her face was on fire, but she rested her fingertips on his shoulders. "I'm scared," she said, the admission falling from her lips before she realized what she was saying.

"So am I." His eyes filled with tenderness. "I have only kissed one other woman, and nearly four years have passed since then. For a very long time, I did not think to ever have the privilege again." His head came forward, but instead of kissing her, he merely leaned his forehead against hers. "And now that I have it, now that I have you in my arms, I am very much afraid. I want this to be a beautiful moment for you, Helen. And for me, I don't want it to end."

It doesn't have to. "It is beautiful already," she whispered, then smiled. "I thank you for not making me share it with Christopher."

Samuel chuckled as he pulled back to look at her. "We most definitely will not share this with your brother." He leaned forward again, this time with intent in his eyes. Helen felt hers flutter closed as his soft, warm lips brushed against hers, then lingered, moving gently, filling her soul with a sweet warmth.

I love you, Samuel. She must have only thought it, as her mouth was too occupied to speak, but she longed for him to hear the words, to know that the pretend had become so very real for her. He'd said he did not want this moment to end.

But it did. He pulled back, head still tilted slightly as he studied her with inquisitive eyes. "Well?" A corner of his mouth quirked up as if certain of her answer.

"Well yourself," she said, feeling suddenly bold and fixing him with what she imagined to be a rather heat-filled stare.

"Did you enjoy your first kiss?" he asked, sounding slightly less confident.

She hesitated. "Yes. But . . ."

"What?" His brows wrinkled with worry.

Helen bit her lip to keep from laughing. Then feeling she had tortured him long enough, she set out to do the opposite. "I do not think my hands should be on your shoulders. Because I have no intention of pushing you away." Never taking her eyes from his, she moved closer, sliding her hands over his shoulders to the back of his neck.

Now Samuel's eyes were wide with astonishment, and Helen felt an entirely new emotion, as if she were in possession of a great power she had just discovered. "And I think it ought to be the lady who decides when a kiss is ended, especially if it is her first. Your kiss was quite good until you ceased it abrupt—"

His mouth covered hers again, and she closed her eyes. *Absolute bliss.* His arms tightened at her waist, and Helen sighed contentedly. But still Samuel's lips caressed hers. *What have I done?* She realized it would be up to her to pull away, and she wasn't at all sure that she could.

As for me, I don't want it to end. Could that possibly mean—

"Papa, Miss Helen, what are you doing?"

They broke apart at once, and Helen wasn't sure whose face appeared redder—hers or Samuel's. Beth danced at their feet—her own bare, and no cloak or winter wrap about her.

"What are *you* doing?" Samuel scolded, then snatched her up.

Instinctively, Helen stepped forward, took Beth's feet in her hands, and began rubbing them briskly. "She's frozen."

Samuel unfastened his coat and wrapped it around Beth. "Where is Mary?"

Beth shrugged. "She told me to stay out of mischief while she went to take my dress downstairs to be washed. I used my paints on it, and she was very cross with me."

"Oh dear," Helen said.

"Your *paints*?" Samuel asked.

"This is my fault. I gave them to her." Helen tensed, awaiting his reaction. "Beth is very creative, and I thought—painting might be a good outlet?"

"Her creativity has never been the problem," Samuel grumbled, but Helen thought she could see the start of a smile beneath his gruff words.

"It wasn't a very pretty dress," Beth said. "So I decided to make it better. Miss Helen says if there is something about ourselves that we do not like, we must work to improve it. Is that not right, Miss Helen?"

"Yes, but . . ." Helen covered her mouth, partly to keep from laughing and partly because she knew that no amount of explaining would fix this. Somehow, Grandfather's advice had taken on a whole new meaning for the little girl.

"You should have listened to Nanny when she told you to stay out of trouble," Samuel said, both sounding and looking exasperated.

"I did," Beth said. "I am not in mischief now, and Nanny did not say *where* I must stay out of it."

Helen turned away, but not fast enough. A burst of laughter surfaced, followed quickly by another.

"Now you see what you have done," Samuel grumbled behind her. "Miss Helen was supposed to be having a delightful moment at sunset, but instead, she is overcome with hysterics."

"It *is* a most delightful moment," Helen assured him, turning to look at them once more.

"*Is* or *was*?" Samuel's brows rose in question.

"Both," Helen answered, meeting his gaze and feeling her heart soar.

"Altogether too short, if you ask me," he complained, but Helen did not miss his smile.

"Come." Shifting Beth's weight to one side, he extended his arm. Helen stepped up beside him so that he had his arm around her shoulders.

"At least we will not cheat you of the sunset." He turned them toward the west and the glorious pinks and oranges still painting the sky over the brilliant white landscape. "My favorite time of day," Samuel said.

"More so than your morning walks?" Helen asked, then wished she had not.

Just because he may be starting to care for me does not mean I should ever ask him to cease loving Elizabeth.

He looked at her carefully. "Yes. More than my mornings in the garden. Especially tonight, as you are here." He gave her shoulder a gentle squeeze, and Helen leaned against him.

Together the three stood, basking in the sun's last light and the possibilities of a future brighter than any Helen might have ever pretended.

CHAPTER 24

Samuel followed Christopher into the study and closed the door behind him. Aware that he was wasting precious minutes that could be spent saying goodbye to Helen, he seated himself quickly and motioned for Christopher to do the same. "What is it that cannot wait until we meet again?"

Christopher withdrew a sheaf of papers from his coat pocket. "The solicitor we hired has had some success." His tone, while not completely solemn, was at least more serious than usual.

Samuel leaned forward and took the packet. "It is as we feared?" The knot already formed in his stomach grew tighter. "Have you discovered that Crayton paid your father for the privilege of wedding Helen?"

"Whether or not marriage was the plan is questionable," Christopher said. "But yes, money was exchanged in the bargain—£3500 to be exact."

Samuel grimaced. It was worse than he'd thought. "And

that in addition to whatever Nicholas was coerced into paying your father to compensate for Helen's *unmarriageable* status."

Christopher nodded. "No one ever said Father wasn't sly."

"I'll have the funds withdrawn directly," Samuel said, only too eager to pay Crayton and have the matter done with. "Have you an address where the man might be reached?"

"I do, but I wouldn't suggest paying him—not yet, at least."

"What do you mean?" Samuel leaned closer, intent on getting through to Helen's brother the importance of removing this threat to her well being.

"As of yet, Crayton is unaware of Helen's whereabouts. If he suddenly receives a bank draft from a Mr. Samuel Preston, where do you think that will lead him?" Christopher stared at him pointedly.

He brought up a good point, but it also seemed that if there was no longer money owed to Crayton, then Helen might at least be free of obligation there. *But possibly not free from threat.* Samuel recalled the possessive look in Crayton's eyes that night at the theatre. "You don't believe he wants the money, then?"

"Oh I'm sure he wants the money." Christopher leaned back in his chair, a thoughtful expression upon his face. "But it would seem—at least from the dialogue our man was able to discover—that Crayton wants Helen more. That Father did not deliver his end of the bargain likely contributed to his untimely death. And now that there is now a price on my head—"

"*What?*" Samuel rose from his chair and walked over to stand before Christopher. "You are acting far too casual about this entire situation. Crayton is not only looking for Helen now, but for you as well?"

"And with intent to harm us both, no doubt." Christopher continued to recline in his chair, as if this did not particularly bother him.

"Yet you do not think it prudent to pay the man off and be done with him?" As he had at times before, Samuel felt himself becoming irritated with Helen's brother.

"Oh I think it prudent," Christopher assured him. "But only *after* Helen is safe. When the law would be on her side and Crayton would have no legal right to touch her—because she is already married."

The suggestion settled over Samuel, and he wondered that he had not seen it coming earlier. He glanced once more at Christopher before returning to his seat. "I daresay you have some of your father's shrewdness about you. And I do not mean that as a compliment."

"I don't take it as one," Christopher said, a smile on his face nonetheless. "But be that as it may, I have done my best to use any cleverness I am in possession of to guide my sisters to happy futures. Do you see that anyone has been harmed in the process?"

"No," Samuel said, his tone surly. "Not yet, anyway."

"Nor will they be. Grace shall soon be wed, and she and Lord Sutherland will be most happy together." Christopher's grin broadened, as if the prospect pleased him greatly. Turning his look directly upon Samuel, he said, "You must admit, after weeks of *pretending* to care for one another, that you and Helen make a fine match as well." He rose suddenly, before Samuel had a chance to reply. "Hold off on your payment to Crayton until after the weddings. Then I shall deliver it myself, if you'd like."

Weddings? He thinks there are to be two? "You'd be so foolish as to meet with him when the man would like to see you dead?" Samuel rolled his eyes at Christopher's audacity. "You are both unwise and have assumed a great many things. Even *if* Helen is safely settled—" *If she were to agree to marry me*—"Crayton is not likely to forget the incident at the theatre."

"I should hope not," Christopher said, rubbing his hand absently. "It has taken me a rather long time to recover. I expect his face has suffered at least as much. It would be a good idea to keep tabs on him for some time yet, but it does appear that he sticks mostly to crimes the crown approves of, or at least chooses to ignore. Once married, Helen should be safe enough. And unless Crayton plans to chase me overseas, I think in a few months' time I shall be free of him as well."

"And where do you think to go?" Samuel asked, not surprised to hear that Christopher had adventurous plans.

"America." He spoke the word almost reverently. "The land of opportunity. Where my father's name will neither follow nor condemn me, and where I shall be able to make my own fortune and even purchase my own land." His face lit with animation, and his fists clenched and unclenched at his sides, as if they were overly eager to get started working toward this vision.

"And do your sisters know of this grand scheme of yours?" Samuel well imagined what Helen and Grace might have to say about it.

Christopher shook his head. "Of course not. As with the situation with Crayton, timing is everything. I shall tell them both after they are happily wed and have little time for thought of me."

"You grossly underestimate your sisters if you think they will give little thought to you sailing off to another continent."

Christopher shrugged. "Nevertheless, I must—Crayton being just one of the many reasons. But I will talk to Helen and Grace when the time is right. I trust you and Lord Sutherland will help them to understand."

"*If* I happen to be around when that time comes, I will do my best to aid your cause—so long as it does not overly contribute to Helen's unhappiness. Her well-being must come first, you understand."

"Just as your daughter's welfare had to come first when we began our plot to reunite Lord Sutherland and Grace?" Christopher raised his brows knowingly.

"Yes. *Much* like that." Samuel stood and faced him. "Why don't you be more direct? What, exactly, do you expect me to do? All this speaking in circles is wasting valuable time which I might be spending with your sister."

"You know what I want." Christopher headed toward the door. "Lord Sutherland will be obtaining a license to marry within the week. Why not accompany him to fill out the paperwork and complete your own license at the same time?"

"I should like to be more certain of the lady's favor before I take such a leap of faith." Samuel scowled at the papers in his hand, then threw them on the desk behind him. He didn't want a threat to Helen's safety to be the cause for a rushed wedding. *Or a wedding at all.* He wanted Helen to marry him because she loved him.

Curse Crayton. Samuel was tired of obstacles and misunderstandings and even the situation between Nicholas and Grace right now. *I just want to be with Helen. Can the rest of it not all go away?*

Christopher reached the door and looked back. "You can be certain of Helen's affection. Though if you have not figured that out after the kiss you shared yesterday . . ." He smirked.

"I think I shall be glad to see you go," Samuel said, only half-jesting. "Can a man not have a bit of privacy—"

"Not when he is courting my sister," Christopher replied, his tone serious. "But I promise you will not be wrong in declaring your feelings—just as surely as I know that it would not be safe for her to have banns posted anywhere. It wouldn't do to alert Crayton of her whereabouts."

"No," Samuel agreed. "It would not." *Has Helen, perhaps, confided in her brother her feelings for me?* His heart lightened. Today's parting with Helen need not be a true parting. He *could* ask her to marry him when he next saw her again. He *would*. His mouth curved upward, and he gave a short laugh as he studied Christopher. "If I didn't know better, I would say you have plotted this entire situation from the very beginning."

"*Do* you know better?" Christopher asked as he pulled the door open. "After all, our grandfather charged me with finding my sisters good husbands. I have been aware of every man they have come in contact with since his passing—and even before. I knew who held the theatre box beside us long before you knew of the occupants of ours."

"Truly?" Samuel said, bemused at Christopher's boasting. "And what of Lord Sutherland? Did you know him as well?"

A sly grin spread across Christopher's face. "Perhaps. Perhaps not. But I *was* known—in my youth—to have tampered with a carriage wheel a time or two."

Helen stood at the sitting room window, staring pensively out through the pouring rain as Harrison and two other servants secured her trunk onto the back of the coach. Packing the last of her belongings and closing the lid this morning had seemed such an act of finality. *I am really leaving. Will I ever return?*

Beth skipped into the room, spied Helen at the window, and rushed over, nearly knocking her over with one of her headlong, impulsive hugs. "Papa says you must go, but I don't want you to."

"I do not wish it either," Helen said, patting Beth's hair. "But my sister needs me."

"*I* need you," Beth cried, clinging even harder to Helen's legs.

And I need you. And your father. Helen pried Beth's small fingers from her and knelt at the child's height, where she might properly return the little girl's affection. Gathering Beth in her arms, Helen held her close. "I love you, dear Beth." Helen felt her heart would burst with it—or break if she was not allowed to maintain this relationship. She looked up through tear-filled eyes and discovered Samuel watching them.

He stepped close, extracted Beth from Helen's arms, and helped Helen to stand.

"I wonder . . ." He patted Beth on the head, then watched as she ran over to the window. Slowly his gaze returned to Helen. "I wonder if *I* might ever hear a similar sentiment fall from your lips."

What is he saying? Her heart pounded so loudly she was certain he must hear it. "If it was something you wished to hear—"

"The weather has turned worse." Harrison appeared in the doorway behind Samuel, water dripping from his hat and already pooling at his feet. "Best not to tarry any longer." Helen followed his gaze toward the window and outside, where the rain was beginning to turn to sleet.

"Roads are already muddy. It'll be slow going, and if we don't leave at once we'll risk being stuck somewhere before nightfall." He wiped his sleeve across his brow, flicking droplets of water across the rug. "And I don't care to have another accident in the middle of the night."

"There will be *no* accidents," Samuel said, speaking more to Helen than to Harrison. "Your brother's presence ought to assure that." His mouth twisted in a wry grin Helen did not understand. "And this time you are traveling with a proper escort."

She nodded, grateful for the two extra men Samuel had employed to see she and Christopher safely home. *Except that it will not feel like home.*

"Your brother is already outside," Harrison said.

"Gallant of him to wait for me," Helen said with uncharacteristic sarcasm.

Harrison coughed into his hand and cleared his throat. "He asked that I inform you that Lord Sutherland will not be here to see you off. Due to the inclement weather he has decided to stay home this morning. And so Mr. Thatcher said your earlier *requirement* before departure is no longer necessary."

"Christopher is already outside because he is fearful I'll strangle him," Samuel muttered.

"No longer necessary." Helen shook her head. "Do not worry. I have seven hours before me to make him pay." She turned to Harrison. "Thank you. Please inform Christopher that I shall be along shortly."

"He asked that I wait for you," Harrison said, his face a perfect mask of respect, yet Helen sensed his own mischief lurking below the surface.

Samuel and Helen glanced at each other, then back at Harrison. Helen silently wished him to go away. Regardless of whether or not Lord Sutherland was here, she wanted a goodbye kiss.

"I'll just wait—over there." With a nod, Harrison turned from them and walked exactly five steps away, no longer in the sitting room doorway, but close enough that he might still see what was going on inside. Helen sighed inwardly.

Samuel moved closer, took both of her hands in his and leaned close. "It seems we are destined to be forever interrupted."

"Not forever, I hope," Helen said, then immediately

worried he would misinterpret her words. "Not interrupted, I mean."

"I know." His voice held a confidence that had not been there a few minutes earlier. "I will miss you, Helen, but I shall see you next week." He leaned forward and placed a chaste kiss upon her cheek.

Her eyes must have betrayed her disappointment, for Samuel's mouth quirked upward. "Patience," he whispered, then glanced at Harrison, pretending to study some point on the wall beyond them and Beth, busily licking her fingers and trailing smudges on the window pane. "This is not goodbye. And this is most definitely not our moment alone. But it shall come."

CHAPTER

Helen sat at the one dressing table in the tiny upstairs bedroom of the cottage. She brushed her long hair, then began the process of plaiting it, while across the room, near the fire, Miranda did the same for Grace.

"If you'll but wait a minute, I'll take care of that for you," Miranda said, censure heavy in her voice as she looked over at Helen.

Proper ladies *do not plait their own hair.* Helen silently repeated the admonition that had been spoken to her many times. "Of course." She allowed her hands to go slack and stared forlornly into the mirror. The face reflecting back at her did not appear worried or frightened as it had so many times in the past. Rather, the deep blue eyes were filled with acute longing, and the pouting mouth confirmed impatience and displeasure. *Not a pretty look.*

Helen sighed and turned away from the mirror. "I think this must be what it feels like to be homesick."

"You mean lovesick," Grace corrected, then winced as Miranda pulled her braid tight.

"That too." Helen rose from the chair and went to stand before the window, looking down at the dark and unfamiliar yard below. "I miss Samuel terribly, but I also miss Beth. I miss the breakfast room and the nursery and the gardens. I think that I have never cared for a place so much—even Grandfather's home was not so dear to me."

"I know what you mean," Grace said, a slight catch in her voice.

Helen closed her eyes and heart against her sister's silent plea for comfort. *I promised not to say a word of Lord Sutherland or his plans.* Oh, but it was difficult to keep her promise when she knew she might end Grace's misery now, or at least give her something to hope for.

"I promise you will have that feeling of being home again one day," Helen said, praying she had not hinted at too much yet had somehow offered the comfort she longed to give. She turned from the window to assess Grace's reaction and saw her smile bravely—if not falsely.

"I know I shall come to feel the same about this dear old house quite soon," Grace said.

"Old it certainly is," Miranda grumbled. "Fireplaces that don't air properly. Windows that don't shut or open. Floors squeak. Water has to be pumped outside. Drafts something terrible in every room. Your grandfather is like to haunt me for letting you girls live in a place like this."

Helen and Grace exchanged surprised looks then Grace's smile turned genuine. "Oh, Miranda. We are used to this and worse."

"*Much* worse," Helen said, thinking of the hovel they'd grown up in. "Here the air is sweet, the meadows wide around us, and everything inside is neat as a pin."

"Not room for much more than a pin." Miranda tied a ribbon at the bottom of Grace's braid. Helen returned to the dressing table and allowed Miranda to finish her hair and continue her muttering. "Nothing is as it should be. Your brother's working outside like a common laborer. Harrison's putting on airs and bringing me trinkets."

"What?" Grace and Helen exclaimed together. Helen caught Miranda's eye and blushing face in the mirror.

"What trinkets has he brought you?" Grace asked.

"Do tell us—or better, show us." Helen turned in her seat to appraise their blushing maid.

"Nothing. Forget I said it." Miranda resumed her task with a strong hand that soon had Helen feeling tears in her eyes.

"Not so tight, please," she begged. "I am only going to sleep. Not out riding."

Grace, safe now—having had her braid finished already—seemed not about to let the matter rest. Leaving her chair by the fire, she came over to sit on the bed, only a few steps away from the dressing table in the crowded room. "If you will not tell us, we shall guess."

"*Hmpf*," Miranda said, sounding decidedly like the person she did not wish to discuss.

"Did Harrison give you a special piece of jewelry, perhaps a family heirloom he's held onto all these years?" Grace asked.

Miranda made no reply but continued plaiting Helen's hair in a torturous manner.

"Or perhaps he picked a bouquet of wildflowers for you," Helen suggested.

"In February?" Miranda rolled her eyes, but Helen had the strangest feeling that their maid was rather enjoying this attention and game.

"He brought you a sweet?" Grace guessed.

Miranda shook her head, and her lips remained pressed together.

Helen sighed dramatically. "If she will not tell us, we shall simply have to ask Harrison."

"Splendid idea." Grace clapped her hands and rose up on her knees on the bed. "We shall tell him how Miranda was speaking of his gift in such loving terms."

"Oh no, you won't." Miranda pulled the ribbon on Helen's braid with finality. "That's all I need is the man thinking I'm so taken with him that I talk about him."

"Well, aren't you?" Grace asked.

"He is quite taken with *you*," Helen said, remembering her conversation with Harrison months earlier. "He admires your strength of character and your caring, giving ways." She grimaced as she ran a hand over her braid, wishing Miranda had been a bit *less* caring with it.

"Harrison said all that? He admires my *character*?"

Helen nodded. "That and more. He cares a great deal for you, Miranda."

"He does," Grace agreed. "If I had someone as good as Harrison who cared for me, I would do my best not to lose him." Her voice had grown quiet, and Helen came over to the bed to sit by her, putting her arm around Grace's shoulders.

"Will that be all?" Miranda asked, considerably subdued from moments earlier.

"Yes," Helen said, answering for them both as she sensed Grace no longer felt like talking. "Thank you."

Miranda gave her usual curt nod, then turned to leave the room. She opened the door but paused before going out to the hall. "Harrison brought me the fixings for a hat, as mine became crushed during the move. He brought me ribbons and flowers and such so I could make it new."

"That was quite thoughtful," Helen said.

"It was, wasn't it?" Miranda spoke as if this was revelation to her.

"Very," Grace added as Miranda left them, closing the door behind her.

"Harrison loves her." Helen rested her head upon Grace's shoulder.

"Yes," Grace agreed. "But will they ever be together? Or will they keep doing the same circles around each other as they have been all these years?"

"I don't know," Helen said, wondering why love had to be so complicated. "Do you think if Harrison told Miranda he loved her it would change anything between them?" She waited, but Grace did not answer, so Helen asked another question, one she had wondered about lately. "When did Lord Sutherland tell you that he loved you?"

"*After* I had taken a chance and declared my feelings."

Helen lifted her head and turned to Grace. "After? You spoke the words first?"

"I did not exactly say that I loved him . . ." Grace smiled wistfully. "It was more that I asked him to hold me and admitted that I would like to be kissed."

"*You did?*" Helen felt properly shocked. She could not imagine admitting something like that to Samuel. *Yet didn't I do as much—by meeting him at the gazebo?*

"I do not regret it," Grace said, sounding quite stoic. "When I am an old maid I shall always have that memory to look back upon and treasure."

"You shall *not* be an old maid." *Why did I ever give my word to not say anything?*

Ignoring Helen's prediction, Grace asked, "Has Mr. Preston declared his feelings for you?"

"No—not really." *I am still not entirely sure what was real and what was pretended.* Helen fell back on the bed. "But we have kissed."

"Goodness!" Grace flopped down beside her, then rolled to her stomach. "Tell me everything." She placed her hands beneath her chin and waited expectantly.

"It was perfect." Helen sighed, remembering the feeling of being in Samuel's arms and those moments of bliss. "He teased me from my nervousness, then instructed me to place my hands on his shoulders so I might push him away if I wished."

Grace laughed. "That sounds like Samuel."

Helen's smile vanished. She sat up. "Did he ever kiss *you*?"

"No. Of course not." Grace leaned away as if offended. "What kind of woman do you think I am?"

"I did not mean—"

"A ruined one," Grace said soberly.

"No Grace. You are not ruined," Helen said, "No matter what the gossips say. Please forgive me for asking such a question."

Grace sat up and hugged her knees to her chest, careful to pull her nightgown over them. "It is all right. Do not worry yourself over it." But she did not sound all right or as if she were not worried.

"Nevertheless, I am sorry," Helen said. *I am the worst sister ever. It is likely Samuel and Lord Sutherland swore me to secrecy because they were afraid I'd open my mouth and bungle the whole thing.*

"I am sorry too," Grace said. "I regret that I ever entertained the possibility of feelings for Samuel. It has made things difficult for you, and it has cost me dearly. And I am sorry I have shamed our family."

"You haven't," Helen said. "It was but a misunderstanding that—"

"—landed me in Lord Sutherland's bed and ruined my reputation," Grace finished. "That is the worst of it, Helen. I have but a kiss to remember the rest of my life, yet the world will judge me for far more."

Helen took her sister's hand and squeezed it tightly. "Let the world think what it will. *I* know the truth—that Miss

Grace Thatcher, age twenty-four, and presently of the run-down cottage at the edge of nowhere, is the most noble, generous, kindhearted, and self-sacrificing woman ever to walk England's soil."

"Oh, Helen." Grace pulled her into a hug. "We have done the best we can, haven't we?"

"Yes," Helen agreed.

But it still remained to be seen if their best would be good enough.

CHAPTER 26

Helen watched from the upstairs window of the cottage as Lord Sutherland's carriage came into view. *They're here!* She felt desperate to see Samuel again; the week apart had been long and had only strengthened her conviction that his feelings for her were also no longer pretended. The carriage turned up the drive, and Helen hurried toward the stairs, then came running down them. Her gathered skirts swishing, she rushed past Grace. "He's here!"

"Goodness," Grace exclaimed. She set aside the book she'd been reading and glanced out the window in time to see the familiar carriage come to a stop before the front walk. "*Who's* here?" She brought a hand to her chest and leaned forward, as if not quite believing what she was seeing.

Helen thrilled to see the look of hope on her sister's face. With each passing day it had become more difficult to refrain from telling Grace that Lord Sutherland was coming. Only the fear that telling her of his plans might ruin a happy outcome for their reunion, along with the promise she'd made, had kept Helen from speaking of it throughout the week.

"Samuel is here." Helen smoothed her skirt before opening the front door. "I saw him waving as they pulled up the drive."

"In Lord Sutherland's carriage?" Grace left her chair and followed Helen to the front door.

Helen raised up on her toes to better see the carriage and clasped her hands, feeling both terribly excited and equally anxious for herself and for her sister and the events that were about to unfold. She glanced at Grace once more, glad her story was to end well.

It is good that Grace should be so happy.

"Restrain yourself, Helen," Grace said. "It has scarcely been a week since you last saw each other."

"A week is forever," Helen said, wondering how Grace had survived two months without the man she loved.

And Samuel has been alone for over three years since Elizabeth's death. Helen did not ever wish him to be so again and knew she would be perfectly content spending the rest of her days doing all she could to bring Samuel and Beth happiness.

A footman opened the carriage door, and Samuel stepped down, the look on his face as exuberant as Helen felt. From the corner of her eye, she watched Grace's hopeful gaze travel past him.

When the footman shut the door behind Samuel and put up the step, it was all Helen could do not to put her arms around Grace in comfort. *Just a few minutes more, dear sister.* She did not understand why Lord Sutherland had insisted upon doing things this way—it seemed cruel—but Samuel had said they must not interfere.

Any more than we already have, Helen thought, her smile growing broader as they hurried down the walk toward him.

He met them halfway. "Helen." He spoke her name with a joy that matched her own, then took her hands and leaned forward to kiss her cheek.

"Samuel!" Helen felt a blush heating her face and remembered how he had complimented her on it before. "You mustn't kiss me in front of Grace."

Grace laughed. "On the contrary, I think he *must*." She held her hand out to him.

He kissed the back of it, and Helen watched as the look in his eyes changed to brotherly concern. She had known it would be so but felt relieved to see it, just the same.

"How are you?" Samuel asked Grace. "How have you been?"

"Well," Grace said, withdrawing her hand. "The country is every bit as peaceful as we hoped."

"I am glad to hear it," Samuel said. "Nicholas said to give you his regards. He hopes you are well and eagerly awaits news of your family."

"How is he? And how is it you came to be driving in his coach today?" Grace blinked and turned aside, pretending a sneeze.

Helen and Samuel exchanged sympathetic looks.

"Ah." Samuel turned his pointed gaze upon Grace before glancing at the carriage. "You thought—"

"No." Grace shook her head. "I would never expect a visit." She took a deep breath and looked at Helen. "You two have much to discuss, I expect. And owing to the compact nature of our cottage, you do not have much place to do it. May I suggest a walk down the lane to the swing in the old oak?"

"Yes, let's. Please." Helen linked her arm through Samuel's and wished they were near another swing, at a place she held dear.

"I'll search out Christopher, and we'll see you at tea," Grace said. "We can catch up then, and you can tell me all of your plans." She turned away, walking in the opposite direction.

"*You* shall be telling us of your plans," Helen said too softly for Grace to hear.

"While Helen and I shall be keeping silent about ours, which have led to this happy reunion," Samuel added. He leaned forward, kissing the top of her nose.

"What was that for?" she asked, secretly pleased at the display of affection when no one was near to observe it.

"I am kissing away your worries," he said. "Your nose wrinkles whenever something is bothering you. It is quite endearing."

"I did not realize," Helen said, touched that he had noticed something like that.

"What is troubling you?" Samuel's own brow wrinkled. "I hope you are not worried about the way Nicholas plans to greet your sister. He loves Grace deeply and spoke of nothing throughout the entire ride but how he might please her—and that with Beth seated beside him."

"Beth has come?" Helen looked over her shoulder, wondering where the precocious child could be. *Certainly she wouldn't have stayed in the carriage. She would have insisted upon seeing me—wouldn't she?* "Such a long journey for her. I did not expect—"

"Yes, well. I thought it might be good if she accompanied me." Samuel increased his pace and ceased looking at Helen. "Let's walk quickly. I would like to have a few moments alone before Grace and Nicholas arrive."

Alone. Helen felt a bit dizzy in an entirely pleasant way as she hurried to keep up with Samuel's brisk steps. "I should think we will have several minutes. Grace and Lord Sutherland have been apart for so long they will have much to discuss."

"I daresay you're right," Samuel said. "But they may have to talk later. Everyone else is already at the church—

including Beth, who is probably busy throwing flower petals about or extinguishing candles, and generally driving her grandmother mad." He grinned, as if pleased with his daughter's mischief.

"Nothing more than Lady Sutherland can handle," Helen assured him, remembering all too well the dowager's stern reprimands. She'd nearly forgotten that she would see the woman today.

But any worrying over what Lady Sutherland would find to criticize her about was quickly eclipsed by the anticipation of having a few moments alone with Samuel.

Will he kiss me again? Will we finally speak of our future? Helen lapsed into silence as they walked, but her heart and step were light, filled with happy expectation. She led Samuel to a grassy knoll at the top of the meadow, overlooking the path Lord Sutherland and Grace should shortly be walking.

"They will not be able to see us here." Helen released her hold on Samuel's arm and sat on the ground, arranging her skirts modestly around her.

"Alas, we are not close enough to eavesdrop," Samuel lamented as he dropped to the ground beside her.

"A *good* thing," Helen said. "I have had enough of eavesdropping to last a lifetime. We need only be close enough to ascertain that Grace appears happy."

"*I* have had enough of fretting over your sister and Nicholas," Samuel said, rather surprising Helen. "It is *you* I am concerned for at the moment."

"What do you mean?" she asked, quietly pleased at his words. "I am perfectly well at this moment—and most others of late." She pressed her lips together to hold back a flirting smile but gazed up at him from beneath her long lashes.

Samuel took her hand in his but did not bring it to his lips; neither did he appear to return her look with the tender affection she had witnessed from him before. Instead a somber mood seemed to have descended on him during their walk, and he sat somewhat hunched forward, as if he carried a great weight upon his shoulders.

A twinge of worry took hold in Helen's mind.

"Is something amiss?" she asked, sensing the answer already. *What is wrong?* She ought to have asked that instead.

"Yes. And there is no easy way to tell you. It is *not* what I wished to tell you this morning, but I feel I must." Samuel met her gaze and held it. "It is about Crayton."

Helen stiffened and instinctively looked around. She did not see the pirate, but Grace and Lord Sutherland appeared on the path, walking together in apparently deep conversation.

"Crayton is nowhere about," Samuel rushed to assure her. "He does not know where you are. I have had a man following him, just to be sure."

Helen relaxed the tiniest bit. "You've hired someone to watch him? Is that not a bit extreme? It isn't as if we are in London."

"And we ought not to go there until the situation is resolved," Samuel said.

"What *situation*? If you mean what happened the evening at the theatre, I have determined not to dwell on it. It was an unfortunate incident on an otherwise perfect evening." She attempted to catch Samuel's eye, hoping to lighten his mood by reminding him of the pleasantness of that excursion. But instead of looking at her, he stared past her, seemingly lost in thought.

"Why are you are so serious?" Helen asked. "And on this morning when we are supposed to be celebrating?" *When I believed we would be speaking of our feelings for each other.*

In the meadow below, Grace and Lord Sutherland had stopped walking and stood facing one another. He pulled something from his pocket and held it out to her.

Beside Helen, Samuel inhaled deeply, as if gathering courage. "I am serious because the situation demands it. Several months ago your father accepted a payment of £3500 from Sir Crayton."

Helen gasped. She pulled her hand from Samuel's and covered her mouth, as if that could contain her horror and the sick feeling washing over her. "A payment—for me?"

He nodded. "The evidence is not entirely conclusive yet, but it also appears that when your father failed to deliver you he met with foul play."

Helen's eyes widened. "You think Crayton had something to do with Father's death?"

"Yes." Samuel rubbed the back of his neck, as if the whole business pained him.

As it must. She felt a lurch of fear. *Samuel is involved now—and Beth.*

"I have made arrangements for Crayton to be paid the £3500," Samuel said. "And I should like to have it done with as quickly as possible."

"Such a large sum," Helen exclaimed. "We shall never be able to repay you."

"I did not tell you this so you would fret about the money," he said. "That is the least of my concerns, as it should be yours. I would gladly pay ten times that much to see that you are safe." He looked at her directly, as if to make certain she understood.

"I thank you." *Still . . .*

"I suspect it was against my better judgment to mention any of this to you at all and cause you more fear and heartache, as I see I have done already." Samuel stood and brushed the dirt from his trousers, then held his hand out and helped Helen to her feet, studying her face closely. "But I felt you had a right to know, that I ought to be honest and you to be made aware."

"It is good you have told me." She folded her arms

across her middle and looked out at the meadow, where Grace and Lord Sutherland stood facing one another and holding hands. *I hope their romantic moment is going far better than ours.*

Helen thought of the kiss she and Samuel had shared in the gazebo and wanted to cry. She had been gone but one week, and now it seemed as if that place and those memories were taken from her, destined to remain only as some magical figment of her imagination.

Sir Crayton has purchased me. The chilling thought worked its way from her mind to her heart, sending a cold numbness spreading through her. "Paying Crayton will not satisfy him," Helen predicted. "He was put off once before, and it cost Grandfather dearly to get him to go away." She remembered that time, the guards they had posted to keep her and Grace safe, and the enormous sum of money—far more than £3500—Grandfather had spent to be rid of Crayton.

"I have heard the story," Samuel said. "And you are likely correct. He has already put a price on your brother's head, and he has men searching the city for you. Sooner or later one of them is bound to learn who accompanied you that night at the theatre. Mrs. Ellis had learned of it already, by the time we attended her ball."

Helen felt herself pale. She turned to Samuel. "You are in danger. Beth too." *That's why he brought Beth with him today,* she realized.

"Shh." He pulled Helen close, wrapping his arms around her, yet she could take no comfort from his embrace. Every minute she stayed near him was another that might lead Crayton closer.

Oh, Samuel. All of her dreams and hopes seemed swept away in the swift current that was Crayton's hunt.

Samuel leaned back to look at her but still kept hold of her shoulders. "Listen to me, Helen," he said, somewhat sternly. "You are safe. My men will alert us if Crayton draws near."

When, Helen thought. *Not if.*

"It is probable that his interest will cool somewhat when he receives the anonymous payment, sent with a simple note, telling him you are married to another." There was nothing romantic in Samuel's tone or what he was suggesting.

Married. The word she had longed to hear, and now it terrified her.

"The law will be on our side, then, with you as my wife, and with the crown's good favor Crayton has worked to gain, he would be foolish to go after any of us."

"You speak as if everything has already been settled." Helen pulled away from him and folded her arms once more.

"You are right, of course," Samuel said, sounding and looking at once repentant, as he reached a hand out to her, which she declined to accept.

"I'm sorry," he said. "I knew we would have little time to speak this morning, and I have felt burdened with this knowledge all week. I did not like knowing you were here, and unaware. And I suppose I still have your brother's practicalities in mind."

"You have discussed all of this with Christopher?" Helen felt stung, imagining them speaking of her. *Of what to do with me, is more like.*

"I have," Samuel admitted.

"And he agrees that the best thing to do to ensure *my* safety is for you to marry me and thereby put *yourself and Beth* in danger?" Helen stared at him, waiting for his answer.

"We have Christopher's blessing, if that is what you are asking."

She was not surprised. This entire solution seemed so like Christopher. "Indeed. I am surprised he did not suggest it to begin with."

Samuel did not offer a response to this; neither did he hide the flash of guilt that crossed his face.

"Christopher *did* suggest that you marry me," Helen said, reeling backward as if she had been struck. At the moment she was not certain which feeling was worse—her fear of Crayton and her worry for Samuel and Beth, or the hurt and disappointment from realizing Samuel's feelings were not of the depth she had imagined.

"He only spoke first what I had been contemplating for some time." Samuel stepped close again. He reached out, touching her face. "How the decision was arrived at does not matter so much as that we are able to marry, and quickly. I want to know you are mine and as much out of harm's way as possible."

"While I shall know that our marriage has brought trouble to your doorstep?" Helen turned away from his touch. "I cannot marry you, Samuel," she said miserably. "If the man has murdered my father as you believe, what is to stop him from pursuing you? I cannot put you and Beth in such danger."

"So you intend to offer yourself up to him instead?" Samuel shook his head as if disbelieving. "Or do you plan a life of solitary hiding? Or maybe you wish to travel abroad with Christopher."

"Abroad—" *I should have known he would want to do something rash like that.* But now was not the time to worry about Christopher. She would think on that later.

"Marry me, Helen, and let me take care of you," Samuel pled, his voice softer.

It was not the proposal she had hoped to hear. But even through her keen disappointment she berated herself for feeling hurt. *A trite matter considering our far-more-serious problem.* But it seemed she could not forget Samuel's proposal to Grace, how he had knelt on bended knee and proclaimed he would spend the rest of his life in the pursuit of her happiness. *That is what I wish, not to have him bound to paying for my safety—and his and Beth's—for the rest of his life.*

A joyous shout came from the meadow below, and Helen and Samuel watched Lord Sutherland gather Grace in his arms and swing her around. Grace's gentle laughter echoed across the valley, and a moment later the couple stopped turning about and kissed.

A well of sorrow pushed its way through Helen's numbness to the surface, and tears sprang to her eyes. *Lord Sutherland is not marrying Grace to protect her. He adores her.*

"Helen?" Samuel asked, calling her from her troubled thoughts. She looked at him and found his expression as tender as it had been that evening at the gazebo. *And so many other occasions.* "I promise Crayton will not hurt us. Not any of us. I'll hire as many guards as necessary. Nicholas will want to be involved too. We will find a way to be rid of Crayton and to live undisturbed. You will be safe."

"Safe or happy?" Helen said, hating herself for the cutting edge to her voice. "They are not synonymous." *Love me, Samuel. It is more than feeling compelled to offer your protection.*

"Can it not be both?" Samuel asked, sounding hurt.

Yes, she wanted to answer, though her heart still ached. She loved him enough that she felt willing to accept whatever affection he could offer. But she could not forget the night Christopher had first suggested they pretend engagement and Samuel had been so adamant that nothing be done that would hurt Beth.

Marrying him could hurt them both.

"I am sorry," Helen whispered. *I have never been more sorry in my life.* The exact words Grace had used when she rejected him. "But I cannot marry you."

CHAPTER 27

Helen had been inside the small chapel only once before, just a few days earlier for Sunday services. Today the room looked remarkably different, and a quick glance at the front of the chapel explained why. Lady Sutherland was practically running to and fro, instructing a small army of servants, who were busy placing flowers and ribbon, adorning the simple church in finery, the likes of which it had probably never seen and never would again. It was a wonder that the dowager had agreed to her son being married in such a place at all.

But somehow she had, and here they were, Helen and Grace, standing in a side room at the back of the chapel, dressed in the gowns Grandfather had bought them shortly before his death. Grace looked splendid in hers, the pearls at her neck matching the ivory gown perfectly.

Helen did not own pearls but loved the ruby comb and necklace Grandfather had given her every bit as much. They had been locked safely away, so Father might not gain access to them, until their shortened visit to London, when

Christopher had retrieved them from the bank box, believing that she needed a bolster of courage after the incident with Sir Crayton.

It did seem that whenever she wore them, she felt that courage. The night of the Ellises' country ball, she had worn the rubies, and she had not been at all frightened the entire evening, though she had danced with several men she had not previously met. Now, as she stood at the brink of Grace's happiness and her own uncertain future, Helen recalled Grandfather's words once more, desperate for their calm reassurance.

There is magic in the ruby that few know of. Outwardly, it is remarkable, a stunning blood-red stone and one of the hardest gems, able to withstand great pressure, much as you have, my dear Helen. But it is the inner fire of the ruby that allows this protection and where its real value lies. Seen only by a few who pause to examine it closely, the ruby's center emits a light of its own, bringing much joy and happiness to those who take time to appreciate its value. You have that inner fire. It burns strong. Use it wisely. Take courage from it.

I am *strong—strong enough to do this.* This, being to stand beside Grace, watch her speak vows and then embark on a life of happiness. *While I am about to embark on—*

"Excuse us a moment, Grace," Christopher said as he appeared in the doorway. He looked sharp in his suit as he strode forward, taking Helen's arm and leading her outside.

Grace looked after them curiously as Helen shrugged. *Who knows what Christopher is about now?* She had a few words for him after this was all over, but she dared not start on those now, fearing her emotions would overwhelm her and ruin Grace's day.

He led them past the open church doors and down the steps. Helen squinted against the sun—she'd taken off her cloak and bonnet already but could not muster enough emotion to care that she was outside without either. Instead she tried to feel grateful that Grace was to be married on such a beautiful day. Crocuses pushed through the ground, revealing bursts of color all around the small stone building, and the air felt especially spring-like, given that it was only the last day of February.

"You might try to appear happy," Christopher started in, scolding her. "What will Samuel think if he sees you looking as if you're about to cry?"

"I don't suppose he will think anything," Helen said. "And if you are scolding people for appearing dour, perhaps you ought to speak with Samuel as well. He has been in quite a serious mood all morning."

"Why do you suppose that is?" Christopher asked, sounding exasperated as he ran his fingers through his hair, making a mess of it.

"I don't know," Helen lied. *I don't wish to discuss it with you.* "Perhaps he feels as I do—somewhat envious of their happiness."

"There is no need for you to *be* envious." Christopher glanced heavenward. "Would that you were here, Grandfather, to shake some sense into my sisters. At times like these, I fear what you've asked of me is too much."

"What on earth are you talking about?" Helen reached out, placing her hand on Christopher's forehead. "Are you ill? Have you a fever?" First Samuel spoke to his deceased wife, and now Christopher was speaking to Grandfather? Did all the men she knew speak to the dead?

"I promised that I would see you and Grace happily wed and that I would protect you from Father and any other man who would do you harm. You've no idea the task it has been."

"Well, I am sorry," Helen said, feeling anything but. She placed her hands on her hips. "You needn't worry over taking care of me or finding me a husband to keep me safe. I am quite capable of looking out for myself."

"Then do it!" Christopher said, loudly enough that those inside likely heard. More quietly, he added, "Open your eyes, and quit hiding behind your fear. Samuel loves you. He will still marry you, but now *you* will have to ask."

"*I* will—" She broke off, giving a harsh laugh. "I am not Beth. I cannot simply ask a man to dance—or to marry me." *Especially when it would affect his life so terribly.*

"Then you should have said yes when he asked you," Christopher said.

Helen narrowed her eyes at him. "No, I should not have. I cannot bring Samuel—and his daughter—into our situation. It will be bad enough worrying for my safety and yours. I cannot comprehend worrying for them as well. Not to mention that it was *your* idea he marry me." Helen turned away with a flounce of curls.

"Comprehend this, dear sister," Christopher said, taking her arm and turning her around to face him once more. "Samuel is *already* part of this situation, and by virtue of that, so is Beth. From the moment Crayton saw us at the theatre, they became involved."

"It doesn't have to stay that way," Helen argued.

"You're right," Christopher said. "But he wants it to. He loves you so much that he's ready to risk his life for you. But you wouldn't let him get that far. You crushed his heart the minute he offered it."

"It wasn't an offer—" *Not the one I hoped for.* "I do not want him marrying me to protect me. I want his feelings to be real, too."

"They *are*," Christopher insisted. "He's shown it at least a dozen times that I have seen. I've never known a man more besotted with a woman, save perhaps Lord Sutherland over Grace."

"You *asked* us to behave as if we were in love," Helen reminded him. "And Samuel has done so remarkably well."

"I asked you," Christopher said, "not only to help Grace

and Lord Sutherland reunite, but so you and Samuel might realize your feelings for each other. I assure you, his are no more pretend than yours."

"Then why has he not told me he loves me?" Helen asked, wanting to believe but still fearing Christopher was wrong, that Samuel had somehow been coerced into this entire situation.

"Consider this," Christopher said. "Samuel has known the loss of his wife, and he has known the sting of rejection from Grace. And this morning he has heard nothing but frustration and resentment from you, simply because of his efforts to keep you safe. Might it not be fair for you to declare your love to him first? And if you do not—today—" Christopher forged on without allowing her a chance to speak—"you may lose him, and his precious Beth, forever. They will go home, and you will be here alone. Is that what you want?"

Helen turned away, brushing at the tears suddenly spilling from her eyes. "If your intention in talking to me was for me to appear cheerful, you have failed miserably."

"I have failed at much more than that if I cannot get you to speak up and declare your feelings to the man you love," Christopher said quietly.

Helen made no response. Such a declaration would not be the simple thing he made it out to be.

"In fifteen minutes, I will walk Grace up the aisle to stand beside Lord Sutherland before the vicar," Christopher said. "I would like to walk you up that aisle too and be witness to *two* weddings today."

"*What?*" Helen whirled to face him. "Are you completely mad? That is impossible. Banns have not been posted, and—"

"Samuel obtained a special license at the same time Lord Sutherland did, earlier this week. I certainly did not force him to that, just as I did not force him to kiss you in the gazebo or to dance three times with you at the Ellises' ball. He does love you, Helen."

She brought her hands to her pounding heart as a dozen evidences of Samuel's caring flooded her mind. *Safe or happy . . . Can it not be both?*

"Oh, Christopher." She turned her anguished gaze upon him. "I am such a wretched fool."

"Yes, you are," he readily agreed, but his lazy grin appeared. "We are making some progress at last."

Helen wrung her hands. "But I would still worry for his safety, and that is such a lot of money to pay Crayton, and I thought Samuel only felt compelled to offer his protection and—"

"I know." Christopher seized her arms and looked directly at her. "I have already heard from him the whole miserable conversation. And do you know what he said after telling me of your refusal?"

Helen shook her head.

"He said he did not regret that he had opened his heart to you, because love was always worth the price. And he was sorry you did not feel the same."

"But I do," Helen said, anguished over her earlier, harsh words and the unkind way she had spoken to him. "What must he think of me?"

"Right now I would guess that he is trying *not* to think of you and is rather miserable, believing, as he must, that you do not care for him after all—and this after I had assured him repeatedly that you did. You rejected not only his protection and money this morning, but his love as well."

"I cannot face him," Helen said, unable even to raise her head to look at Christopher.

He took her hand and gave it a quick squeeze. "Find your courage, Helen. It is not too late to fix this. Tell him how you feel." He pulled a paper—the special marriage license—from his pocket and waved it at her. "I will be awaiting your decision." Christopher turned and hurried back up the steps and into the chapel.

Helen remained outside, left alone to contemplate her choices—marriage or loneliness, courage or misery. Or perhaps it might be courage *and* misery, if Christopher and Samuel were wrong and something terrible happened.

Love is always worth the price. Find your courage, Helen.

She wiped her face and dried her tears as best she could, careful not to muss the sleeves of her gown. *Beth, at least, will be pleased to see me in it.* Helen had not worn it since the day she'd met Samuel in the garden and she and Beth had played Camelot.

The ladies of old were brave and bold. How many times had she and Beth sung that as they skipped across the lawn? Helen smiled, remembering those carefree afternoons when she had regaled Beth with the stories of women who had lived in perilous times. *And the brave acts they had to do— often in the name of love.*

They had *to be bold. So why shouldn't I?*

CHAPTER

The few guests were seated in the pews. Miranda and Harrison sat together, Helen noted happily. When she'd done what she could for her own situation, she resolved that she would do what she could for theirs. It would likely be much easier than remedying her own mistake.

"I did not quite believe that Nicholas was serious about getting married *today*," Grace said, looking pensively at the solemn vicar waiting at the head of the chapel. "But at least I had an hour's notice." She glanced at Helen. "You have had only minutes to decide. Are you certain this is what you wish to do?"

"She's certain." Christopher came to stand between them, taking each by an elbow.

"Eager to be rid of us, are you?" Helen asked, smiling at him nonetheless. She didn't want to remember this as the day she and Christopher quarreled.

"You've no idea." He kissed each of them on the cheek.

"Though I fear my life is about to become dreadfully boring without you two to keep watch over."

"It will serve you right," Grace said. "Perhaps, in our absence, you will learn to appreciate female company."

"Perhaps," Christopher said, but his faraway gaze spoke of travel and adventure. "Are you ready now? We should begin before the vicar decides I have not paid him quite enough for our change of plans."

"I am ready," Grace said. They stepped from the side room to the back of the chapel. Grace focused at once on the front and Lord Sutherland's striking figure, waiting there.

Helen looked for Samuel and noted that he sat beside Beth, who was already squirming on the front pew.

The organ sounded its opening note. Helen exchanged smiles with Grace and felt her heart nearly burst with happiness for her.

This day could not be more perfect for her wedding, Helen thought as they began walking. She only wished she knew if it would end that way for herself as well, or, if in a few minutes' time, she would be returning down the aisle—alone.

The march to the front of the chapel seemed to take less than a minute. Christopher turned to Grace and kissed her cheek lightly. He faced Helen next, kissing her cheek and whispering, "Trust me."

She gave the barest nod and released his arm, then clasped her trembling hands in front of her. Christopher stepped back from their view.

"Hello, Miss Helen," Beth whispered loudly from the front pew. Helen sent a warm smile her way, then felt it falter as she took in the little girl's awkwardly shorn hair. But Beth's grin only widened, as if to ask if Helen liked her new style.

If there is something about ourselves that we do not like, we must work to improve it. Beth's logic rang through

Helen's mind as she imagined the child taking scissors to her hair to *improve* it, much as she had tried to improve her dress by painting it.

Yes, we must, Helen silently answered. *I must be more courageous.* Bending low beside the pew, she whispered to Beth. "You look beautiful today." And she did. Somehow the randomly cropped curls gave Beth an impish look that perfectly suited her. Helen felt a swell of love for the little girl—and the man seated beside her. It was the bolster she needed.

I cannot lose them.

Her eyes traveled from Beth to her father. "I love you, Samuel," Helen whispered. His gaze rose to hers, and she felt crushed at the disbelief she read there. He did not say the words back, or anything else, and Helen had no choice but to stand and face the vicar—alone.

"Gentlemen—" The vicar looked from Lord Sutherland to Samuel. "Please take your places next to your brides." Astonished gasps and whispers rippled through the audience. They were expecting this even less than she had been.

Lord Sutherland came to stand beside Grace, but Helen remained alone. She kept her gaze forward and counted in her head, resolved to wait several seconds before she would slip, humiliated, into the closest pew.

One. Two. Three. Four. The seconds ticked by in agonizing slowness. Tears were building behind her eyes while her chest and throat tightened, making it difficult to breathe. *Five. Six. Seven . . .*

He will not join me. I was too late.

Eight. Nine. Ten.

A hand clasped hers, its familiar warmth flooding her with both relief and joy. Helen turned to Samuel as the first tear escaped and slid down the side of her face. "I'm sorry," she whispered.

He merely offered a tentative, fleeting smile, and the vulnerability Helen read in his eyes pierced her all the more—much more than she had felt wounded by him that morning. *How could I refuse him, when he has lost so much before? And after all he has given me.*

Helen wanted to talk to him, to explain why she had initially refused but stood here now. *But first, we must be married!*

She faced the vicar. Samuel released her hand but stood close enough that their shoulders touched.

"Dearly beloved," the vicar began, and Helen felt his words touch her soul. She wanted Samuel to know he was beloved, and she felt a sort of desperation to show him. But the ceremony seemed to go on forever and—times two—even longer than that.

When the scriptures had all been read, Lord Sutherland presented Grace with a wedding band and spoke his vows, then the two of them knelt. The vicar then turned to Samuel and Helen. She swallowed, uncertain what to expect. *What shall we do without a ring?* But Samuel withdrew one from his coat pocket, took her hand, and slipped the silver band onto her finger. Helen glanced down and felt her throat constrict as a small ruby shone at her from the center of the band. It was a gift that had nothing to do with protection and everything to do with love.

"With this ring I thee wed, with my body I thee worship, and with all my worldly goods I thee endow." Samuel took her other hand, and they knelt together.

Keeping you safe is but part of the bargain, she imagined him thinking.

The vicar returned his attention to Lord Sutherland and Grace.

Helen leaned closer to Samuel. "My feelings have never been pretend," she whispered. "I have loved you for so long. Please forgive me my lack of courage and faith."

He didn't have time to answer, for the vicar's gaze was upon them again as he led the prayer. At last they were blessed, and the ceremony was done. Samuel helped Helen to stand. She felt suddenly shy of him. *We are truly married.* She turned to congratulate Grace and was shocked to find her sister enveloped in her new husband's embrace right there for all to see.

"If it is good enough for Nicholas . . ." Samuel pulled Helen close as a smile lit his face. She felt relieved to see it.

"Samuel," she began to scold when he tugged her closer yet; then she thought the better of it and kissed him instead. Lady Sutherland's shocked gasp echoed through the chapel.

"You were right," he said, drawing back and grinning broadly. "You are *not* shy."

"You had best take good care of my little sister," Grace said, seeming somewhat surprised at Samuel's forwardness and Helen's acceptance.

"I intend to take excellent care of her," Samuel said. "Loving Helen shall be our new life's purpose, won't it Beth?" He reached down, picking his daughter up as he winked at Helen. "I imagine it shall be a most fulfilling endeavor."

CHAPTER 29

June

"Wake up! Wake up! The roses are blooming." Small, slightly sticky hands pressed upon Helen's cheeks, smashing them inward. She opened her eyes and found Beth's quite close.

"The roses are blooming. Come see them." Releasing Helen's cheeks, Beth grabbed her hand, attempting—without success—to tug her from the bed.

"Where do you think you're taking my wife?" Samuel growled as he sat up suddenly, hands raised in the air as if he were a madman. He made a grab for Beth but not before she'd jumped out of reach, shrieking loudly.

"The evil king demands an explanation at once," Samuel said. "Explain this rude awakening, or he may consider eating you for breakfast."

"Oh, Papa." Beth giggled behind her hand. "You told me to watch for the roses to bloom, and I have. It's time to show Mama her surprise."

Surprise? For once another word eclipsed the sweet thrill of Beth's loving endearment. Helen rolled over to look at Samuel. "What have you two been plotting?"

"You'll have to wait and see." Samuel kissed the top of her nose, then whisked the covers back so that it was Helen who shrieked and jumped as she hurried to pull her nightgown to a more modest length.

"Come. Get on your wrap, and we shall all go down." Amid Helen's protests that she could not go downstairs if she wasn't wearing at least a morning gown, he swept her from the bed and hurried her into her robe.

"How will we cover her eyes?" Beth asked as Samuel tied the sash at Helen's waist.

"A very good question," he said. "But one I have thought of already." Reaching behind him, he pulled the previous night's hastily discarded cravat from a chair and proceeded to wrap it around Helen's eyes.

"I do not think it will be much of a surprise when I fall down the stairs because I cannot see," she muttered good-naturedly, having no doubt that Samuel would steer her safely to wherever the surprise happened to be.

"*Tsk.* Such little confidence in me," Samuel said, sweeping her into his arms again and carrying her. Helen felt, rather than saw, them leave the room. She could tell they were moving through the hall and then down the stairs to the foyer below.

She worried that her reaction to the surprise would not be appropriate. If it had to do with Samuel's—and Elizabeth's—roses, she was not certain her response would be at all what he hoped for. Since mid-spring nearly two months ago, he'd spent a great deal of time with the roses— at least as much as he had spent staying appraised of Sir Crayton's whereabouts and planning with Christopher and Nicholas what was to be done about the man.

Samuel had first transplanted the roses that had been

indoors all winter, then trimmed and replanted some already growing along the drive. If that wasn't enough, he had planted even more bushes from the wagon-full that had been delivered. At times, as she watched him laboring diligently, Helen's heart felt a peculiar catch. It wasn't that she was jealous, exactly. Rather, she wondered if Samuel's love for her could ever equal that which it seemed he still felt for his first wife.

His unwavering love and devotion to Elizabeth had been one of the things that had attracted Helen, and he had been nothing but loving and devoted to her since the day they'd wed. Still, Helen was not certain what to make of his continued and considerable dedication to the garden.

She smelled the roses before she saw them, their sweet scent heavy beneath the mid-morning sun. *How many must have opened at once for their fragrance to be so strong.*

A draft of spring air sent a chill rushing up her gown, reminding Helen that she'd been in the foyer and was now out in the yard, with only a dressing gown to cover her. Samuel wore no more clothes than she, and Helen felt her cheeks heat as she worried that someone might see them gallivanting about in such a state of undress.

"Blushing already." Samuel stood her on the ground and placed a kiss upon her cheek. "It becomes you as much as ever, but you needn't feel embarrassed. The servants all know I am besotted with you, and as for our neighbors . . ." He chuckled. "I am fairly confident that Nicholas and Grace would not judge us being in the garden dressed as we are."

"*Under*-dressed, you mean," Helen chided, but she could not be angry.

With gentle hands, he untied the cravat and let if fall from Helen's face. Her eyes blinked as they adjusted to the sun, then widened as she took in the glorious bursts of red and yellow encircling them.

Elizabeth's yellow roses still grew along the drive, but

beside them now, interwoven in a lovely pattern, were dozens and dozens of *red* roses in bloom. What had to be hundreds of new plants filled the garden, their bursts of crimson the most glorious sight she'd ever beheld.

"Oh, Samuel." Helen turned and threw her arms around him.

He chuckled. "I take it you like the addition."

She clung to him, her face buried in his shoulder. "They're perfect. How did you think of it?" With such evidence before her, how could she ever doubt that she held Samuel's heart?

"I thought of *you*," he said. "As I do every day from the moment I wake to my very last thought before I fall asleep with you in my arms. You hold my heart in your hands, Helen. No one else."

Standing beside him in the morning sun, in the glory of the garden, with Beth skipping a circle around them, Helen wondered how she had ever doubted. She was home, and she was loved.

Dear Reader,

Thank you for reading *Loving Helen*. I hope you enjoyed Helen's journey to courage and love.

The book you just read is the second in the Hearthfire Historical Romance series. A third novel, *Marrying Christopher*, will be coming Summer 2015 and will continue the story of the Thatcher family. Watch for previews and teasers on my website: MichelePaigeHolmes.com

Reviews are always appreciated, by authors and readers alike. Thank you in advance if you are able to take a few minutes to post one.

If you would like more information about my other books and future releases, please visit MichelePaigeHolmes.com. You can also follow me on Twitter at @MichelePHolmes.

Happy reading!

Michele

ACKNOWLEDGMENTS

I continue to be grateful for the talents of so many who have contributed to this novel. Their dedication and skill make my stories into what I have imagined them to be.

I am especially grateful for fabulous editors Heather Moore, Annette Lyon, Cassidy Wadsworth and Kelsey Down, whose combined efforts shaped *Loving Helen* into a story worthy of publication, and for the beautiful cover designed by Rachael Anderson. I am also grateful to Heather Justesen for her work formatting the e-book.

Much gratitude goes to my husband and children, all of whom are neglected when I am in the final stages of writing a novel. Thank you for your patience and Pepsi. Thank you for understanding (or pretending you do) my need to keep writing the stories in my head. I hope you know, I write them for you.

ABOUT MICHELE PAIGE HOLMES

Michele Paige Holmes spent her childhood and youth in Arizona and northern California, often curled up with a good book instead of out enjoying the sunshine. She graduated from Brigham Young University with a degree in elementary education and found it an excellent major with which to indulge her love of children's literature.

Her first novel, *Counting Stars*, won the 2007 Whitney Award for Best Romance. Its companion novel, a romantic suspense titled *All the Stars in Heaven*, was a Whitney Award finalist, as was her first historical romance, *Captive Heart*. *My Lucky Stars* completed the Stars series.

In 2014 Michele launched the Hearthfire Historical Romance line, with the debut title, *Saving Grace*. *Loving Helen* is the companion novel, with a third, *Marrying Christopher*, to be released in summer 2015.

When not reading or writing romance, Michele is busy with her full-time job as a wife and mother. She and her husband live in Utah with their five high-maintenance children, and a Shitzu that resembles a teddy bear, in a house with a wonderful view of the mountains.

You can find Michele on the web:
MichelePaigeHolmes.com
Facebook: Michele Holmes
Twitter: @MichelePHolmes

www.ingramcontent.com/pod-product-compliance
Lightning Source LLC
LaVergne TN
LVHW010157070526
838199LV00062B/4405